'Not a wallflower, surely, Miss Northcott?'

'Come, we shall attract attention if we hide in this corner. We shall dance, and you may tell me all about your sister.'

'Thank you, Lord St Ervan, but I do not care to dance.'

'Do you not? Didn't they teach dancing at that school of yours?'

'Of course they did. But I am too tall to dance gracefully, and besides...'

'Besides, what?'

Sarah laughed, her ready sense of humour getting the better of her. 'Besides, being so tall, I was always called upon to take the man's part in dancing lessons.'

He gave a shout of laughter. 'So you tried to lead? Well, you shall have no chance of leading me!'

'I fancy no one has ever been able to do that, my lord,' she retorted drily.

'No woman, certainly,' he returned carelessly.

THE DEVIL'S OWN LUCK

Petra Nash

MILLS & BOON LIMITED
ETON HOUSE   18-24 PARADISE ROAD
RICHMOND   SURREY   TW9 1SR

*First published in Great Britain 1989
by Mills & Boon Limited*

© Petra Nash 1989

*Australian copyright 1989
Philippine copyright 1989
This edition 1989*

ISBN 0 263 76424 9

*Set in Times Roman 10¼ on 12¼ pt.
04-8905-69509 C*

Made and printed in Great Britain

CHAPTER ONE

A CHILL wind ruffled the surface of the canal, and Sarah Northcott shivered, huddling her cloak more tightly around her. Old and shabby though it was, she was glad of the warmth of the good Flemish cloth on this late October day when, as so often, the salt-scented breeze had swept straight in from the North Sea over the few flat miles of land that stood between Bruges and the shore. English visitors complained as it tugged at their bonnets, skirts and umbrellas, but Sarah had lived with it for many years. The cold did not prevent her from lingering by the canal to watch the last of the pale winter sunlight on the Béguinage that stood over the water, miraculously reflected in every detail, on the bridge that separated the canal from the Minnewater lake.

The air grew colder as the light failed, and with another shiver Sarah turned and set off along Wijngaardstraat, the package of lace firmly clutched in one hand while the other held her cloak tightly to her. She nodded as she passed to the old lady in the Godshuis, or alms-house, from whom she had bought the lace. Times were hard in Bruges among the lacemakers now, for by this year of 1853 the ever-increasing industrialisation of textiles meant that their once prized product was being superseded by the cheaper machine-made item, and Sarah was glad of her commission. Agathe, at least, would feel the cold a little less this winter.

As she turned into the broader thoroughfare of
Ketelijnestraat, Sarah began to hurry, realising that it
was later than she had thought. She still had some way
to go before she reached the hotel where her erstwhile
charge, Mademoiselle Adélie Tessier, was staying with
her mother before returning home to Brussels. Adélie
had insisted that she must have some Bruges lace to trim
her petticoats and nightgowns now that she was a young
lady, and Madame Hortense, the head of the school
where Adélie had been a pupil, and Sarah was still a
teacher, had offered the services of her least regarded
member of staff to carry out the transaction. Madame
Tessier would be impatient to return to Ostend. She had
made no secret of the fact that she found Bruges dirty,
uncomfortable and full of beggars.

It was at this moment that she heard a faint cry.
Stopping, she peered through the gathering gloom down
a small side street from which she thought the sound
had come. It came again, the voice of a girl, young and
frightened, calling for help in breathless tones and, to
her surprise, in English. Without stopping to think, Sarah
dived into the alley, pushing the package of lace into the
waistband of her skirt to leave her hands free.

Around the corner of the alley she found a group of
young lads, hardly more than boys, jostling and threat-
ening a short delicately made girl dressed in the height
of fashion, as even Sarah's inexperienced eye could see.
A silk dress, heavily trimmed, an equally decorated velvet
mantle with a deep fringe, and a bonnet that might as
well have had the word 'Paris' pinned to its ribbons, all
of these proclaimed her to be a young lady of
considerable means, if not of taste. She had not been

hurt, though the wide silk skirts were spattered with mud, but she cowered timidly away from the jeering urchins and continued to call for help.

Sarah was tall for a girl, nearly five foot nine, and the voluminous cloak helped to hide the slenderness of her figure. Trusting in the near darkness to hide her youth, she strode forward, laying about her with a heavy hand, and uttering a few pithy phrases in Flemish which expressed her opinion of the boys and their behaviour. They drew back, and one or two muttered that the girl was rich, and foreign, and therefore fair game. A few terse words disposed of that idea, and a very idiomatic remark concerning their ancestry had them running off with shrieks of laughter to find more mischief.

The girl was brushing ineffectually at the fine silk of her skirts, doing more harm than good. She was still whimpering and sniffing, and the hand which came out to clutch at Sarah was trembling.

'*Merci, merci, mademoiselle*,' she said in a pretty, breathless voice.

'It is all right. I am English,' said Sarah, putting back the hood of her cloak. There was little light in the dark alley, and the girl stared up at her. Sarah was used to her surprise. Her mother had been Italian, and from her Sarah had inherited the black hair and dark eyes that contrasted so strongly with the white skin that was her fair father's gift.

'Why, you are quite young. How brave you are! I was so frightened, I didn't know what to do.'

'I do not think they would have harmed you. They were only teasing. You should not have been out on your own at this time of day. Whatever can you have been thinking of?'

Unconsciously Sarah's voice took on the firm, commanding tone she was used to using with her charges at the school. The other girl drooped her head meekly.

'Indeed, I know it, and I did not intend to be alone. But something...' She paused, unwilling to confide, and Sarah deduced an assignation of some kind. It was not surprising, for even in the darkness she could see that her new acquaintance was remarkably pretty, as well as, quite obviously, well to do. Her companion seized the opportunity to change the subject. 'Besides, there was a gentleman here, and I thought he would come to my aid. But he just stood and watched, and did nothing. See, he is still there!' Her tones had risen to an affronted wail, and she pointed. Peering into the gloom, Sarah could just make out the tall figure of a well-dressed man lounging nonchalantly against the wall. As they looked at him he straightened, walked lazily towards them and removed his hat, bowing in what Sarah, quick to make judgements of others, felt to be an odiously condescending fashion. He paused, looked both of them up and down, then calmly continued his walk past them.

'Well!' gasped the girl. 'What a very unpleasant man!'

'Perhaps he is afraid of the boys,' said Sarah in a carrying voice which she hoped would reach him, and he stopped.

'The young lady was in no danger,' he drawled in an unmistakably English voice. 'I saw no necessity to spoil their fun. They get so little.'

Sarah was outraged. 'A young girl, dressed as she is, and out alone, and you saw no need to help her! You astonish me, sir!'

'A young girl, as you say, who goes out alone dressed like that—I drew the obvious conclusion.'

'And that was?' the girl asked before Sarah could prevent her.

'That she was a little lovebird out for customers,' he responded with brutal frankness. 'I had no wish to become entangled in such a situation. For all I knew it could have been merely a way of attracting my attention.'

The girl burst into tears, but Sarah was rigid with anger.

'I take leave to tell you that you are no gentleman, sir!'

'Take anything you like, if you will take her away. Snivelling females bore me. Since you do not scruple to give me your opinions, I need not hesitate to remind you that if I am no gentleman, your language just now, admirably to the point though it was, was certainly not that of a lady. Good evening.'

He turned the corner and was out of sight. Sarah blushed with fury, and also with shame at the memory of the words he had heard her use. It occurred to her to wonder how he could have understood her, since she had spoken in the coarse dialect that local people used, and which she had learned from the servant who had nursed her since her infancy. It was curious. In spite of what she had said, he was obviously a gentleman, and at home here, and yet she had never seen him before. Even in the gloom his face had been striking, handsome even, with dark hair and strongly marked dark eyebrows above an aquiline nose and a well-boned face. But what an unpleasant man! She put the memory from her and turned once again to her companion.

'Come, it is getting very late, and your friends must be alarmed for you, as I fear mine will be for me. Where are you staying?'

The girl named a hotel near the Wollestraat, and Sarah realised with relief that she would not have to go out of her own way to take her back. They set off at a brisk walk, and to distract her companion from the memory of her indignities, Sarah asked her about herself. It was easy, and the girl was soon chattering cheerfully while Sarah, scarcely listening, nodded and encouraged with an occasional word.

Her name, it appeared, was Emily Yarcombe. Her father, now dead—poor Papa—had been Mr Jeremiah Yarcombe. Here she paused, and eyed Sarah expectantly. Sarah racked her brains fruitlessly, and admitted that she had never heard of the gentleman, explaining tactfully that she lived a very retired existence, and that it was many years since she had set foot in England, not since she was quite a child in fact, and then only for a short time.

'But you are English?' asked Miss Yarcombe, eyeing her in some alarm. Sarah smiled and reassured her.

'Yes, as English as you are. That is to say, my father is English, and I was born in England, although my mother was Italian.' Reassured, Emily continued her recital. Poor Papa had done very well, it seemed, and had made a great deal of money in railways. He had been so busy doing this that he had not married until he was well into middle age, and Emily was therefore his only child. He had been dead for two years, and Emily missed him dreadfully, poor Papa, he had always been so good to her, and they had been such friends!

Seeing tears on the way again, Sarah turned the subject. Mama? Oh yes, Emily still had Mama. She had been so much younger than Papa, of course. Indeed, she sometimes said that she had been only seventeen when Emily was born, although she, Emily, did not quite believe that. Mama was here, at the hotel. Emily had been for a year to a school in Paris, and Mama had come to fetch her home. Mama was planning for her come-out, and they had bought gowns—so many gowns Sarah would hardly believe it—in Paris, and bonnets, and everything. Why, this very bonnet was one of them. Did Sarah not think it pretty?

'Very pretty, but perhaps not quite suitable for the occasion?'

'Is it too grand? I was afraid it might be. But I particularly wanted to wear it, because it is my favourite, and I wanted to look especially nice this afternoon. Only, please, I do not look like—like that dreadful man said, do I? I have never heard anything so shocking in my life!'

Sarah reassured her, and tactfully refrained once again from asking for whom this favourite bonnet had been worn. It was, after all, none of her business if Emily was making assignations somewhere—by the Minnewater probably, since that was a well-known beauty spot for lovers. Let Mama beware, though.

'Mama had a headache—she always does, after travelling. We are stopping here for one or two nights—just to see the sights, you know—and then we are to spend a few weeks in Ostend before we go to England. Mama thinks it will be a good idea. We do not know many people in London, you see, and we might make some friends in Ostend.'

Sarah thought she could make a pretty good assessment of the situation. Mama, to judge by the overdressed child by her side, had a great deal more money than taste, and was probably bent on launching her only daughter into society on the back of her late husband's fortune. Without any aristocratic or well-connected acquaintance, however, it was most unlikely that money alone, even allied with Emily's pretty face, would admit them to that tightly-knit group, polite society. Ostend, though, was becoming popular with the English, and even in winter there was a sprinkling of minor aristocracy and country gentlemen. In the more intimate atmosphere of a seaside town, away from London and its close-knit society, it might well be possible for Mrs Yarcombe to find someone to sponsor her daughter—possibly at a price, since it was the less well off who generally chose to live abroad. Who should know that better than she, the daughter of an impoverished second son?

They reached Emily's hotel. Sarah, sighing, gave her a short and, as she feared, useless lecture on the evils of secret meetings and going out unattended, particularly in Bruges where so many of the inhabitants lived by begging. Emily ignored the first part of the lecture, and replied spiritedly to the second.

'You are out on your own yourself, and you are young,' she pointed out.

'I am twenty-two,' replied Sarah austerely, 'and I have been used to take care of myself for many years. Besides, I have nothing worth stealing, as anyone can see. Now go in, for I am very late.'

'But stay!' called Emily after her retreating back. 'You have not told me your name.'

'I am Sarah Northcott, but I do not suppose we shall ever meet again. I am a teacher at the school of Madame Hortense Duval, in Ostend.'

'But I have not thanked you...'

'You have, several times, and I am so late. Please, Miss Yarcombe, you must let me leave now.'

Sarah saw the younger girl's hand hover over her reticule as she clearly wondered whether to reward Sarah with a gift. To her relief the purse was not taken out, and Emily simply offered her hand and her cheek, with the simplicity of a child. Sarah felt a sudden liking for her.

'Do not spoil your happy life by a foolish action now,' she advised, more gently than before. 'Your mama is doing her best for you, I am sure. She will see that you are safe, and happy. Now go in. Goodbye!'

Sarah hurried away, almost running. Emily watched her out of sight, then made her way up to her chamber. To her horror, she found that it was not empty.

'Mama!' she gasped. 'I thought you were... Are you better, then?'

'I am. Or I was, until I came into your room and found you had vanished. Are these the manners they taught you at that fancy French school? If so, I can see I've wasted my money, and I'd have done better to keep you at my side. Where have you been?'

Emily burst into tears.

'I am sorry, Mama. I just went out to see the sights, and to take the air, and I went further than I should, and got lost.'

'Taking the air, and in that good dress and your best bonnet! You must think I was born yesterday. Whom did you meet? And I tell you straight, my girl, if there's been any funny business going on, I wash my hands of you, and that's straight.'

'Mama!' Emily blushed hotly. 'It was nothing like that. I met no one, truly.' She paused, thinking gratefully that it was no lie.

'And what have you done to your dress? I forget how much I paid a yard for that silk, but it looks to me as though it was ruined. Look at you, girl, covered with mud and I don't know what else.'

'I am sorry, Mama, but when I was lost some horrid boys came and teased me. I was so frightened, you can't imagine, but then such a nice girl came along and saved me! She hit them, and shouted at them, and they ran away! She was so brave.'

'Hmm. It's a pity she didn't come sooner, and save your skirts from the dirt. I suppose she wants paying, does she? How much?'

'Oh, no, Mama, she's not like that at all. She's an English girl, and a lady, I think, though she was dressed so drably. She teaches at a school in Ostend, I forget what it's called, but she spoke very kindly to me, and told me off for being out on my own.'

'You are too simple for your own good, Emily. No doubt she did not ask you for money because she knew very well she would get more from me—at least she might think that. She will think again after I've had a word with her.'

Emily turned sulkily away and began to take off her bonnet and mantle.

'Well, she won't think it, or anything else, because she's not going to meet you. She's gone. And she said we would probably never meet again. And I don't care what you say, Mama, because I should like to see her again, for she was truly a lady. It's what you sent me to Paris to learn, and I did. I know how a lady should talk, and walk, and behave. And she is one.' She finished on a defiant note, and was both pleased and surprised to see that her mother was almost convinced.

'And what might this paragon's name be?'

'Sarah Northcott.'

'Northcott. Northcott? Now, what does that remind me of?'

'I don't know, Mama.'

'Be quiet, Emily, I am thinking. Northcott. And she lives in Ostend? Well, that might be interesting, it might indeed. Emily, I think I should like to thank this Miss Sarah Northcott, after all. We shall go to Ostend tomorrow. And now for heaven's sake ring for your maid, and take off that dress. You look like a peasant girl.'

She swept from the room, leaving her daughter open-mouthed behind her, and not a little relieved to have escaped with so little scolding.

CHAPTER TWO

IN SPITE OF her haste, Sarah was too late. On reaching the hotel, the proprietor met her with a long face. Madame and her daughter? No, they had left. Madame had waited, but she did not wish to drive back to Ostend in the dark, so she had left at least half an hour before. Madame had been—agitated. Well, yes, Madame had in fact been very angry.

'Did she leave any message for me?' Sarah tried to hide her anxiety. Madame Hortense would be annoyed if Sarah had upset Madame Tessier, who had two other daughters younger than Adélie and was a valuable customer. And Madame Tessier, as Sarah had soon learned, was easily upset.

'I regret, mademoiselle, that she left nothing. She said only that I was to tell you to bring the lace at once to her hotel in Ostend. She intends to leave for Brussels in the morning.'

He was blandly indifferent, but Sarah had to push down a rising feeling of panic. She had virtually no money with her, except a small amount left over from buying the lace, which in any case did not belong to her. If she did not get back to Ostend that evening, not only would Madame Hortense probably disown her, but her father would be alone, and she tried never to leave him alone in the evenings. It was some years since the gambling fit had come upon him, and she hoped and believed that it had gone at last, but she worried constantly when she was not with him. An evening alone, with no one but Madeleine for company, and who knew what he might do.

'I—I must return to Ostend this evening,' she began to the hotel-keeper, who could not have been less interested in her problems.

'If you have the money, you can hire a conveyance, mademoiselle. But if not...' He shrugged.

'I have not enough money, but I think that Madame would pay when I reach the hotel.' She was not, in fact, at all sure of it, and neither, by his face, was the hotel-keeper. He had seen Madame's annoyance with this poorly-clad young lady, and he also had a vivid memory of how carefully she had checked the bill for their luncheon. He was anxious to be rid of this troublesome young person, for he did not want to find himself obliged to take any responsibility for her. Nevertheless, he was not an unkind man.

'If you have some friend with whom you can pass the night, you will surely find some means to get to Ostend in the morning. One of the travellers then might convey you as a kindness. I myself will ask for you.'

He beamed at her, amazed at his own generosity. Sarah thought. There was old Agathe in her Godshuis, who would probably shelter her. It would be quite easy. But there was her father... Accustomed for many years to regard her feckless parent with the fond anxiety of a mother with a dear but delinquent child, Sarah could not consider it.

'No, I must return tonight,' she insisted. The hotel-keeper shrugged, affronted.

'In that case, mademoiselle, I am unable to help you. And unless you intend to take a room here, I must ask you not to keep me from my duties. I am a busy man.' He turned away, and Sarah gripped her hands together to stop herself from grabbing at his arm. Taking a deep breath to keep her voice from shaking, she prepared to humble herself and beg.

'In trouble again?' drawled an unpleasantly familiar voice from behind her. 'Try swearing at him. It seemed to work last time.'

Sarah felt her cheeks burning with rage and embarrassment. She had not heard him come in, so intent had she been on her thoughts. Now he stood just behind her, looking down at her with a bland expression that was somehow deceptively penetrating. Seen at close quarters, he was taller than she had realised. Accustomed to finding herself almost at eye-level with many of the men she met, it was pleasant to find herself looking up at him, as she did with her own tall father when he held himself straight and did not stoop, as he habitually did. This man, she felt, had never been bowed by sorrow, or want, or loss of self-respect. She could almost have hated him for that upright, commanding stance when she thought of her father as she had last seen him that morning, hunched over his breakfast and staring unseeingly at a week-old English newspaper.

'Since you declined to help last time, it will be no hardship to you to leave me to manage my own affairs now,' she said, with an attempt at coolness.

'But you are not managing, are you? No money, no means of travelling, nowhere to stay.'

For a horrible moment she thought he was going to offer her accommodation in return for her favours, and she shrank from him.

He laughed. 'Don't worry, I have no designs on your virtue. I do not need to buy that sort of friendship.'

'I don't know what you mean.' She tried to recover her composure, but knew that she blushed.

'Don't be coy. You know perfectly well what I mean. I prefer my women gentler—and plumper, too. You look as if you've never had a square meal in your life.'

'I am naturally charmed by your compliments, but you cannot imagine the depth of my indifference to your opinion of me. Good evening.' Seething with rage, she tried to brush past him, but he seized her arm and held it in a strong grip that she could not break without an unseemly struggle.

'Don't rush away—you haven't heard me out yet. I was about to tell you that I am on the point of returning to Ostend myself. If you wish to accompany me, you may.'

'Travel with you in a carriage, alone, and at night? You must be mad!'

'Quite possibly. I think that must be the explanation. I have never known myself perform such a kind action before.'

'A kind action? But I should be ruined!'

'Not at all. Perhaps you were not quite attending, but I have already informed you that your virtue is safe with me. I do not find you at all attractive.'

'*Merci du compliment!* But you must know as well as I do that if it were known that I had spent an hour and a half alone with you, in a carriage, my reputation would be in shreds. I have my living to earn, and my father to support. Madame Hortense is most strict that the teachers she employs for her girls have the most spotless of reputations.'

'But if you do not return this evening you will lose your place in any case, will you not?'

'No, for I do not reside at the school. But why are we discussing this? It is impossible.'

The hotel-keeper, suddenly obsequious, advanced, bowing and rubbing his hands.

'If I can be of assistance to Monsieur le Marquis ...?'

'I was not aware that your assistance had been requested. It is not I, but this young lady, that is in need of your help.' He waved a dismissive hand, but the hôtelier, still bowing, did not retire.

'I, my lord, have a daughter!'

'You are doubtless to be felicitated.'

'My daughter, my lord, has for some time been expressing a wish to visit her aunt in Ostend. If it would be of service to my lord, and to this young lady whose plight I pity so sincerely, I would permit her to travel, *en chapéron*, with you.'

'For a consideration, of course?'

'But naturally! My daughter helps in the kitchen, and it will make much extra work for the other girls. But for Monsieur le Marquis, and the young lady ...'

'You are a scoundrel! Still, if she can be ready in ten minutes, which in my experience is a feat of which no female is capable, she may have her free ride. And perhaps a small gift at the end of it, if she does not annoy me by talking all the time. Tell her to make haste.'

'But I have not said that I will travel with you!'

'No, but since your only objection has now been solved, I can see no reason why you should refuse my very kind offer.'

'I do not wish to be uncivil, but I do not care to travel with you. You are altogether too high handed.'

'What very curious notions of civility you do have, to be sure,' he returned equably. 'I believe I could almost find you amusing!'

'I would not travel with you, even if you provided fifty chaperons to lend me countenance!'

'That would certainly be quite out of the common way. We should have to hire a special train, I suppose.'

'I said I would not!'

'Imagine my relief! I do not know where to procure fifty chaperons. It has always been my concern to be rid of such creatures, not collect them. Now stop being childish, girl, and consider. You say you must return to Ostend tonight. I am offering you the means to do it, and with your reputation unsullied. Do you really think there is any other choice open to you? You do not like me, but you can surely spend less than two hours in my company for the sake of reaching home tonight. Think of it as an act of charity.'

'I thought *you* were dispensing the charity.'

'I am, and it is so novel an experience that really it is almost amusing. Do not, I beg of you, deny me my first, and possibly my last, opportunity to help a fellow being.'

She could only give in, and accept with as good a grace as possible. She still did not understand his motives, but no doubt he was acting on a whim, as men so often did, in her experience. She collected the rags of her dignity around her and dropped a small curtsy.

'Your lordship is very kind.'

'How did you...? Oh yes, the landlord. I suppose we had better introduce ourselves. I am Anthony St Ervan.'

'The Marquis of Berrington?'

'I see my fame has, as usual, gone before me. And you are?'

'Sarah Northcott.'

'Any relation to Lord Henry Northcott?'

'He is my uncle.'

'Good Lord, then you must be Matthew Northcott's daughter. I thought he was dead?'

'Only to his family.' She could not keep the bitterness out of her voice.

'Well, I don't recall that I ever met your father, but I once met your uncle. One of the most boring men I've ever spoken to. You're not missing much.'

'Your lordship is all consideration.'

'Yes, I am, aren't I? Ah, here comes the girl. Good God, I hope she's not going to giggle like that all the way.'

The hotel-keeper's daughter was short and plump. Her shiny round cheeks were scarlet with excitement, and she seemed incapable of uttering more than a shrill giggle in answer to any question. The carriage drew up, and with many protestations the hotel-keeper ushered them into it, adjuring his daughter to behave herself, and not to annoy my lord. She bade him farewell with another volley of giggles, and no sooner was the door shut than the coachman set off at a smart trot.

The girl, Marie-Rose, seemed content to stare around her at the luxurious inside of the carriage that was revealed by fits and starts as they passed by the lighted doorways of the town. Sarah sat as far back into her corner as she could, and kept her head resolutely turned to the window. There was not much to see, particularly as they were soon free of the houses, but the road followed the canal and there was enough moonlight for her to see a gleam of water, and pick out the occasional building silhouetted against the sky.

About twenty minutes passed in silence. Sarah, though exhausted, was unable to doze as Marie-Rose did opposite her. Trying not to move her head towards him, she stole a glance at her male companion, sitting to her right in the other corner of the seat. She could see his profile against the gleam of moonlight that was the window. Studying it, she thought absent-mindedly that it resembled a Roman general on an old medal her father possessed. He had thrown his hat carelessly on to the opposite seat, and his dark hair sprang thickly from above the wide, smooth brow.

He did not look towards her, but as though he had felt her glance, he spoke quietly. 'It is dull stuff to travel in silence when there is not even anything to look at outside. Shall we not beguile the time with more of our edifying conversation?' His voice in the darkness was teasing, but gentler than before.

Sarah said stiffly, 'I am afraid I have not been very polite to you, my lord.'

'My dear girl—forgive me, just a turn of phrase—do not start being too polite to me now. You cannot imagine how refreshing it is to have my faults pointed out to me with such candour. And don't put "my lord" in every other sentence. I prefer to be criticised. You remind me of my nurse. She was the only person who ever told me off.'

Sarah thought about the little she knew of her companion's early life. The only son of elderly parents, he had been indulged and doted on, and on inheriting the title and a fortune on his father's death, he had at the age of seventeen proceeded to scandalise society by his riotous career. His mother's death the following year had removed the last vestiges of restraint. He had gambled away his fortune by the age of twenty, and as quickly gained another one by the same means. His reputation for drink and women was appalling. It was true that recently he appeared to have settled down and learned discretion with the advancing years, for apart from his habit of making unpredictable and solitary journeys, he now led a fairly blameless life. Nevertheless Sarah wondered whether even the presence of Marie-Rose, snoring happily opposite her, would be enough to save her reputation if this escapade ever became known. Not, she reminded herself, that anyone but Madame Hortense was very interested in her reputation or lack of it. If she had been Emily Yarcombe, now, setting herself up for a good marriage, it would be a different thing. But she, Sarah, was unlikely ever to marry now. She gave a small sigh.

'Am I boring you, Miss Northcott?'

'Not at all,' she replied politely. 'Did your parents never correct you?'

'Of course not,' he replied carelessly. 'They thought me perfect. In fact they nearly gave my nurse her notice for scolding me, but I told them not to.'

Startled, she stared at him. 'Poor little boy!' she exclaimed.

'Not at all! They gave me everything I asked for,' he replied simply.

She was appalled. Everything, she thought, except love—the proper love of parents for children that makes them strict when it is necessary. She remembered her own upbringing, cared for throughout her childhood by Madeleine, after her mother's early death. Madeleine, who was no more than a Flemish fisherman's widow, but who had loved her enough to chastise her, and to teach her that this, and this, was the right way, and that was not. She remembered the security, against her father's restless life, of knowing that Madeleine was there and could always be depended upon.

Haltingly, she tried to express some of this. He heard her out in polite silence.

'I am sure you are quite right, and I would probably have been a better person had I been less indulged.'

'I did not mean...'

'Yes, you did, and I agree with you. Sometimes I even shock myself! But I am as I am, and at more than thirty I am too old to change. And I must tell you, Miss Northcott, that I have had a great deal of enjoyment! Also, whatever you might have heard, I never deliberately harmed anyone.'

'Sir Nigel Utkinton?'

'You *do* know about me. I had no idea I was so famous! But that was a duel, and no female understands duels. Besides, he recovered. Now, since you are so remarkably well informed about me, it is only fair that you tell me about yourself.'

To her surprise, she found herself telling him. Perhaps because he himself had led such a wild existence, there was no embarrassment in telling him of her own father's excesses. As a younger son he had disappointed his family by refusing to enter the church, a career which had been planned for him since there was a good living in the parish which was to be held for him. He had then alienated them further by marrying an Italian dancer.

'I scarcely remember my mother, but she was very beautiful, and good as well. They were very happy together, I believe, although my grandparents would not acknowledge her. After I was born they lived abroad, in France, Belgium and Italy. She died when I was three. My father brought me to Ostend, for they had been in Brussels when she died, and he wanted to take me home and try for a reconciliation with his family. He found Madeleine to care for me, and she is still with us. By the time we reached Ostend, he was ill with sadness and worry. He wrote to his father, but the letter was never answered. He took me to England, and tried to see them, but they would not let him into the house.'

She paused. She had a faint recollection of that last visit, when she had been about four.

'In the end they agreed to see him. They said he could return home—alone. I was to be placed with a family abroad, or in a school. They would pay for me, but he was not to see me any more, or think of me as a member of the family.'

She felt him stir beside her, but he did not speak.

'He refused,' she continued proudly. 'He said I was all he had left of my mother, and he would not be parted from me. They have never acknowledged our existence from that day to this.'

Sarah said no more. She remembered the wandering years of her childhood, her father, sad and lonely, going to gambling-dens for company and, later, as a means of gaining money. Sometimes he was successful, and she had new frocks and they ate like lords. Sometimes, and more often as time passed, he was not, and they shivered over the endless bowls of soup that Madeleine conjured out of bones and vegetables.

'Later, my father's health broke down. We came back because Madeleine's family are here, and he likes it. The Northcott land is in Norfolk, you know, and he says this reminds him of home, with the wide beaches, and the flat land. I teach English to the girls at Madame Duval's seminary, and French to the English girls. My father and I are happy together. But I do not like him to be alone all evening, without me. He gets sad, and when he is sad, he goes...out.'

He nodded, too familiar with such a life to be ignorant of the fact that 'going out' meant drinking, or gambling, or both. They were both silent, and to her surprise Sarah saw that already there were lighted windows to be seen outside. They were in Ostend. She looked out to get her bearings.

'If you would be so kind as to let me out at the next corner but one,' she requested.

'By all means. I will not offer to take you to your door,' he smiled sardonically.

She found herself smiling back. 'No, that would never do. You must perform your good deeds in secret, Lord St Ervan.'

He tapped to attract the coachman's attention, and the coach drew to a halt.

'It is barely half-past seven,' he said, consulting his watch. 'I do not think your father will have had time to miss you.'

The coachman opened the door and prepared to hand her out. She turned to St Ervan and held out her hand.

'You have been very kind. Thank you,' she said stiffly.

He grinned as he shook her hand firmly. 'How annoying for you to have to say that! I feel sure you would rather box my ears, as you did those boys.'

'Why must you keep reminding me of that?' she said crossly, pulling her hand away. 'I was quite in charity with you before.'

'Yes, I know, but you are more amusing when you are angry.'

'Without giving her time to answer, he signed to the coachman to shut the door. A moment later the carriage was gone, leaving her standing on the corner staring after it. She pulled herself together, and hurried home.

CHAPTER THREE

TO HER RELIEF, Sarah found her father at home. He had begun to be concerned for her, but she soon made him comfortable with a drink of brandy and hot water, and beguiled him by telling of her little adventure with Emily Yarcombe. He was much diverted, for she told him all that she had said. Used as he was to mixing with all kinds of people, and with all nationalities, he was not shocked, and indeed congratulated her on her presence of mind. Sarah was pleased to see him sit down to their simple fish supper and eat with more appetite than usual. Madeleine's cousin was a fisherman, and they ate fish nearly every day.

'Yarcombe,' he said as he carefully dissected a sole. 'Yarcombe. If her "poor papa" was old Jeremiah Yarcombe, she must be worth a fortune. He put everything he had into railways, and they did him proud. His father was an engineer, I believe, quite a humble sort of man, but clever, very clever. And so was Jeremiah, but not clever enough to keep out of the way of that wife of his! I heard she was very pretty, and much younger than he was.'

'Emily was certainly very pretty. And her clothes, Papa! So unsuitable for a place like Bruges. You would have thought her on her way to make calls in Park Lane, at least.'

'And out to meet someone, you say?'

29

'So I thought, though she would not admit to it, naturally. But she did not seem the sort of girl who would be interested in looking at a place for its history or its architecture. I can certainly think of no other reason for her to slip out alone in her best bonnet. I tried to give her a word of warning, but I doubt she was listening.'

'Girls of that age are all the same. Except you, of course, daughter.' His face clouded. 'At that age you were already at work, teaching those wretched children. I wish you *had* been slipping out in your best bonnet to meet some handsome young man.'

'Well, I do not,' she rallied him, hating to see the defeated look appear on his face again. 'For one thing, no handsome young man would have looked at me twice then, for I looked like a boy with long hair, as that nasty little Dutch girl once told me. And in any case, where would I find a man as handsome as you, or one that I could care for half as much? We do very well as we are, my dear.'

He could not but be pleased by the compliment, for he had always been a well-favoured man, and proud of his looks. He would not have it, however, that his daughter had ever been anything other than a beauty. 'For you resemble your dear mother, child,' he said with finality. Sarah, who had a looking-glass and perfectly good eyesight, could see that she was not a patch on the miniature of her mother that was her greatest treasure, but she would not argue with her father on such a subject. Sarah herself could see well enough that though her eyes were large and well spaced, fringed with thick dark lashes, her mouth was too wide for beauty, and her chin too strong to fit the submissive, helpless female face that was currently in fashion. It showed her for what she was: strong willed, decided, used to making her own decisions and acting on them. She thought herself un-fitted for marriage, for she could not imagine subordi-nating her own ideas to those of someone else. In the fullness of time, if she could find enough money, she thought she would probably open her own school some-where. She was good with children and young girls, understanding their problems and knowing when to be strict and when to use kindness. It was not, perhaps, the full and happy life she might once have hoped for, with her own home and children, but she would be indepen-dent, and useful. While her father lived, she would not be lonely, and afterwards... She refused to let her mind dwell on 'afterwards', for she could not bear to imagine it.

'Well, Miss Yarcombe did not meet her young man, for whatever reason, and I doubt whether she will have many opportunities in future. If her mama intends her to make a brilliant marriage, as I suppose she does, she will doubtless keep a close eye on her. Poor little thing, I wonder what will become of her? I hope she will be allowed to make a happy marriage, as well as a good one. I don't suppose we shall ever know, unless we see her wedding announcement in the paper. I doubt we shall ever see her again.' With this, Sarah changed the subject, and taking her work-basket, engaged herself on a piece of prosaic sewing, a new shirt for her father. He read to her, as was their custom, and presently Madeleine came in with a tray of tea. Sarah persuaded her to join them, for she was more like one of the family than a servant.

The following morning Sarah delivered the packet of lace, intact but a little grubby on the outside, to Madame Tessier's hotel. It was early, and Madame was still abed, so Sarah wrote a note of apology to wrap round the extra money from the purchase, and departed with speed. She had to be at the school by half-past eight to help to oversee breakfast. Madame Hortense met her with a face of thunder.

'I wonder, mademoiselle, that you dare to show yourself here today! Did I not expressly tell you that you were to help Madame Tessier in every possible way? And yet she tells me that when you had shown her a little of the town—which by the way she did not find impressive—you vanished off with the money and did not return for two hours! She was late leaving Bruges, through having, in her kindness, awaited your return, and then had the discomfort of doing the latter part of the journey in the dark.'

'I think Madame Tessier must, in her boredom, have felt the passing of time slower than it actually was. I can assure you, Madame, that I wasted no time in buying the lace. Madame had given me very exact instructions as to what she wished me to purchase, and as you know it is not quick work to find the best quality in the right lengths.'

Madame Hortense was not to be mollified. 'The fact remains that you kept her late at the hotel. Madame Tessier suggested that you were meeting some friend on the sly, but I assured her that this would not be the case. I trust I am correct?'

'I have been with you now for five years, madame. I cannot believe that you would really suspect such a thing.' Sarah hid her annoyance in an attitude of distress. Madame Hortense, who knew that she would not easily find an English gentlewoman who could also teach good French, and who was prepared to reside in Ostend, retreated at once.

'My dear mademoiselle, I would not have thought it for a moment. But you have not yet explained why you were, after all, so very late in returning?'

'On my way back to the hotel I met a young English girl who was being teased by a gang of boys. They would not have hurt her, I suppose, but she was very frightened, having ventured out alone and become lost while visiting the town. I could not leave her in such a plight, and accompanied her back to her residence.'

'A young girl out alone?' Madame Hortense was suspicious. 'It sounds very shocking.'

'A piece of foolishness, no more. She was returning to England after completing her education in Paris. I imagine she was eager to see a little of the country before leaving.'

'Well,' Madame was dismissive, 'I suppose you could not have done otherwise. But it was unfortunate that you upset Madame Tessier. I do not need to tell you that if she were to remove her other daughters from my care it would be a serious loss—a very serious loss. All the extras, even the harp, and never a day late with the bills! It would not do to annoy her, and you may have noticed, my dear, that she has a—a very high spirited way with her.' She paused, admiring this masterly understatement. 'Under the circumstances, it would be as well if you do not meet her. She is coming this morning to permit Adélie to say her farewells to her friends. You may take the morning off, and return in time for the afternoon's classes. Everything will be disrupted by Adélie's leaving, in any case, so there will not be much work done this morning.'

'Thank you, madame. You are most generous. I am so sorry that I have caused this trouble.' Sarah had learned that in her position it was important to show a great deal of gratitude. She made a small curtsy indicative of submission and overwhelming gratefulness, and went on her way.

'It is a half-holiday, Papa!' she announced joyfully when her father looked up in anxiety to see her returning at such an unwonted hour. 'I have been told to keep out of Madame Tessier's sight. What shall we do?' She was excited. It was rare for them to be able to spend time together during the day, for even on Sundays she was expected to help at the school, accompanying those of the young ladies who were not Catholics to the Protestant church, and supervising their activities in the afternoon.

'It is such a fine day, I think we should take a turn by the sea, like people of leisure,' she suggested. 'Should you not like that?'

He brightened and nodded.

She dropped a kiss on the top of his head as she passed. 'Then let us dress in our Sunday clothes and put everyone to shame,' she joked. 'They will wonder who such a handsome couple can be!'

They did indeed make a striking couple as they left the house a little while later. Sarah's sober walking-dress of dark blue wool was carefully fitted to her slender figure, and the skirts were spread as widely as her four petticoats could hold them. It was a little out of fashion, to be sure, but although the sleeves were tightly fitted to the wrist instead of widening, as they had begun to do, still the lace that set off her slender hands was of the finest. On such a warm day she had no need of her cloak, but threw round her shoulders a fine silk shawl that had come to her from her mother. Her father, for once holding himself to his full and impressive height, wore his neatly-brushed coat with an air, and Madeleine had polished his shoes until they could have been new. With his hat worn at a precisely fashionable angle on his still thick hair, he looked every inch the gentleman. In high good humour they made their way to the sea front.

The broad promenade was thronged with well-dressed people, tempted out by the unusual warmth of the sunshine. The cold wind of the day before had vanished, and they were able to walk slowly, enjoying the brightness of the day, and deriving much amusement from watching the people that they passed, and the antics of children and dogs on the golden sand below.

On the corner of Christinastraat they paused to admire the new Casino, just completed. While she deplored its existence, for it was a constant temptation to her father, Sarah could not but admire the handsome façade. Elegant tall windows and a pillared portico supporting a balcony were flanked at each end of the building by charming little octagonal pavilions, and every turret was surmounted by a flagpole whereon colourful pennants fluttered in the breeze, topped by a bigger flag above the central clock tower. There was no wonder, thought Sarah, that Ostend was becoming a fashionable place.

No wonder Mrs Yarcombe had chosen to begin her daughter's assault on the bastions of society here.

She was just voicing the thought to her father when she heard herself hailed by the very person of whom they spoke.

'Miss Northcott? It is Miss Northcott, isn't it? I thought I could not be mistaken.'

Emily Yarcombe was approaching, with signs of genuine pleasure, and behind her a handsome woman, obviously her mother, was smiling and giving her a stately inclination of the head.

Sarah was surprised. 'Miss Yarcombe! I had not expected to see you here. When did you arrive in Ostend? May I present my father to you? Mr Matthew Northcott. Papa, this is Miss Yarcombe, of whom I told you last evening.'

'How do you do, Mr Northcott? Oh, Miss Northcott, we came here the first thing this morning. Mama would so much like to meet you. She is so grateful to you for helping me!' Correctly interpreting Sarah's enquiring glance, she added, in a lower voice, 'She was in my chamber when I returned, and I told her how very kind you were to me.'

Emily was as finely dressed as before, Sarah noticed, and Mrs Northcott, though still in mourning, also presented an elegant and fashionable appearance to the world. Her dress, though black, was of the finest silk. Sarah reflected that she could well have abandoned black, after two years of widowhood, and moved into grey, or lavender. Then she saw how well the darker colour set off Mrs Yarcombe's still fine skin and determinedly golden hair.

At Emily's words her mother approached, offering her hand with the utmost graciousness.

'My dear Miss Northcott!' Only the most critical observer would have noticed the faint coarsening of the vowels in her carefully cultivated voice. 'I have longed to meet you, to thank you for your care of this silly girl of mine. To be going out alone, and in Bruges of all places, where there are so many unemployed, idle persons! A very lucky girl she is, that no harm came to her, and so I told her. But there! We can't expect old heads on young shoulders, as the saying goes. Accept a mother's heartfelt gratitude, Miss Northcott.' She pressed Sarah's hand warmly, and surged irresistibly forward. 'Will you not present me to your father, my dear? He must be proud to have such a brave, noble daughter!'

Torn between amusement and embarrassment, Sarah presented her father. He bowed over her hand and, since she seemed to expect it, raised it to his lips in the continental fashion. To Sarah's amazement, and Emily's too by the look on her face, she gave what in a less stately person could only have been described as a giggle.

'Why, Mr Northcott, how very gallant!' she almost simpered. 'I declare that you make me feel quite young again! I have lived so very retired, since my poor husband died, that I am quite unused to such things!'

He followed her lead and complimented her boldly on her youthful appearance, rallying her that if it were not that her daughter's beauty so resembled her own he would never have believed it possible that she could be the mother of so grown up a young lady. She was clearly delighted, raising a tightly-gloved hand to her cheek to indicate the blushes that she obviously hoped were there.

'Mr Northcott, you shouldn't say such things to me, you shouldn't really. Of course I was very young when I was married to Mr Yarcombe, hardly out of the schoolroom, you know, but that was long ago. I have no thought of my own appearance now.'

Emily stared, and stifled a giggle. Sarah frowned slightly. She could not understand why this rich and formidable lady was making such a blatant attempt to flirt with her father who, though she loved him dearly, was not in the least the sort of man she thought Mrs Northcott would usually choose to favour.

If he was surprised, he concealed it, and offered his arm to his new acquaintance. 'May I be so bold as to request the indulgence of a stroll together? It is a long time since I have had the pleasure of the company of three attractive ladies at one time.'

Sarah thought that if Mrs Yarcombe had carried a fan she would have hidden her face behind it, or playfully tapped him with it. As it was, she simpered again and laid her hand on his arm. They continued their walk. Sarah and Emily walked behind, and conversed in low tones.

'I am glad your mama was not angry with you when she found you had been out on your own.'

'Oh, but she was—very angry. She thought I had been out to meet somebody, because I had put on my best bonnet.' Sarah, who had thought the same, said nothing, but gave her a quizzical look. Emily blushed. 'Well, I suppose I had, in a way. At least, nothing was arranged, but I knew he was in Bruges, and I just hoped... But I did not see him, so it was to no avail.'

'Who is he? I suppose your mama does not approve of him?'

'Well, she doesn't know about him, but I expect she would not, for he is a younger son. His sister was a particular friend of mine at the school in Paris, and he is spending a few months travelling abroad because he goes into the army.'

'You had made no actual assignation, then? I am glad to hear it. It is not at all the thing, you know. If he thinks seriously of you, he would not consent to such clandestine behaviour.'

Emily pouted. 'You sound like the teachers at school, and Mama.'

'Well, I am a teacher. Your mama really does know best, in this instance. You should be guided by her in such matters.'

'But it's so stuffy! And so is he, for he would not meet me in Paris, or in Bruges, though he knew I was going there. He says he is too poor to think of matrimony. As if I cared for that! Why, Papa left me simply pots of money! We are very rich, you know.'

'I do, but you should not talk so,' said Sarah repressively.

'Why not, if it is true?'

'Because it is vulgar, and people will not like it,' said Sarah firmly, feeling every minute more and more middle-aged.

'Oh, pooh! I don't care for that. Papa was vulgar, and he was the best person I ever knew. Why pretend? I'm not well born, so why should I try to fool people that I am? They know I'm not, anyway,' she finished shrewdly. 'If they don't like me as I am, that's too bad.

It's better than having everyone pretend to like me, because I'm rich.'

Sarah pondered. 'Though you may not be a lady by birth, you may be one by behaviour,' she said finally. 'I do not remember my own mama at all well. As I told you, she was Italian, and though her father was from the aristocracy she was not——' she paused, '——not legitimate. She was brought up in the country, very simply, yet from what Papa has told me, she was most truly a lady. You are what you make of yourself,' she finished earnestly.

Emily gazed at her, wide-eyed. 'How romantic!' she breathed, with tears in her eyes. 'Thank you for telling me.' She was thoughtful for a while, then returned doggedly to her previous contention. 'I still don't see why I may not marry—him—since I have enough money for both of us.'

'A man has his pride,' explained Sarah gently. 'He might not wish to live only on his wife's money, and be thought a fortune-hunter. And,' she added firmly, 'he might not wish to marry someone who constantly talks about how rich she is!'

'I had not thought of that!' exclaimed Emily, much struck. 'From now on, I shall take care not to speak of it!'

Sarah could only hope that her lesson would be heeded.

CHAPTER FOUR

AT THE END of half an hour's strolling, when Mrs Yarcombe showed no signs of wishing to separate, Mr Northcott proposed that they should visit a nearby establishment for a cup of chocolate, and perhaps some of the sugared waffles that the town was famous for. Mrs Yarcombe seemed pleased, and once again Sarah wondered why. She was not deceived by the fluttering exterior that Mrs Yarcombe was presenting, for she had more than once seen a look of cold calculation in those blue eyes. It was beyond her to imagine what use they, an impoverished couple with no connexions at all but a family who refused to acknowledge them, could be to the wealthy Yarcombes. She ceased to worry, however, when her father took the opportunity of mother and daughter speaking together to give Sarah the ghost of a wink, and a droll look.

The chocolate and the waffles were enjoyed amid an atmosphere of cheerful badinage, and the party broke up only when Sarah declared that she must positively return home and prepare for school in the afternoon. They parted with many protestations of pleasure and, on the lady's side, strong hints that the walk should be repeated, and that they should all meet again in the near future.

Sarah could not risk being late for school, and they walked home too fast for any conversation to be poss-

ible. At the end of the day, she was scarcely inside the
door before she began to question her father.

'If she were not a widow, Papa, one would have said
that she was flirting with you!'

'Yes, she was, wasn't she?' he responded com-
placently. 'One could almost have said she was throwing
herself at me.'

'But, Papa, why? Whatever does she want from us?'

'I have no idea, but it is certainly most entertaining.
Never has anyone, even you, my dear, so hung on my
every word. She treated my lightest pronouncements as
if they were graven in stone, and the merest pleasantry
was accorded as much laughter as if it were wit incar-
nate. It was quite extraordinary.'

'I do not trust her, Papa.'

'No more do I, but I own I cannot resist repeating the
experience. I shall give her a day to cool off, and then
I shall invite her to take tea with me in the afternoon.
And the daughter, of course. Maybe I shall find out what
she is after. I do not think she is clever enough to hide
her purposes completely. Besides, she is an attractive
woman, in her way.'

Sarah had her misgivings, but she could not deny her
father the chance of enjoying himself. He certainly did.
Afternoon tea was succeeded by luncheons, dinners, and
even, to her horror, a visit to the Casino.

'You need not worry, my dear, I did not place a single
bet. I advised the lady on hers. And, wouldn't you know
it, she had the devil's own luck!' Mrs Yarcombe paid
for all these little outings, Sarah heard, in the most discreet manner possible. 'She calls it a recompense for your
help with her daughter,' he said airily.

At the end of a fortnight, he was less amused. 'Dash it all, Sarah, this is more serious than I had thought. She's started to drop hints. I think she means to marry me!'

'Are you sure, Papa? I admit she does seem to have been pursuing you, but it seems so...so unlikely. I mean,' she amended hastily as he looked a little offended, 'she seems to have formed the idea before she had even met you. I was sure she was coming to Ostend to meet people who would be useful to her when she takes Emily to London. But how could we be useful to her? We have not set foot in England for years.'

'I've half a mind to put the question to her, and see what happens.'

'Papa, you would not, would you? Have you formed an attachment to her?'

'I could never love another woman as I loved your mama, my dear child. But at my time of life, you know, a man does not look for romance in marriage.'

'But even so, Papa, I am convinced that she would not continue to be so pleasant.'

'Very probably not. But we should live comfortably, and you would be able to leave that wretched woman's school and take your place in society, as I have always wanted you to do.'

'I do not think of that, Papa. Indeed, I am perfectly happy living as we do. I do not wish for a different life. Do not take such a rash step for my sake, I beg of you.'

He looked obstinate, and her heart sank, for she had never been able to move him when that closed look came over his face.

'You must allow me to do what I think best for both of us, Sarah. I know that there have been times when I have been a burden to you,' he waved away her quick disclaimer, 'but for this once I am trying to think of *our* future, yours and mine. Whatever you may say, I cannot believe that you want to spend the rest of your life drudging for other people's children. And as for me, I am getting tired. I was not brought up to live like this. When you are young, it is different: you do not notice the discomfort, or worry about the next meal. But now I am older, I do not want to die in this place and leave you alone. If by marrying this woman I can win some comfort for my last years, and some security for your future, I do not grudge it. And I would see that she did not regret it, either. I have come to know her a great deal better than you in the last weeks. She has many good qualities, and there is no doubt that she is devoted to Emily. Since Emily is disposed to like you, I see no reason why her mama should not be prepared to treat you well.'

She had never heard him speak like this, and was alarmed. 'Papa! You are not ill, are you?'

He reassured her. 'On the contrary, I have not felt so well in a long time. I suppose I had forgotten, until these last two weeks, how very pleasant it is to take good food for granted, and servants, and comfort. Do not look like that! I am not complaining, and I know how hard you work, and how much you do to keep this little home of ours pleasant. But there is another world out there, Sarah, one that I was born and brought up to, and to which I belong. I would like you to know that world, too, while you are still young.'

Sarah was not convinced, but she still could not believe that Mrs Yarcombe was actually serious. She herself was not present at their meetings, for she had to be at school all day and knew only what her father told her. Once, on a Sunday afternoon, she was given a few hours off, and she accompanied her father to take tea with the Yarcombes at their hotel.

November had set in with a vengeance, and Sarah had to appreciate the comfort of the warm rooms and blazing fires as they came in, cold and damp from their walk. She sank into the softness of a well-upholstered armchair, and watched in amazement as her father, quite at home, ordered cakes, and Mrs Yarcombe smiled coyly over the teapot.

Afterwards Emily took Sarah off to her room to show her, at Mrs Yarcombe's suggestion, some of the clothes they had purchased in Paris.

Sarah admired, and praised, and even tried on a bonnet, but her heart was not in it. At length she blurted out, 'Miss Yarcombe, what is happening here? Why is your mama so friendly to us?'

'Oh, will you not call me Emily, and let me call you Sarah? For I think—do not you?—that the time may soon come when we may call one another sister!'

'It is so, then?' Sarah was still amazed. 'I cannot understand it. Forgive me, Emily, but I had not thought that your mama was the kind of woman to wish to marry a man like Papa. Do not misunderstand me—he is the dearest person in the world, and any woman would be proud to wed him, I think—but he is poor, and without friends in the world. Your mama must know this. Yet she seemed decided on him from the very first moment they met.'

'Oh, yes, and even before,' responded Emily blithely. 'The moment I told Mama your name, she said we should come to Ostend at once. And until that moment, forgive me, Sarah, but she had been saying that you would want money from her, and had only helped me for a reward. I told her it was not so, of course, but she said I was simple, and was so very angry that I was quite frightened. Mama can be very—very alarming, you know, and I had scarcely seen her for a year, while I was in Paris.

'So it was the name, then. How very curious,' Sarah mused. 'For I do not scruple to tell you, Emily, that though it is a proud name, and an old one, we have been quite cast off by my father's family. Papa was too proud to accept help from his friends, and after his marriage he lived entirely abroad. We only visited London once, after Mama died, and there was a worse quarrel than ever. There has been no word from them, or to them, from that day to this.'

'It is all very romantic,' remarked Emily happily. 'However, I expect Mama knows what she is about. She usually does. Shall you mind it, Sarah?'

'I hardly know. I have known no other life but this, and I have never expected anything to change. I cannot imagine how it would be.'

'Well, I think it will be lovely. Your papa is a great dear, and so kind, and I am sure I love you already quite as if you were my own sister. What fun it will be! You will be able to tell me how to go on, and teach me how to behave, and Mama, perhaps, will be too busy to bother us.'

'I am hardly the person to teach you how to behave, my dear. I am glad you want me for a sister, and I hope I shall always love and care for you as a sister should. But you must not take your pattern from me.'

'Well, whatever you say, you are a lady,' said Emily firmly. 'And so I told Mama, when she said you wanted her money. I think it will be famous. We shall go to balls, and the theatre, and everywhere. How fortunate that you are not blonde, too!' she finished naïvely. Sarah laughed.

'I certainly make an admirable foil to you, though you make me feel like a beanpole. But maybe you are romancing, and it will never happen.'

'Oh, I think it will. Mama is quite decided on it, and she always gets her way.'

It seemed that Emily was right. When they returned to the private parlour where their respective parents were, Mrs Yarcombe surged to her feet and came to them, her face wreathed in smiles.

'My child! My Emily! How can I find words to tell you of the great happiness that has befallen us. Behold—your new Papa!' As Emily ran forward to kiss him and exclaim over him, Mrs Yarcombe turned to Sarah. The smile remained fixed to her lips, but her eyes were cold and wary. 'And Sarah, my new daughter! What a joy to call you by that name.' Their eyes met. There was a momentary pause, unnoticed by the other two, then she leaned forward and offered her cheek to be kissed. Sarah touched the discreetly powdered surface with her lips, and mechanically offered her good wishes. The moment passed, and the room was full of bustle and chatter, but

Sarah could not forget the calculating look she had seen in those blue eyes.

The marriage, it seemed, was to take place as soon as possible. Now that it was settled, some of the coy flirtatiousness vanished from Mrs Yarcombe's manner and a hint of steel began to show. Sarah and her father found themselves being hustled. New clothes were the first necessity, for Mr Northcott and, as somewhat of an afterthought, for Sarah. She, reluctant in any case to accept too much from this woman whom she found herself unable to call Mama, discovered that she did not have to refuse very hard. One or two serviceable day dresses and a simple evening dress were all that she took. For the rest, Mrs Yarcombe offered some of her own dresses, from before her widowhood, to be made over.

'I understand your feelings, Sarah, and they do you credit,' she said in her most stately manner. 'You do not wish to be beholden, and in your situation there is really not much need for too much finery. At your age you can scarcely be expecting to make a come-out, like my little Emily.' She fixed Sarah with a gimlet eye as she spoke, and Sarah agreed meekly. She was bewildered by the speed at which events were happening, and in any case she truly was not much interested in cutting a dash in society.

In what seemed to Sarah a miraculously short space of time a special licence was procured, an Anglican divine found, and in a quiet ceremony attended only by their two daughters, Augusta Yarcombe and the Honourable Matthew Northcott were made man and wife.

Only one battle had marred the preparations for the wedding. It concerned Madeleine. Mrs Yarcombe had said that she had servants enough, and that she could see no need for Sarah to have her own maid when she could perfectly well share Emily's. Sarah as stubbornly insisted that she would not be parted from Madeleine. A stalemate was reached, broken by Emily, who informed her mama that she did not like her French maid. Mrs Yarcombe's objections were silenced when Emily was able to show that the girl had been pilfering from her. The maid was dismissed without a reference, and Mrs Yarcombe reluctantly agreed to keep Madeleine on to look after both girls. Sarah proudly offered to pay her old servant herself.

'With what, pray? My own money, I suppose?' said Mrs Yarcombe disagreeably. She had eventually agreed to allow Mr Northcott to make his daughter an allowance out of the money he would have from her. Sarah, who had some of her wages saved up, privately determined to pay Madeleine herself while this lasted, and to find some means of earning some more when it finished.

After the wedding it was decided that they should stay only two days in Ostend before proceeding to Paris and thence to Italy for the wedding trip. Sarah was pleased, for she had always longed to visit her mother's country. It was with disappointment, therefore, that she came down to breakfast on the morning they were due to leave and learned that they would, instead, be returning directly to England. Her father, looking very pale, was reading and re-reading a short official-looking letter, and her stepmother was looking triumphant.

'What is it, Papa? What has happened?'

Silently he held out the letter to her. On expensive paper, it was headed Abercrombie, Crouch and Abercrombie, Solicitors. She read:

> Dear Sir,
>
> It is with regret that we have to inform you of the death of your brother, the Honourable Henry Northcott. Your father, Lord Northcott, is very ill. If you wish to see your father alive, you should return at once. Lord Northcott has expressed a wish to see you again.
>
> We beg to remain, Sir, your very obedient servants.

The signature was illegible.

Sarah looked at her father. 'Oh, Papa, I am so sorry! Shall you go?'

'I must,' he said simply. 'We shall leave at once. It is fortunate that we had not yet departed for Paris.'

Sarah looked again at Mrs Northcott, whose face still held a look of satisfaction. She spoke her thoughts aloud. 'If my grandfather should die, Papa will be Lord Northcott of Northcott Hall, unless... Papa, has your brother any children?'

Mr Northcott looked up absently. 'Children? No. That is, his wife had two daughters, but they both died in infancy, and she herself was killed on the hunting field, I believe.' He returned to his letter, oblivious of his surroundings.

Sarah turned to her stepmother. 'Did you know of this?'

'Of course I did. Why else do you think I would marry a man in your father's position? I have a friend in Norfolk, not far from Northcott Hall. She told me that Henry Northcott had married to please his parents, but that the marriage was unhappy and he was drinking to excess. The family tried to hush it up, but it was common knowledge in the village that he was drinking himself to death.'

Sarah's lip curled. 'Servants' gossip. No wonder you were in such a hurry to tie the knot! As a Northcott of Northcott Hall you would not have found him so easy.' She spoke from the bitterness of her heart.

A flush of anger stained Mrs Northcott's cheeks an unbecoming brick red. 'Northcott of Northcott Hall he may be,' she snapped, 'but it's me that holds the purse-strings, and so I'll thank you to remember, miss.' They glared at one another, completely ignored by Sarah's father, who continued to stare unseeingly at his letter. Emily looked, appalled, from one to the other of them. Her shocked gaze recalled Sarah to herself.

'I beg your pardon, ma'am,' she said stiffly. 'I am afraid that the shock made me forget my manners.'

'For your father's sake, I accept your apology,' was the equally stiff reply.

Looking at her, Sarah knew that there would be nothing but war between them in future. Going to her father, she gently removed the letter, and took his arm. 'Come, Papa, we must make ready to leave. There is a boat quite soon, I think, and we must not miss it.' Still talking softly to him, she led him from the room.

Emily looked at her mother. 'Did you really know all of this, Mama?' she asked.

'Of course I did, you ninny! Weren't you listening?' She walked to the looking-glass over the fireplace and looked at herself, smoothing her hair.

'Lady Northcott,' she said musingly. 'Lady Northcott of Northcott Hall. I think that will do very well.'

CHAPTER FIVE

THE JOURNEY was a nightmare. The voyage, on a sea that was far from calm, seemed interminable. The ship hugged the French coast until they came almost to Calais, and then made the crossing at the narrowest place. Even so, the motion of the ship seemed terrifying to the three women. They lay in their cabin, and Sarah, who was sure that she would have been better out in the fresh air with her father, was forced to remain, for Emily seemed really very ill, her slight form racked by ceaseless nausea and her head spinning. When at last they reached Dover, they were all exhausted, and it was as much as they could do to crawl into bed in the first hotel they found.

A night's sleep, however, did much to restore them, although Emily still looked pale and Sarah owned to a headache. The train journey to London was accomplished in silence, and Mr Northcott waited only to see his new family safely to a hotel before taking a cab to the offices of Abercrombie, Crouch and Abercrombie. Emily and her mother retired at once to bed, but Sarah could not rest until she had heard what her father had to say. It was two hours before he returned.

'It is all too true,' he said in answer to her anxious enquiry. 'My father is a little improved, but he is still very ill. The shock of my brother's death brought on a heart attack. Henry was always his favourite. He put all his hopes on him, for I was always wild and disobedient.

Henry married to please him, and look what happened! She spent all their money on horses, they had no living children, and in the end he started to drink. Abercrombie was quite open with me on the subject, for he has been the family's solicitor since I don't know when. They managed to keep Henry's condition from my father for a while, but it was not possible to do so for long. Poor Father, it is a sad disappointment for him. It almost makes me glad that my mother died when we were young, though maybe things would have been different had she not.'

'What will you do?'

'I must journey down there at once, as soon as may be. Abercrombie says my father has wanted for years to make his peace with me, but he was too proud to admit he had been wrong. Poor Father! If we had been better friends when I was younger...but I suppose it was not in him. I cannot but pity him. My life has not always been happy, but at least I have a daughter I can be proud of!'

'And a wife, Papa,' reminded Sarah.

'Good heavens, yes, I had almost forgotten! What is to be done? It is too much to expect him to receive a whole new family just yet. I must see him on my own first. I want to make it quite clear that I expect my daughter to be greeted with all the respect that is due to her.' For the first time ever, Sarah saw a look of firmness and determination, as opposed to obstinacy, on her father's face. Always before, it had been she who made the decisions. Now it seemed that she need no longer do so. 'You three must stay in London,' he continued. 'I believe Mrs—that is, your stepmama—wishes to take a house. She wants to take Emily into society as soon as may be, and I think she had best do so. If my father should die—and it seems all too possible that he might— we should all have to go into mourning, and that would delay you. Emily can afford to wait, but you should make your curtsy to the polite world as soon as may be.'

'Yes, Papa.' Sarah's voice was unwontedly meek. There was no point in telling this new, managing father that she had little wish to make her curtsy to society. In time, she supposed, she might be permitted to remove to Northcott Hall, where she thought she could make herself tolerably useful and happy. The new Mrs Northcott would certainly welcome her departure, of that she was quite sure.

He was gone within half an hour, leaving only a word of farewell for his new wife and daughter. Mrs Northcott could not be said to have been desolated by his absence. With her usual energy she inspected houses, and within three days had them installed in a commodious establishment in Mount Street. The following evening found them at the Opera. Well aware that she might have but a short time to launch her daughter before Lord Northcott's death made it ineligible for them to attend any but the quietest of functions, she was determined to make her mark. A box was engaged, mother and daughter arrayed themselves in all their Paris finery, and even Sarah was persuaded to borrow a demure string of pearls from Emily.

'I do not want people to think that you are neglected, my dear,' Mrs Northcott said with a vinegary smile. She nodded with approval at Sarah's evening dress of dove-grey silk, cut less low over the shoulders then Emily's,

and trimmed only with narrow bands of ribbon. Emily
was enchanting in white tiffany, the bertha and the
floating skirt trimmed with rows of lace and little clusters
of white silk rosebuds. Fresh rosebuds were set in her
hair, and diamonds flashed from her neck and wrists.

Sarah frowned. 'Are you not a little young to be
wearing those, Emily dear?' she asked gently.

Her stepmother bridled. 'Nonsense! Of course she
should wear them. What is the point of having them,
otherwise? We're not in Ostend now, and I'll have none
of your shabby provincial ways, miss.'

Emily looked worried, but said nothing. Sarah bit her
lip and did likewise, and the journey to Covent Garden
was accomplished in silence. As they took their seats in
the box, Mrs Northcott looked round the assembled
company and took care to point out to Emily that there
were many ladies present wearing diamonds, though
none, as far as she could see, as fine as hers. Sarah refrained from pointing out that all these ladies were of
mature years, and that the other young girls were less
vulgarly bedecked.

They had arrived in good time, for Mrs Northcott's
aim was to see and to be seen. She scanned the other
boxes with anxious attention, waving occasionally so that
people should think that she knew somebody. At length
her careful vigil was rewarded. As new arrivals entered
a box not far away, she looked closely at them, and
stiffened with excitement.

'Why, I do believe that is Lady Esher! You may remember me telling you, my dear, that your papa and I
met her, once, at the Assembly Rooms in Harrogate. A
charming woman, simply charming!' She set herself to

waving, bowing and smiling so many times in the direction of Lady Esher's box that that lady finally noticed her, and gave a bewildered smile and bow in return.

'You see! I thought she would not have forgotten me, for I am sure we must have talked for all of ten minutes at the Ball! Emily, my dear, we must be sure to pay our respects in the interval.'

Sure enough, at the end of the first act, Mrs Northcott was on her feet, her eyes fixed on Lady Esher's box.

'See, they are leaving their box, they are coming out. Quickly, my dear, we must not miss them!' In high excitement she pulled Emily to her feet, and with Sarah trailing dutifully behind, managed to intercept the other party in the corridor.

'My dear Lady Esher! What a pleasant surprise! Can I hope that your ladyship remembers me—it is some time since our last meeting in Harrogate?'

Lady Esher looked blank for a moment, but quickly covered her confusion with practised social ease. 'But of course! Harrogate, to be sure! You must forgive me if the name escapes me just for the moment; my memory, you know...'

'Mrs Yarcombe, your ladyship, as I was then. But your ladyship is not to know...' she gave an affected laugh, 'that I am but recently married, and my name is now Northcott!'

Lady Esher was startled. 'Northcott? But I thought Henry Northcott died some time ago?'

'Ah, your ladyship is referring to my poor late brother-in-law. I am Mrs Matthew Northcott. Mr Northcott and I were married only the week before last, abroad, before he had heard of his brother's demise. My husband is at

present at Northcott Hall, with his father Lord
Northcott. I am left with my two girls. Emily, Sarah,
make your curtsies to our good friend!'

The girls were introduced. Lady Esher's good-natured
indolence was no match for Mrs Northcott's determined
assault. Weakly she introduced her friend Mrs
Abbotsleigh, who was with her son Andrew, and the
whole party walked on together. Sarah was mortified by
her stepmother, whose conversation was liberally
sprinkled with references to 'my poor father-in-law, Lord
Northcott', and 'Northcott Hall'. Sarah walked quietly
behind them, and Mrs Abbotsleigh turned to her.

'You do not go into mourning for your uncle, Miss
Northcott?'

Sarah put up her chin. 'Under the circumstances,
ma'am, I do not at present go into full mourning. I never
met Mr Henry Northcott, and he was no friend to my
father or to myself. I shall follow my father's wishes on
the subject, and if he tells me to go into black, I shall
do so. Until then, as you see, I intend to keep to half
mourning shades.'

To her surprise, Mrs Abbotsleigh nodded in approval.
'I am sure you are quite right, Miss Northcott.' Sarah
was surprised, for the acidulous tones had quite vanished from Mrs Abbotsleigh's voice. She was watching
in some approval as her son Andrew, a tall, spindly man,
chatted to Emily. 'Miss Yarcombe is the daughter of the
late Jeremiah Yarcombe, is she not?' Sarah assented.
'An only child?' pursued Mrs Abbotsleigh, eyeing the
clear sparkle of the fine diamond necklace that Emily
wore.

'Yes, and I believe he doted on her,' said Sarah innocently, and smiled to see Mrs Abbotsleigh's nod of satisfaction.

'You must come to a little party I am giving tomorrow night,' said Mrs Abbotsleigh decidedly. 'Quite small, just a few friends, you know, and a little dancing for you young people! I shall send a card to your stepmother in the morning.'

'Thank you, I am sure my sister and her mama will be delighted to accept,' said Sarah. 'I am not sure whether I... I am waiting to hear from Papa. It may be that he will want me to join him.'

Mrs Abbotsleigh made civil but insincere protestations of regret. Her son was a young man of expensive tastes, and she was not a wealthy woman. A fortune, wherever it came from, was not lightly to be passed over, and she was determined that Andrew should have a good chance of gaining it before the girl's pretty face attracted other suitors. She decided to have a word with her son before he left, as was his wont, to join his cronies for the night's gambling session.

Mrs Northcott was delighted with the success of her evening. As they drove home, while Emily and Sarah stifled yawns, she could talk of nothing but Lady Esher, Mrs Abbotsleigh and the delights to come.

No word came from Northcott Hall the following day, and the invitation from Mrs Abbotsleigh duly arrived. Sarah would have preferred not to attend, but Emily looked so disappointed that she had not the heart to refuse. To Emily's disapproval she insisted on wearing the same grey gown she had worn the night before, though she did allow her to embellish it with a few of

the hothouse flowers that had arrived from Andrew
Abbotsleigh (at his mother's suggestion) late in the
afternoon. Emily tucked a cluster of white gardenias into
the heavy chignon of Sarah's hair.

'There, you look very elegant. Oh, Sarah, think, our
first party!'

She herself looked ravishing in white lustring. Sarah
reflected how wise her stepmother was to dress Emily in
white. Not only was it most appropriate for her youth,
and the bereavement in the family, but it suited her. Not
many young girls could wear white, but Emily's bright
hair and pretty colouring glowed against the shim-
mering paper-fine fabric.

Mrs Abbotsleigh's 'small party' turned out to be much
grander than they had expected. Nearly a hundred people
crammed the rooms. Emily looked intimidated as they
arrived, but as she soon found that young men were
queueing up to ask her to dance, she was soon happy.
Sarah danced once or twice, but did not enjoy it. She
was aware that her partners for the most part found her
disconcertingly tall, and that in general they asked her
only because they were unable to get near Emily. She
was unfamiliar with the events and affairs that preoccupied the London set, and knew that her conversation
was stilted and dull. At last she took refuge in a quiet
corner behind a large arrangement of plants, from where
she could keep an eye on Emily, lest the pleasure of
finding herself all the rage at her very first party should
lead her into unbecoming behaviour. Mrs Northcott was
collecting new acquaintances as fast as she could, so as
to transform them into old and dear friends overnight.

Half hidden behind the foliage, Sarah relaxed and allowed herself to enjoy the spectacle.

She was pleased to see that Emily was a success, not only with the gentlemen, but with the mamas as well. Though her background might be vulgar, she had been carefully taught, and she was neither over-shy nor disagreeably pert. She smiled impartially on all her partners, handsome or plain, and Sarah noticed that she showed no inclination to flirt with any of them, and in fact showed plainly in her manner that she did not care to be made love to. Sarah heard her called a very prettily behaved girl and was satisfied, reflecting that Mrs Northcott might well have cause to thank the unknown second son who seemed to have stolen her daughter's heart.

'Not a wallflower, surely, Miss Northcott? Or do you disapprove of dancing? Perhaps you are setting up as a Quaker.'

The mocking tones made her jump, but after one start, she turned and spoke calmly enough. 'Lord St Ervan! I had no idea I should meet you here.'

'Why should you? I am surprised to find myself here. Someone told me there was a new beauty, fabulously rich, invited this evening, and I came to cast my eyes over her. I expect rumour has lied. It is too much to hope that she can be both rich and beautiful. In my experience, life is seldom so generous.' His dark eyes passed lazily over the throng of dancers.

'I would be grateful, my lord, if you would not refer to my sister in those terms!'

'Your sister? How does this come about? I thought you didn't know the girl. Come, we shall attract attention if we hide in this corner. We shall dance, and you may tell me all about it. It is thanks to your new sister, I believe, that I find you here? I had not thought to see you in London.'

'Thank you, Lord St Ervan, but I do not care to dance.'

'Do you not? Didn't they teach dancing at that school of yours?'

'Of course they did. But I am too tall to dance gracefully, and besides . . .'

'Too tall? Nonsense. I dare say you are taller than some of the fellows here—did you dance with some of them? But you are not taller than I. Besides, what?'

She laughed, her ready sense of humour getting the better of her. 'Besides, being so tall, I was always called upon to take the man's part in dancing lessons.'

He gave a shout of laughter. 'So you tried to lead? Well, you shall have no chance of leading me!'

'I fancy no one has ever been able to do that, my lord,' she retorted drily.

'No woman, certainly,' he returned carelessly.

He swept her into the dance, and after a momentary embarrassment she found that in his firm clasp she soon forgot her school habits. She was quite in charity with him, until he once again annoyed her by asking about Emily.

'I hear the mother is a dragon, and odiously pushing besides,' he remarked in a conversational voice. 'How do you get on with her? She got her claws into your father, I suppose, before he knew he was likely to inherit the title after all. Lucky for her!'

'You should not speak to me like that of my stepmother.'

'Why not? Isn't it true?'

'Even if it were, how could I possibly say so, to you or to anyone?'

'You disappoint me. I had thought you always said what was on your mind. You were more amusing in Bruges.'

'It may surprise you to hear, my lord, that amusing you is not high on my list of priorities. In fact, it does not appear at all.'

Her voice had risen. His eyes glinted as he looked down at her.

'You should not quarrel on the dance-floor, you know. It is not at all convenable. I venture to give you the hint,' he said kindly, 'as I assume you are just now making your début. How do you find London? Abominably dull, isn't it?'

'When I need to mend my manners, I shall not turn to you for guidance, my lord, for you are the rudest man I ever met! Kindly allow me to return to my stepmother!'

'Oh, I don't think she would welcome you, you know. She is talking to a Duchess, no less. She looks like a cat surrounded by bowls and bowls of cream.'

She bit her lip to keep back a smile, acknowledging the truth of this observation. His arm tightened momentarily round her waist as he swept her into a swift turn, and she thought that she had never known before that dancing could be such a pleasure.

'I do not know why it is that you say such things to me. Why do you make me angry?'

'Call it perversity, if you like,' he replied. 'There is a flash in your eyes, like lightning, when you are angry. I have always preferred thunderstorms to calm, still days.'

'Well, I do not! I have always known that, to some men, women are no more than playthings. But I decline to dance to your piping, my lord. I will not converse with you, even if you will insist on dancing with me.'

'Then let us take a cup of tea. I saw the trays being taken through just now. That might refresh you for another round.'

'There will be no more storms, my lord. Not even in a teacup,' retorted Sarah triumphantly. He flung up his hand in a fencer's acknowledgment of a hit, and in some good humour she allowed him to lead her to the tea-tables.

CHAPTER SIX

'MY DEAREST Sarah, I have been looking everywhere for you! I saw you dancing while I was talking to the dear Duchess—such a delightful woman—and I do not believe I am acquainted with your partner. So remiss of me! Your papa would say I am neglecting you!'

Sarah, who thought that her father was highly unlikely to say anything of the sort, bowed to the inevitable and introduced the Marquis. He bowed over her hand.

'Mrs Northcott,' he drawled in the deceptively lazy voice that Sarah had learned to distrust, 'you must allow me to felicitate you on your recent marriage.' She simpered, but her smile slipped as he continued, 'And so fortunately timed! One would have almost thought... But you could not have known, of course. How foolish of me. It was quite a sudden romance, I suppose?'

Well aware of listening ears ever on the lookout for a breath of scandal, Mrs Northcott was forced to bite back the angry reply that was on the tip of her tongue. 'Was it not a strange chance! You must know, Lord St Ervan, that I had been abroad for some weeks, and before that, as a widow, I lived very retired. I was quite out of touch with what was going on in the world. Naturally I did not wish to marry in such haste, but Mr Northcott was quite insistent, there was no saying him nay!' She gave Sarah a gimlet glance, daring her to deny it. Sarah, torn between amusement and shame, said nothing.

At that moment Emily, flushed with dancing and success, was brought by her partner to rejoin her mother at the end of the dance. Mrs Northcott seized on the opportunity to change the subject.

'Lord St Ervan, may I present my daughter to you? Emily is just returned from Paris, my lord, and is just now beginning to go about in society. Emily, my love, this is the Marquis of Berrington.'

'I am enchanted, Miss Yarcombe.' At the sound of his voice she started, and paled. As if to tease her, he continued, 'I believe we have already met, have we not?' Two pairs of reproachful eyes were turned on him, and he relented. 'But no, of course, I must be mistaken. It is impossible that we should have met, and now I come to think of it, the young lady I was thinking of was not quite the thing, though I should not be mentioning it to you.' He looked blandly at Mrs Northcott, who was eyeing him suspiciously. 'I am afraid she was no better than she should be,' he added in a low, confidential tone.

Mrs Northcott did not know whether to look interested or offended, and her daughter blushed scarlet. 'Then I am sure it was not my Emily,' she announced in affronted tones. 'She has been most strictly brought up. I beg you will not mention such things in front of her, my lord.'

'My dear Mrs Northcott! How could you think I meant...I am sure both the young ladies are patterns of propriety,' he responded earnestly. Sarah gritted her teeth. 'Miss Northcott, show you have forgiven me, and grant me the honour of this dance.'

'I regret, my lord, that I am unable to do so. Being a pattern of propriety, I am well aware that it is not at all correct to dance with the same gentleman twice in succession, and you have already done me the honour of taking me on to the floor. But here is my sister, partnerless for once!'

He had no choice but to turn to Emily and repeat his request. Looking rather alarmed, she would rather have made her excuses, but a sharp nudge from her mother changed her mind. They were soon to be seen revolving rather silently together.

Mrs Northcott followed them with an assessing eye. 'What a very strange man! I thought at first he was about to say something very impertinent. But a Marquis, after all...' She sank for a moment into a rosy dream, then roused herself to practicality. 'Has he any money, I wonder? Not that it signifies, precisely, but I should not like it if he were in debt. Or,' she turned horrified eyes on Sarah, 'if he were married! Tell me at once, Sarah, is there a Marchioness?'

Sarah was amused. 'I have not the least idea, ma'am! That is to say, he did not mention a wife. I cannot imagine that anyone would consent to marry him, for I think him quite odious.'

'But Sarah, he is a Marquis! Besides, you were talking with him for some time, and he approached you quite as if he knew you. I thought you must have met him before.'

'I did meet him once, in Belgium,' said Sarah with careful truth, 'but our acquaintance was of the slightest. You will have to ask someone else about the state of his finances, and his marital status, for I cannot help you. And I very much hope never to know any more about than than I do today.'

Shaking her head at such improvident behaviour, Mrs Northcott bustled off to sound out one of her new acquaintances.

'Anthony St Ervan? No, he is not married. I believe he was engaged, and she died or something, but it was many years ago when he was very young. He is very eligible, and all the mamas were after him for a while, for he is very wealthy. He is fickle, though. He would make a great fuss of a girl for a whole evening, and then ignore her the next time he saw her. He gained quite a reputation for breaking hearts, and now the careful mothers warn their girls against him. He is dancing with your daughter? I should not encourage her to look in that direction, if I were you. He may look as high as he wishes for a bride, when he does choose to marry.'

Lady Esher's words of warning were not lost on Sarah, standing silently behind her stepmother. Mrs Northcott looked thoughtful. When St Ervan brought Emily back to her at the end of the dance, she encouraged him to stay and talk. He chatted unexceptionably with them, and Sarah was relieved to see that the younger girl had quite recovered her composure.

Under cover of more general conversation, Sarah was able to draw her a little to one side. 'What did he say to you? Did he tease you?'

'Not at all, he was very kind! He apologised for being so tactless and putting me out of countenance, and assured me he would never refer to the subject again. My heart nearly stopped when he spoke of seeing me before, for I had never told Mama how far I was from the hotel. She thought I had just gone a few steps. And if she knew he had seen me . . .'

'He did not say anything about me?' asked Sarah diffidently. She had never admitted to Emily how she had travelled back to Ostend with him, and had no wish for it to come out now.

'No, why should he? He merely remarked that it must be happy for me to have a sister, and I said it was! I said you are very kind to me, and very strict, and he laughed!'

For the rest of the evening Sarah declined to dance, and Mrs Northcott made no objection to her joining the ranks of the chaperons. For her part, she had no wish to see her stepdaughter, plain though she appeared in her eyes, setting herself up in rivalry to Emily. That Emily was a success she could not doubt, but she had heard more than one person describe Sarah as a well-looking girl, with a sensible and agreeable manner. She was clever enough to realise that Sarah's composure, her intelligence and her wit, polished by travelling and conversing with her father and his friends, would make her of interest to the older, and therefore possibly more eligible, men.

Tired out, Sarah slept late the following morning. She was awoken by Emily, who danced into the room, looking quite enchanting in a pale pink peignoir hastily thrown over her lace-trimmed nightgown. Sarah, scarcely awake, rubbed her eyes as Emily flung back the curtains and announced, in a low but joyful voice,

'Oh, Sarah, he is in London at this very moment!'

'Of course he is,' Sarah responded sleepily. 'We saw him last night.' Emily stared at her.

'Whatever are you talking about, Sarah? *He* is in London! Charles, Lettice's brother.'

Sarah sat up. 'I beg your pardon, Emily. I must have been still dreaming. You mean the young man you didn't meet in Bruges?'

'Of course I do. Charles Dulverston! Why, whom did you think I meant?'

'No one. I am sorry, Emily, I told you I was not properly awake. So your friend's brother is in London? How do you know?'

Emily was happy to return to her own affairs. 'I wrote to Lettice as soon as we reached London, almost. She was my dearest friend at school, but she left a month before Mama came to fetch me, and we have corresponded ever since. I had a letter from her this morning. She is to spend the winter with her family in the country, at least until after Christmas, but she writes that Charles is in London! He has joined the Guards. Only think, I shall see him in his uniform! How handsome he will look!'

'If he is busy with his duties, as I imagine he must be, you are not likely to meet for some time,' Sarah pointed out prosaically. 'You might be lucky enough to come across him at a party, I suppose. Or will his sister tell him you are here?'

'Oh, I shan't wait for that,' retorted Emily blithely. 'Why, that might take three or four days! No, I shall write to him myself.'

'Emily!' Sarah was shocked. 'Your mama would not like that at all. It is not at all the thing for a young lady to carry on a correspondence with a gentleman, unless they are engaged, and even then...'

'Well, I shan't tell her,' Emily interrupted.

'That would not make it any the less shocking,' said Sarah firmly. 'If it became known that you had carried on a clandestine correspondence, your reputation would be in tatters. You know your mama particularly wants you to make a good marriage.'

'Oh, pooh,' replied Emily crossly. 'I don't care for such things. I want to marry no one but Charles.'

'Supposing the gentleman is not willing?' suggested Sarah drily. 'He might not want to marry you.'

'Well, you're wrong there,' Emily came back triumphantly. 'He does wish it. He said so himself.'

'Surely he has not spoken to you already?' Sarah was surprised. It seemed hardly likely that the young man who had declined to make an assignation in Bruges or in Paris should do something so out of the way.

'Not to me, silly,' Emily laughed. 'He said it to Lettice, and she told me!'

She looked triumphant, but Sarah's heart sank. She could only hope that it was not simply a piece of family fun, blown up out of all proportions by a girl's romantic notions. Ten to one, she comforted herself, Emily would find her friend's brother far less interesting now that there were swarms of other young men eager to vie for her favours. She hoped so, indeed, for she was under no illusions that Mrs Northcott would look kindly on a younger son with his way to make in the Guards, as a suitor for her daughter's hand. She set herself to dissuade Emily from writing, and succeeded in the end by reminding her that the young man might be disgusted by such forward behaviour in one whom he had known only as a meek schoolgirl.

'I never was meek!' Emily protested. Sarah could well believe it.

Three days passed in a whirl of activity, then a letter arrived from Northcott Hall. Lord Northcott, Sarah's father wrote, had made his peace with him, and a touching reunion had taken place. Since then, the old gentleman had seemed to take on new strength. He was still very ill, but had rallied enough for him to hope that the immediate danger had passed. He had been surprised to hear of his son's recent marriage, but on reflection not too displeased. Sarah, reading between the lines, thought that Lord Northcott, having lost quite a bit of money through his heir's unfortunate marriage, was not unhappy to have a new fortune come into the family. Nevertheless, her papa deemed it inadvisable for his wife to come to Northcott just yet, and under the circumstances it was more sensible for the girls to stay in London with her. Mrs Northcott was happy to obey. She had no desire to bury herself and her daughter in a cold Norfolk house, and Emily had already attracted several eligible gentlemen.

One of these was Andrew Abbotsleigh. Mrs. Northcott did not feel that she wanted to encourage him as a suitor, for he was a well-known gambler, and had no title. Nevertheless his family was very well connected, and his mother provided several very useful introductions which led to other invitations for Emily and her family. It did not escape Mrs Northcott's notice that the young man seemed to be courting Emily more at his mama's wishes than his own, and she did not therefore scruple to allow him to visit, dance, and take Emily riding in the Park.

The Marquis of Berrington was also a not infrequent visitor. Mrs Northcott was still in two minds about him. At times he seemed almost to be laughing at her, which she was not used to and disliked very much. It had crossed her mind that he might be interested in Sarah, but as that young lady invariably tried to withdraw whenever he was announced and seemed positively to avoid him, her mind was soon put at rest. He did not try to flirt with Emily, but teased her as if she were a younger sister. His title and wealth must make him an acceptable visitor in any household with marriageable daughters, and while he showed himself pleased with their company, he would be welcomed.

Both he and Abbotsleigh, together with several other young men of Emily's train, were sitting with Emily and Sarah on the afternoon when the footman announced, 'Lieutenant Charles Dulverston,' and a tall young man in Guards uniform came diffidently through the door.

Emily gave a squeak and jumped to her feet, almost running to greet him. She would have thrown herself into his arms if he had not forestalled her by catching her hands and holding her at arm's length. At once she became very demure.

'Mr Dulverston! What a pleasant surprise! I must make you known to my new sister, Miss Northcott.' Sarah, reflecting that it was fortunate that Emily's mama was not present, rose sedately from the corner whither it was her custom to withdraw when, as so often happened, she was forbidden to leave the drawing-room, but was told by her stepmother to remain as chaperon for Emily. Looking at Emily's young man, she found herself surprised into thinking that Emily must really be

in love after all. The handsome soldier she had pictured
gave place to an open, boyish face with an engagingly
freckled snub nose and a friendly grin. Seeing that Emily
was surrounded, and that he was unlikely to be able to
get a quiet moment with her, he stayed chatting with
Sarah with cheerful good manners. She decided that she
liked him very much, and began to think that Emily had
chosen better than she would have expected. She was
afraid that he might be made unhappy by the number
of Emily's admirers.

'Emily is quite the rage,' she remarked brightly. 'There
are young men and bunches of flowers arriving at every
hour of the day, but I do not think that she regards any
of them.'

He gave her a sharp glance, and grinned again so in-
fectiously that she had to smile back.

'Of course she doesn't,' he replied cheerfully. 'She's
just enjoying the novelty. I am glad, for after a few
months of this her mama can hardly say she has not had
any opportunities, can she? But I wanted to thank you,
Miss Northcott, for being so kind to Emily, and for
helping her when she was so scatterbrained as to wander
round Bruges looking for me.'

'Oh, so you knew that, did you?'

'Naturally I did! Emily tells me everything. Oh, not
to me, you understand,' he amended as she raised her
eyebrows, 'but she writes to my sister, and my sister
writes to me. It is understood between us that anything
she says to Letty may be passed on to me. I would not
allow her to enter into a secret correspondence, any more
than I would let her meet me alone in Bruges. The trouble

is,' he added sagely, 'that being so young she is very romantic.'

Sarah surveyed the youthful face before her, and suppressed a smile. 'She seems to have the idea that you would like to marry her, Lieutenant Dulverston,' she said carefully.

'Well, I should like to, but you must see that it is quite impossible at the moment, Miss Northcott. I have to make my way in the world, and of course her mama would never give her consent. But, in a year or so, I expect I shall contrive something.'

Sarah regarded him with a fascinated eye, and asked faintly what he expected to contrive.

'I shall have to talk Mrs Northcott round, somehow or other,' he said carelessly. 'Or will it perhaps be your father to whom I should speak?'

'I do not think so. From what she has said, I collect that Emily's money is to come to her on her marriage only if she has the full consent of her mother. Otherwise Mrs Northcott keeps a life interest in it, and on her death it is to be divided among some distant cousins. I think her father was anxious to protect her from fortune-hunters, seeing how young she was when he died, and how impressionable. I know that my father was relieved that she did not have the money outright—he did not want the worry of it.'

'No more do I,' he said ruefully. 'I have no wish to be branded a fortune-hunter, and I have no doubt I can make my way in the world without riding on my wife's skirt-tails. I only wish it were not so much.' He paused, frowning. Then his mobile face lightened and he was giving her his engaging smile again. 'Well, I'll cross that bridge when I come to it. The thing is, Miss Northcott, that while we are in London I should like to be able to see Emily as much as possible. She's a good little thing, but you may have noticed she's liable to be silly if one doesn't keep an eye on her. If I don't show up, ten to one she'll do something hoydenish like coming to visit me, and then the fat would be in the fire with a vengeance.'

Sarah gave her heartfelt agreement. 'I was hard put to it to stop her from writing to you to say she was in London,' she admitted.

'There you are! I particularly told her she must not do it, but when I'm not there I cannot prevent her. That is why I need your help.'

'I will do whatever I can. What do you suggest?'

'The problem is, that if I keep coming and asking for Emily, her mama will soon show me the door. But if it appeared that I was coming to visit you...' He had the grace to look embarrassed.

Sarah laughed out loud. 'You are quite shameless,' she said. He agreed, and continued to look at her hopefully. She was irresistibly minded of a friendly dog hoping to have a stick thrown for it. She could not deny him. 'Very well, sir, you shall play the part of my suitor. But heaven help you if your plan backfires and you end up having to propose to me. I should punish you by accepting, and lead you a dog's life!'

'If I thought that I could aspire...' he said in maudlin tones, rolling his eyes sentimentally. She laughed again and he shook her warmly by the hand. 'You are the best of good fellows!' he assured her. She could not but feel that it was, if unusual, a pleasing compliment.

He made his way back to Emily's side, and his place was immediately taken by Lord St Ervan. Sarah was not best pleased. It seemed sometimes that he had only to speak to her for her to behave in an unladylike way. He teased her without mercy, and delighted shamelessly in raising the spark of anger that was so easily seen in her eyes. At the same time, when he did not speak to her at all, she was annoyed to find herself unaccountably disappointed.

'A new admirer, Miss Northcott?'

'If you like, Lord St Ervan. I fear he admires my sister more than myself, however.'

'Well, she is of course a very pretty girl,' he remarked provocatively.

She laughed. 'You mean, I suppose, that she is a great deal prettier than I am?'

'She certainly is, though I can't imagine why you would think me rude enough to mention it.'

'Then I can't think why you are wasting your time talking to me,' she was goaded into retorting crossly.

He raised one eyebrow. 'Now I have made you angry with me. I gave you credit for more sense. It is true that she is prettier than you, and nobody in his right mind would deny it. Mere prettiness, however, is not always sufficient to attract a man of sense and experience. What you have, and what Miss Yarcombe lacks and will probably always lack, is character. A doll may be pretty. A woman should be something more.'

Sarah struggled to retain her composure, aware that her colour was rising. She was aware that she always seemed to behave her worst in St Ervan's presence. It was partly the embarrassment of remembering their first encounter, and partly something else. She struggled to meet his eyes. His face bore its usual faintly sardonic look, but there was a warmth in his eyes that she had never seen there before. 'Th—Thank you,' she stammered.

'I had never thought to see you so at a loss for words,' he smiled. 'Now I know how to do it, by paying you a compliment.'

They stood in silence for some moments. The room had been furnished in the latest fashion, according to the new Mrs Northcott's instructions, and Sarah suddenly found it stiflingly oppressive. The patterned carpets, rich velvet curtains and the profusion of small tables and ornaments seemed to press in on her. She could hardly breathe, and longed for the solitude and the wide skies of Belgium. If only he would go away! His presence was definitely disturbing. St Ervan, however, continued to stand at her side, looking completely at ease and making no effort to start up a new conversation.

'Did you visit the Great Exhibition?' she asked in desperation. 'I should so love to have seen it. It must have been wonderful!'

'It was certainly interesting,' he agreed kindly, humouring her. 'Some of the objects on display were decidedly bizarre, but there was a great deal to inspire, to instruct and to entertain. As a schoolmistress, you would have found it of great value.'

'What a shame that it should have lasted for so short a time.'

'But the benefits will be lasting. You know that the profits have been used to buy land in South Kensington?

I believe work has already started on a new museum there. Meanwhile, there is still Mr Wyld's model of the earth, if you have not already visited it.'

'In Leicester Square? No, I have not. It is very large, isn't it?'

'Very large indeed,' he concurred solemnly. 'Should you like to visit it?'

'I should love to!' she exclaimed. 'Only I'm afraid it's not the kind of thing that Emily or Mrs Yarcombe likes.'

'Must you always do only the things that they want to do?'

She looked down, absent-mindedly pleating the fine cambric of her dress with her fingers. 'I am their— guest—in a way,' she said quietly. His eyes followed hers, and she hastily smoothed away the creases she had made.

He was surprised to find himself annoyed. It seemed wrong to him that Sarah should be at the beck and call of her new family, and yet what was it to him? He had grown out of his wild-living days, it was true, and gambling no longer had any appeal, but he had no intention of tying himself down as yet. He made an excuse and left her abruptly, only to find that he could think of no one else for the rest of the day.

CHAPTER SEVEN

FOR THE REST of his visit, Lieutenant Dulverston joined the group that formed around Emily, moving from sofas to piano as they amused themselves with music and conversation. Sarah wondered if she were the only one who noticed that somehow, as if by chance, he always seemed to be the one to sit next to Emily, or to turn the pages of her music. When Mrs Northcott returned she had, perforce, to join the group herself. Her stepmother's suspicious looks were banished when she saw that this unpromising second son, with whose name she was already slightly familiar as the brother of Emily's friend, spent most of his time talking to Sarah. Sarah, for her part, was well enough entertained, for he was far too polite to behave as though he wished himself otherwhere, and he was an amusing companion. She could only be thankful that he was tall, for she foresaw that she would be dancing with him whenever the occasion arose.

Emily was inclined to pout at the attention he paid her, but Sarah was soon able to set her mind at rest. When the guests had departed, and the two girls went upstairs to change for dinner, Sarah followed her stepsister to her room. Madeleine, while well able to care for their clothes, was not skilled in arranging hair. Sarah had always been used to manage for herself, for she preferred a simple fashion without any of the drooping curls and ringlets favoured by many young ladies. Emily, with her smooth oval face, looked pretty in the current fashion, and Sarah was accustomed to arrange her coiffure for her each evening.

'You and Charles seemed to have plenty to say to each other,' Emily remarked sulkily, dropping her afternoon dress on the floor. Sarah automatically picked it up and shook out the folds of silk before laying it over a chair. Madeleine, who regarded such duties as peculiarly her own and who hated to see Sarah perform menial tasks, took it up crossly and shook it out again.

Sarah smiled at them both. 'We certainly did,' she agreed cheerfully. 'Can you not guess what we were talking of?'

'I am sure I have no idea.' Emily took up a sponge from the wash-stand as Madeleine poured hot water into the bowl. She made a great business of washing her face and lathering her hands with scented soap, refusing to look at Sarah.

'Why, we talked of the subject closest to his heart, of course,' teased Sarah. Emily dropped the cake of soap into the bowl with a splash. 'And that was you, you goose!'

Abandoning her search for the soap, Emily whirled round and flung her arms round Sarah. 'Wicked one, to tease me!' she exclaimed, oblivious of the fact that she was dripping soapy water all down her sister's dress. 'Is he not wonderful?'

Sarah gently removed the wet arms. 'I generally wash *after* I have removed my dress,' she mentioned, dabbing at a soapy splash on the lilac cambric.

'I beg your pardon, but it is your own fault. Now tell me at once what you think of him.'

'He is certainly a young man of considerable charm,' admitted Sarah. 'I should say that he will probably go far, for he certainly has plenty of effrontery! He suggested that he should pretend to be my suitor, so as to have an excuse to visit the house.'

'What a good idea!' Emily glowed with pride. 'He is so clever, I knew he would think of something. Mama will certainly not object to that.'

'*She* may not, but what about me? Imagine my feelings, when I am pointed out as the girl who was courted by a man younger than herself—which I think he must be—and then callously abandoned by him for her younger sister! I shall be an object of derision!'

Emily looked at her, much alarmed. 'Oh, Sarah, I never thought of that! Then you must not do it, and we shall think of some other plan. Not for worlds would I have you made uncomfortable, when you have already been so good to me.'

Sarah was quite touched at the gesture, and returned immediately, 'I was only joking, you dear child! I am sure he will be everything that is discreet. So careful as he was with your reputation, he will surely not wish to damage mine.' She took up a brush, as Emily sat at her looking-glass and took out the pins that held up her hair. 'Sit still, now, for it is getting late, and I must change, too. We go to the theatre this evening, do we not, with Mr Abbotsleigh?'

'Yes. I wish we did not have to. I do not like him at all, Sarah. He is full of pretty speeches, but there is something horrid in the way he looks at me. And when he touches me, I want to shiver.'

'I know what you mean. Still, your mama will be with us, and his too.'

'I wish we were going with Charles.' Emily was downcast, but brightened when Sarah pointed out that they would be seeing him very soon, for he had promised to attend the soirée they were going to the following evening, and to call as often as his not very onerous duties would permit.

The evening was not a pleasant one. Andrew Abbotsleigh, whose financial affairs were in a more serious state than he had admitted to anyone, especially his mother, was forced to become much more particular in his attentions, in so very marked a fashion that his own mother smiled approvingly, and Emily's was alarmed, though she did not wish openly to show her displeasure. His compliments were fulsome enough to make Emily blush, and fall silent. In an attempt to shield her, Sarah drew his attention by talking much more than she usually did, and succeeded so well that she several times made him laugh, so that he drew his chair nearer to hers and away from Emily, to whom he had been sitting so close that she had to fight not to shrink away from him.

Her efforts, though they brought her a look of gratitude from Emily, brought her none from her mother. During the interval, several people visited their box, and under cover of the noise of conversations Mrs Northcott scolded her fiercely for her behaviour.

'What you can be after, pushing yourself forward in that fashion, I cannot conceive!' she hissed. 'It is most unbecoming to be drawing attention to yourself in this way. Kindly remember that in this household you are a nobody!'

'I am Papa's daughter,' Sarah was moved to retort, regretting the words the instant they were out of her mouth.

'And what is that, pray? The daughter of a ne'er-do-well who can scarcely make ends meet, and a foreign person of whom the less said the better. Let me remind you, miss, that every morsel you eat, and every stitch on your back, are paid for by me! I am generous enough to allow you to join us when we go out, so kindly see that you repay me by remembering your place!'

Sarah bit back a furious rejoinder. She could, with some justice, have pointed out that since her marriage every penny of her stepmother's money was the legal property of her husband, Sarah's father. It was true that he would never have pressed for his rights, but they were there. A married woman's property, income or earnings belonged only to her husband. For Emily's sake, she kept a dignified silence. They were interrupted by a voice which, for once, Sarah welcomed.

'My dear Mrs Northcott! And Miss Northcott! I hope I find you well?'

For once Mrs Northcott's usual welcoming manner forsook her. 'Very well, Lord St Ervan,' she replied shortly and with heightened colour, as she wondered how much he had heard. She kept up the polite fiction that she and Sarah were devoted to one another. Sarah also looked at him, but his face gave nothing away.

'I see Miss Yarcombe is busily engaged with her many admirers. Since I cannot hope to compete with them, may I have the pleasure of your company, ma'am, in a short stroll? And Miss Northcott's too, of course,' he added carelessly.

Mrs Northcott was all smiles again, sure that she had not been overheard. 'I am sure your lordship has no need to worry about those other gentlemen,' she fluttered, 'but I own that it is a trifle warm in here. I should welcome a stroll. My stepdaughter will doubtless wish to remain with her sister,' she added firmly.

Nothing loath, Sarah returned to her chair and saw her depart with relief. She, for her part, was sure that Mrs Northcott's angry words had been overheard by the Marquis, and she had surprised what she could only think of as a look of anger on his handsome face, a look that was gone almost before she had recognised it. The Marquis must have employed considerable address, for when Mrs Northcott returned to the box, she was in a much better humour.

As they drove home in the carriage alone, after declining Mr Abbotsleigh's offer of escort, she said stiffly, 'I believe I may have been a little severe with you, Sarah. I am sure it is only your lack of experience that led you to offend, and not a vulgar wish to put yourself forward.'

Sarah tried to think that this was an apology, and not another insult, and replied suitably, but Emily was upset. 'I am sure if you were unkind to Sarah, it was most unfair of you, Mama. She was trying to protect me from that odious man's advances. If you had heard some of the things he said, you would not wish to accept his invitations in the future. He quite put me to the blush, and he would keep trying to take my hand, and stroke my arm, till I could have slapped him.'

'I own that I cannot, now that I know him a little more, think that he is at all a suitable companion for you. I have heard that he is shockingly in debt, and then his mother is so very patronising. Though what she has to put on airs about, with a son who lives for gambling, I cannot for the life of me see, though her aunt was married to an Earl!'

It seemed to Sarah that it was St Ervan who had put her stepmother on her guard, and she could not but be grateful to him, though she was at a loss to know why he had bothered. Could it be that he was forming an attachment for Emily? He certainly visited them often enough, and made some small attempt to be agreeable, though for the most part he contented himself with the occasional dry quip which Emily frequently did not understand. Until that afternoon he had seldom spoken to Sarah, for she followed her usual policy of distancing herself and keeping her hands and eyes occupied with a piece of needlework, but occasionally she had looked up and seen his gaze fixed on her. When their eyes met, he would generally look away, but once or twice when Emily or Mrs Northcott had said something silly, she fancied that she could see a gleam of humour that could almost have met the secret laughter in her own.

The following morning Sarah and Emily resolved to spend quietly. Mrs Northcott was out visiting a new crony, so they instructed the butler to deny them, and settled to a pleasant time in the small sitting-room that was cosier, now that December had come, than the drawing-room. Sarah was writing to her father, who wrote two or three times a week from Norfolk. She had never been parted from him for so long, and she missed him abominably. Emily had borrowed from the house-keeper a collection of old society clippings which she was avidly reading, for, as she admitted to Sarah, she often found herself at a loss in company by not knowing who was married to, or related to, whom.

'Listen to this, Sarah!' she said for about the tenth time, as Sarah tried in vain to concentrate on her letter. 'It is headed "Marriages in High Life", and it is all about Lady Constance Leveston-Gower's wedding just this year.'

'To Earl Grosvenor? Yes, it was a very grand affair, wasn't it?' Sarah tried to show an interest.

'Yes, very, and she was only seventeen. Only fancy, a year younger than I am, and a Countess! And married in the Chapel Royal, too, which hasn't been used since the Queen married there.'

'Don't be silly, dear,' said Sarah absently. 'It must have been used every Sunday, surely.'

'I mean for a wedding. I don't believe you are really attending, Sarah.'

'I beg your pardon,' said Sarah meekly, laying down her pen and folding her hands demurely in her lap. 'You see me agog.'

Emily gave a giggle. 'Well, you should be, for it is most interesting. Just think, she had eight bridesmaids, and it says they were all "beautifully attired in white glacé silk dresses, with jackets to correspond, and white lace bonnets. The bride",' she continued, warming to her theme, '"wore a dress of rich white satin flounced with guipure lace." How lovely. "A wreath of roses, myrtle and orange blossoms and a veil of guipure lace completed the costume." Imagine that!' She subsided into a happy reverie, and Sarah took the opportunity to continue her letter.

Before Emily could find any other choice snippets with which to regale her, the butler entered and trod his stately way to Emily's side. 'Excuse me, Miss Yarcombe, there is a message for you.'

'Thank you, Johnson.' She waited for him to deliver it, but he said,

'The messenger is waiting below, miss,' and held the door for her. Emily reluctantly put down the scrapbook and accompanied him, while Sarah continued her description of the plays and parties they had attended, with any amusing incidents that she thought her father would enjoy. When the door opened again, she did not look up.

'Please, I beg you, allow me only to finish this letter. It is nearly done, and then I shall attend to everything you have to tell me.' There was no answer, and thankfully she signed her name. Looking up she saw, not Emily, but St Ervan. 'My lord! Why do you always turn up just when I least expect you? And why did you not say you were here?'

'You told me not to,' he pointed out with the utmost reasonableness, 'and you know how obedient I am.'

'I know nothing of the sort. You should not be up here with me alone. Where is Emily?'

'I believe she is busy.' His voice was casual.

'Busy? Does she know you are here?'

'Yes. That is why she is busy. I particularly requested her to go and find something else to do.'

'Is that why Johnson fetched her? And why he did not announce you?'

'Yes, I bribed him,' he said, not without pride. 'I wanted to speak to you alone, and I knew your stepmother would be out this morning. Of course, I couldn't be sure the place wouldn't be crawling with Guards officers and riff-raff, but I took my chance, and as you see, here we are.'

'Yes, we are, but I am sure we shouldn't be. I cannot conceive what you can possibly wish to say to me that you could not say in the presence of my sister—or anyone else, for that matter. It is most improper for us to be alone together like this.'

'Well, we have done it before,' he pointed out.

'How could you! I had thought that any gentleman with the least delicacy of feeling would refrain from even thinking of that unhappy evening, let alone mentioning it. Besides, we were not alone. There was that girl with us.'

'Ah, but she was asleep,' he pointed out.

Sarah shuddered. 'You have no need to remind me. When I think of how she snored! But why are we talking of this? I never want to think of it again. And I do not want to be alone with you. Or in company with you, come to that,' she added. She was beginning to feel flustered by his presence, and by the intent look on his face as he looked at her.

'That is most unfortunate, in view of my errand. I came to ask you to marry me.'

The sudden announcement took her breath away, and she gaped at him speechlessly. He waited.

'You must be mad!' she gasped.

'It is quite possible, of course. I must say I even find I have surprised myself, so perhaps you are correct.'

His coolness enraged her. 'How can you be so cruel, even if you are joking? It is not a subject to jest upon, my lord.'

'I have told you before not to call me "my lord". And you must have a curious sense of humour if you think this is a joke. Most married men say that deciding to get married was the most disastrous step of their lives. If it is a joke, I doubt if they would see the funny side of it.'

'If it is as bad as all that, why do you want to do it?'

'I suppose I thought it was time to settle down.'

'And I was the first woman you happened to run into?'

'Dash it all, Sarah, I'm asking you to marry me!' He was losing his pose of cool self-control. 'You surely can't pretend you are happy here, with that harpy? When I heard what she said to you last evening...'

'So you did hear that? I thought you did. Well, my lord, you have no need to marry me out of pity. I am well able to fend for myself, and if I were not, I have a father who can care for me. However desperate I were, I wouldn't marry you if you were the last man on earth!'

'Is that your final word?'

'It is.'

'Then I will wish you, Miss Northcott, a very good morning.'

The door closed behind him. Sarah uttered a good many Flemish words that he might have recognised, had he still been there, and sat down to a hearty burst of tears.

CHAPTER EIGHT

THE MARQUIS of Berrington strode from the house, passing the butler without a word and leaving him gaping after him as he left. He would have gone bare-headed into the street had not that worthy, with a belated memory of his duties, run after him with his hat and gloves. Outside, it was the very reverse of fine, for the air was thick with fog that looked as though it would not clear all day. Regardless of this, St Ervan waved away his carriage with a peremptory hand and strode off to walk away his ill-humour.

He was surprised and chagrined. Accustomed for many years to being flattered by hopeful mamas and courted by their even more hopeful daughters, it had never really occurred to him that when his fickle choice alighted on a lady, she might refuse the honour. Unusually for him, he had made an almost spur-of-the-moment decision. His first betrothed had been his cousin, and they had been children together, their marriage a clearly understood thing long before it was announced. He had been fond of her, as if she had been a sister, for they had many shared memories. When she had died, suddenly, of cholera, he had been sad, very sad, but not for a moment would he have said that his heart was broken. On the contrary, he had welcomed the chance of a few more years of freedom. The only son of a widowed and doting mother, and blessed with good health and an excellent income, he knew that as long as he married within his own class there would be no one to say him nay.

That had been many years ago. Since then, he had enjoyed several seasons, flirting casually with this girl and that, being careful never to give rise to hopes that he had at present no reason to fulfil. He entered into a series of light-hearted affairs with married women, discreet liaisons which were entertaining enough, but made him suspicious of the married state. None of the women he had met had ever tempted him to abandon the single state, and he had more or less decided that he was not going to. Then he had met Sarah.

From the first he had felt that she was different. Outspoken, brave, intelligent, he felt that in her was a spirit to match his own. She would not flinch from the life he had led, nor would she subside into tears and vapours if he decided, at a moment's warning, to take a trip up the Nile, or to any of the other out of the way places he had in the past visited as the wandering urge took him. Seeing that her life was at present in turmoil, he had been prepared to bide his time, content to see her now and then but making no effort to woo her, for he told himself there was time enough for that when her father returned. Nor did he doubt that he would be able to charm her into his arms. His life had brought him no experience of failure in that direction.

Then, the evening before, he had heard that vulgar, pushing woman who was her stepmother speaking to her, and he had thought he could have killed her with rage. That she, a parvenu, a mushroom, should speak so to the woman he had chosen... He refrained from speaking then, but had been unable to resist the temptation to speak out today, to show this woman how he valued her despised stepdaughter. Sarah should be a Marchioness, and let her see whether that over-dressed doll of a daughter could do as well for herself, money or no money!

Then came the fiasco of the proposal. He had handled it badly, he knew. He was amazed to find himself so maladroit, with all his experience. The trouble was that always, before, it had been a kind of game. You won, you lost, and if you lost there was always another pretty face instead. This time, thrown into turmoil by feelings he had never experienced before, he had behaved like the veriest clod! That she disliked and despised him she had made only too clear, yet he found to his horror that his own feelings were unchanged. Angry she might make him, yet he could not hate her, still less could he be indifferent to her.

'Damn it all,' he muttered to himself. The fog was growing thicker than ever, and he realised suddenly that he had no real idea of where he was. He had allowed his feet to carry him he knew not whither. Looking about him, as far as he could, he saw that he had left the gracious area of residential streets and was in the narrow, meaner roads that lay behind Piccadilly, but was not unduly worried. Tall and well built, his travels had taken him into many dangerous places, and he was quite sure of his ability to defend himself, if necessary. He walked on, heading towards the busier streets, then turning further west, deciding to go to his club in St James's. He found himself at length in the Haymarket, and coming up to the theatre saw with some distaste that the usual crowd of prostitutes were in the peristyle of the theatre, clustering round the pillars of the portico. It was early in the day for them, but still there were a few men among them, chatting and laughing as they made their choice.

Never having been drawn to this particular aspect of low life, the Marquis would have passed by without stopping, when he heard a familiar voice and looked round to see Andrew Abbotsleigh. He looked drunk and dishevelled, and was being held up by two over-painted young women who stood on either side of him, his arms clasped over their shoulders.

Abbotsleigh saw him, and sneered. 'The noble Marquis! Whither away, my lord?' He removed one arm from its support to make a stage gesture, and reeled. The prostitutes laughed nervously.

'To my club, if it's any of your business, Abbotsleigh.'

'My business? I'll tell you what *is* my business, and that's the Yarcombe girl! Seems to me you've been doing a bit of interfering there, Berrington, and that's something I won't stand for.' He reeled again, and St Ervan laughed.

'Let go of your props, and you'll not be able to stand for anything. Lord, man, you're stinking drunk. Go home and sleep it off.'

'Drunk, am I? I'll show you who's drunk!' He took his arm from the woman's shoulders, and made a wild swing. St Ervan side-stepped without difficulty, and, deprived of support, Abbotsleigh lost his balance and fell, cracking his head as he did so against the base of one of the pillars. The second prostitute picked up her skirts and ran, but the first sank to her knees beside his motionless form and felt anxiously for his pulse. St Ervan, meanwhile, ran his hands swiftly over his erstwhile opponent's head, then looked round for something to use as a pillow before laying it down again. The woman swiftly lifted her skirt and pulled at the tie that held the outermost of her petticoats, pulling off the garment and folding it into a pillow. The Marquis took it readily. It was worn but clean, and had been carefully mended. She seemed capable as well as kindly, and her face was not uncomely. It was hard to guess at her age, but he put it at about twenty-five.

'Do you know this man?'

'Lord love yer, sir—me lord, I should say—we all knows 'Andsome Andrew! That's what we calls 'im, on account of 'e ain't, if you takes me meanin'. 'Andsome is as 'andsome does, and 'e don't, neither!'

'He is a regular, er, customer, then?'

'Well, 'e ain't one o' mine, nor 'e ain't been findin' it so easy to get a girl. It's one thing to 'ave no money, that's a misfortune can 'appen to the best on us, but 'e's a nasty piece o' work, that one. Beggin' yer pardon if 'e's a friend o' yours.'

'No friend at all. I do not like the gentleman any more than you appear to, though with less reason, it seems. What do you know of him?'

She looked nervous. 'Look 'ere, yer lordship, I don't want no trouble. I got enough o' that already. I don't know nothing.'

St Ervan felt in his pocket and pulled out a sovereign. The woman's eyes widened at the sight of the gold, and when he held it out to her she quickly slipped it into the front of her bodice, casting a wary glance around as she did so. No one was paying any attention. Nobody wanted to get involved in anything that might lead to trouble, and the groups of women and men had withdrawn to a distance which rendered them, in the fog, no more than dimly-seen shapes. Still, the woman leaned forward and lowered her voice.

'I did 'ear—and it were no more than a rumour, you understand—that 'e were a bit rough, like, in 'is tastes. You know 'ow it is, me lord,' she gave him a shamefaced look, 'we got a living to make, see, and other mouths to feed besides our own. Most of us can't afford to be too fussy. But I know one girl as is frightened out of 'er wits by 'im, and there was another, a few months back it were, what talked too much about 'im, afterwards. Now that's a thing it don't pay to do, see, an' it didn't do 'er no good, neither.' She shivered. 'Found 'er in the Thames, they did. They put it about as she'd drowned 'erself, but I dunno. I did 'ear she 'ad bruises on 'er throat, like 'and-prints. Like as if she'd bin 'elped on 'er way.'

'That is a very serious accusation.'

'I ain't sayin' it's true, me lord. It's just what I 'eard.'

'I understand. You need have no fear of telling me. Do you believe it to be true?'

'True enough. There's not much you can keep a secret in our life. Us girls stick together, mostly. And I can tell you, there's not one on us'll go with 'im now. That's why 'e was so mad, me lord. Oh, we'd 'umour 'im, right enough, and talk to 'im out 'ere, where there's plenty of us around, but go off with 'im, never!'

St Ervan looked down at the still unconscious body between them. 'What was he saying today?'

'A lot of old talk, as usual. Proper loud-mouth, 'e is.
All about 'ow 'e was going to be rich, and that. Course,
'e was always sayin' things like that, but 'e really seemed
to mean it, this time. Said there was a young girl would
'elp 'im into a fortune. Can't see it, myself. What's 'e
got to tempt a rich young lady, 'specially if she's as pretty
as 'e made out? 'E's no oil-paintin', is 'e? Said 'e'd 'ave
'er, though, whatever. That other girl what run away,
she said as 'ow 'e'd 'ave to kidnap 'er, jokin' like, and
'e said, "Maybe I will." And 'is face as black as
Newgate's knocker. It fair turned me up, I can tell you.'

He looked sharply at her. 'You are quite sure of that?
Quite sure that is what you heard him say?'

''Swelp me, me lord, as true as I'm standin' 'ere. Do
you know the young lady, then?'

'I might do.'

She set her hand on his arm and looked earnestly at
him. 'If you do, me lord, and if so be as it's true yer a
Marquis, like 'e said, then you got to do somethin'. It
ain't right, to let a young thing what's 'ad no experience
get into the 'ands of a man like that. Us lot, we can look
after ourselves, mostly. Got to, ain't we? But a nicely
brought up young girl, that's wicked, that is. You got
to 'elp.'

Once again he studied her face. Beneath the paint he
saw kindness, and decency, and he liked what he saw.
'What is your name?'

'Sal, me lord. They calls me Oyster Sal, on account
of me dad 'ad a barrer down the market.'

'Then, Sal, I want you to be as secret as your name.
Can you do that, do you think? I think I can trust you,
and I will need your help.'

'You can trust me, right enough, me lord. I never was no blabbermouth. What you want me to do?'

'I want you to be my eyes and ears. I want to know what this handsome Andrew of yours says and does. In particular, I want to know if he mentions this young lady again. Can you do that?'

'Reckon I can, me lord.'

He held out his hand, and after a moment's hesitation she put hers in it. He shook it warmly. 'You are a good woman, Sal. Too good for this kind of life.'

'I've got two little 'uns and me old Mum to keep, me lord. This is the only kind of life I knows. Better than wearin' out me eyes stitchin' at shirts, I'd say.'

St Ervan felt in his pocket and produced a card. 'Can you read, Sal?'

'Well enough, me lord. And me Tom, 'e's a wonder at it. Goes to the Sunday School, 'e does. 'E'll 'elp me out.'

He wrote on the back of the card. 'This is where I live. If you show this to the man who opens the door, he will let you in. If you have anything to tell me, and I am not there, be sure to tell them that I have said you are to wait. Is that quite clear?'

'Yes, me lord. Well, fancy me goin' callin' in Belgrave Square! Who'd 'ave believed it?'

'You are not to tell anyone, mind. Not even your mother, or young Tom, unless you have to.'

'Bless you, me lord, I shan't tell nobody. Me visit a Marquis! They'd have me took up for a madwoman!'

Andrew Abbotsleigh was beginning to stir, and his eyelids fluttered.

'It is best that I am not here when he recovers consciousness. Do you stay with him, Sal, but remember, I do not want you to take any chances. Do not put yourself into danger.' She nodded, and hid his card away as she had done the sovereign.

St Ervan bade her a quiet farewell and walked away. He no longer wished to go to his club. Instead he returned to his house. He cursed the fate that had led him towards the Haymarket. Before, he had more or less decided to go abroad again on another of his protracted, wandering tours. Now he could not leave. He had never been much inclined to concern himself with the problems of others, except perhaps those of his few close friends, but he could not find it in himself to leave an innocent little ninny like Emily to the machinations of a man like Abbotsleigh. Besides, and more importantly, Sarah was fond of her, and if Emily were to come to grief, Sarah would be unhappy. Whatever she had said or done, he could not hate her. He was honest enough to see that her refusal of him was mostly due to his own behaviour. Looking back, he saw that he had never made any attempt to win her regard. She had never seen him in the light of a suitor, only as someone who had missed no opportunity to tease her. He wondered that he had ever thought she might accept him.

The object of his thoughts had resisted the impulse to hide herself in her bedroom. She had dried her eyes, and when Emily peeped into the room, she gave her a resolutely cheerful smile.

Emily looked searchingly at her. 'You have been crying,' she said accusingly.

'No, I have not. Well, perhaps just a little,' Sarah prevaricated. 'It is nothing, however, and I desire that you will not speak of it any more.'

'I thought, when he asked to see you alone and told me to leave you together, that he was going to propose to you.'

'Well, he did, and he was quite odious. I do not wish to discuss it.'

Emily ignored her wishes. 'Sarah, never tell me you refused him!' she exclaimed in horror. 'Why ever did you do that?'

'Because he is altogether horrible, and I cannot bear him.' Sarah heard the tremble in her voice, and gritted her teeth. She would not weep again. 'I cannot think he cares for me at all, for he has never shown any sign of it. I think it is merely pique, because I have never made up to him, as the other girls do.'

'But, Sarah, you cannot have considered! He is a Marquis, and so very rich! I have heard he has at least twenty thousand a year!'

'I may be poor, but I have not yet sunk so low that I will marry only for money and a great name,' said Sarah stiffly.

'Of course not, if you truly dislike him. But, Sarah, is he truly so horrid? I had thought, lately, that you did not dislike him so very much. I am sure I have seen you laughing together, though I can never understand his jokes.'

'I cannot deny that he can be an amusing companion, when he chooses. But he is altogether lacking in sincerity, and kindness, and in every characteristic that one would look for in a husband.'

'But he must love you, Sarah, or he would never have asked you. If it were merely pique, as you say, I am sure he might just as well have proposed to me, for I have never made up to him, either. And last time I used that phrase, you said it was horridly vulgar, and scolded me,' she added in parenthesis.

'Love! He doesn't know the meaning of the word. I believe he asked me just to tease me. He certainly did not act the part of the lover. He said I amused him! He might as well marry a freak from the circus!'

'Perhaps he was shy?' suggested Emily hopefully, and with more truth than she knew.

'Shy? St Ervan? He's never been shy in his life! He's about as shy as—as a hyena!'

Emily saw that she was wasting her time, and said no more. For the rest of the morning Sarah kept up a flow of cheerful conversation, at which Emily could have screamed. By luncheon both ladies had a headache, although Sarah would not own to it. They retired with some relief to their bedrooms, where Emily slept and awoke refreshed, and Sarah said that she had done the same. If Emily noticed that her eyelids were still pink and her face pale, she was too thoughtful to mention it. Mrs Northcott, who would undoubtedly not have been so forbearing, was too wrapped up in her own plans, and when Sarah said that she preferred not to accompany them on their evening's jaunts, she was happy not to look for a reason.

CHAPTER NINE

By TACIT agreement, neither Sarah nor Emily referred again to the events of the previous day. When Sarah again pleaded not to accompany them on a shopping trip in the morning, Mrs Northcott was not pleased. She would not have cared to admit it, but she had grown to rely on Sarah's help, not only in choosing clothes for Emily, but in persuading her that the sophisticated, over-decorated styles she favoured were not suited to her age or to her style of beauty. Mrs Northcott might prefer them herself, but she was clever enough to see that Sarah was right, and that under-stating their wealth was more likely to win approval from those who mattered than decking herself in the contents of her jewel-box.

'You had a headache last night. I hope you are not sickening for anything,' Mrs Northcott said in some anxiety. No one knew when the dread spectres of cholera or typhoid might not strike. The new Health Act had brought some improvements, but Mrs Northcott, at least, had clear memories of the last great outbreak, though it was twenty years before, in 1830.

'I am sure I am not, ma'am. It is the air, I think. I have not been used to so much smoke in the atmosphere, and yesterday's fog, though I did not go out in it, was particularly bad. In Ostend we had cold sea winds, but they kept the air fresh. I dare say I shall soon be more used to it.'

'You will not become used to it by cooping yourself up indoors. And have you forgotten the ball at the Duchess's tonight? You will surely accompany us to that?'

Sarah reluctantly agreed that she would, and as an afterthought said that she would go to Bond Street with them. Her headache, though real, was caused by lack of sleep, she knew, and not by the air. It was true that the sulphurous, smoky fumes from the thousands of coal fires burning at this time of year were unpleasant, but she had always enjoyed excellent health. She could not hide herself away for ever, and she was not likely to be so unlucky as to run into St Ervan in a Bond Street modiste or milliner.

It was with some trepidation that she arrayed herself for the ball. At her stepmother's insistence, she did not wear the grey or lilac of half mourning.

'When you go around in those sad colours, it makes people wonder that we are not doing the same,' she complained. 'I do not want Emily confined to them just yet. It will be bad enough when we have to put on our blacks for your grandpapa. Surely for the Duchess's ball you can relax a little?'

Obediently Sarah put on her best ball-gown. Of white silk, it was embroidered with a pattern of ivy leaves and ferns, the same pattern of ivy leaves being repeated across the top of the low-cut bodice and on the little puff sleeves. She had never thought to have so fine a dress, and could not help admiring herself a little, as Madeleine beamed proudly at her. The low V shape of the waist complimented her slender figure, and the wide spreading skirts, held out by no less than six petticoats, gave her slim height a rounder, more womanly, look.

The knowledge that she looked, if not beautiful, at least passably handsome, gave her confidence, and she stepped from the new dress-chariot that had been delivered only two days before. Her cheeks were faintly flushed, and her eyes sparkled. Glancing round the crowded rooms it was impossible to see who might or might not be there. Telling herself that she had not the slightest interest in the Duchess's guest-list, she trod up to greet her hostess in the wake of her stepmother.

Emily's hand was claimed almost immediately by one of her many admirers, and she was swept up into the dance. Then Mrs Northcott was smiling graciously at Charles Dulverston whom, since he had nothing but his birth to recommend him, she was happy for her stepdaughter to monopolise. It had not escaped her notice that he always danced with Emily too, but since he always approached Sarah first and made a point of asking for her when he called, and sitting beside her as often as possible when Mrs Northcott was present, she assumed merely that he had good manners, and smiled upon his courtship.

'Miss Northcott, may I have the pleasure of this dance?'

'Lieutenant Dulverston, you may.'

They danced well together, for he was tall enough to make it an equal partnership, and since there was no spark of sexual attraction between them they were able to enjoy conversing with great ease. They were fast friends, and she had found that his youthful, almost boyish appearance hid a mind that was both sophisticated and clever. He could talk like a man of sense on many subjects, for he was too polite to restrict his conversation to the matter nearest to his heart. Sarah noticed, however, that in the movement of the dance he always contrived to be within sight of Emily.

This evening he seemed a little distracted, and less cheerful than usual. At the end of a disjointed account of an amusing occurrence during his last parade, involving a dog and a sergeant-major, she laughed dutifully and changed the subject.

'Emily is looking very lovely tonight, is she not?'

He glanced to where his beloved was being twirled round the room by the dashing heir to a noble title and no wealth at all. Her many-layered skirt was spangled with silver, and as they watched, one of the silver tissue flowers slipped from her gleaming curls. With practised aplomb her partner snatched it up, and held it above her head as she laughingly begged for it back. It was clear that both were enjoying the game, as she reached for the flower and he kept it out of her way. At length he kissed it and, with a flirtatious smile, slipped it into the breast of his coat. Emily blushed, laughed, and appeared to scold him as they continued their dance.

'Very lovely,' replied Charles gloomily.

'It is all in fun,' said Sarah gently. 'I am very sure that she thinks of no one but you. You must not think her inconstant.'

'I do not,' he groaned. 'But I sometimes think...'

'What do you think?'

'That I am wrong to hold her to what was perhaps no more than a childish passion. I am very sure of my own heart, but she is so young. And what sort of life can I offer her? I would marry her tomorrow without her money, but how could I do that to her? Brought up as she has been, used to every luxury that money can buy, what chance would our love stand if we were obliged to live off my pay and the small allowance my father is able to give me? And yet marry her for her money I can and will not do. It may be years before I am able to rise in my profession, unless there is a war.'

'That seems not altogether unlikely, doesn't it?'

'I think matters must come to a head with Russia and Turkey within a few years. If that should happen, I could get promotion quite quickly. Then I might go into politics, and win myself a position in the world.'

'Or you could be killed,' reminded Sarah with a shudder.

'Yes,' he said soberly. 'I cannot say that at present I have any great faith in our military leaders. They are good enough fellows, but they are so old! Look at Lord Raglan—he was at Waterloo, and to him the enemy will always be the French. They think backwards, not forwards. They're still living with the Iron Duke, and they are so sure we are unbeatable! Not that we have not a great army, one of the best, but an army is only as good as its generals.'

Sarah was to remember his words when, less than two years later, she read in *The Times* of the appalling disaster that befell the Light Brigade. Charles's wounding at the Battle of Inkerman, and his recovery and joyful return, lay as yet in the future, but even as he spoke she felt an icy shiver pass over her skin. He looked at her soberly.

'Can I ask her to accept that? A life of poverty, estranged from her mother, or a long widowhood?'

Sarah thought carefully. 'I do not think that Emily is as childish as you suppose. Oh, she is very young, to be sure, but she was used to spend a great deal of time with her father, and I am sure he was far from being a fool. In her tastes and her interests she is as one would expect, but I think that, underneath, she has a strength of will and purpose that would not fail you. I think you should not give up, at least just yet. My father may be able to talk Mrs Northcott round. If, as seems likely, she becomes Lady Northcott, she will surely be content with her place in society, and less anxious to push Emily.'

'If she becomes Lady Northcott, will she not look even higher for her daughter?'

'Maybe. But I still think you should trust to Emily. Her mother cannot force her into a marriage which she does not wish for. If you are patient, you may win her yet, and her mother's approval.'

They had been speaking as quietly as the noise around them would permit, made oblivious by their conversation of the other people dancing. At that moment someone bumped into them, and Charles looked round in annoyance. There was a mutter of apology, and they continued to dance.

'That damned Abbotsleigh fellow! Sorry, Miss Northcott, I shouldn't speak like that to you, but there's something about him I don't like. You were out with him the night before last, weren't you?'

'Yes, and I can assure you that Emily likes him even less than you. He is a most unpleasant man. I do not think he really likes her, either. He just pretends to.'

'They're saying that it's his mother who's set on his marrying for money. I believe he's run through the family inheritance almost completely. The funny thing is, I've seen him several times while we were dancing. It was almost as if he were following us around.'

'Why should he? He's not interested in me.'

'I don't know, but I hope he did not hear what we were saying.'

The music had come to an end, and he was leading her back to Mrs Northcott. Charles, trying to look non-committal, asked Emily to dance, and led her on to the floor. Sarah sat on her small, uncomfortable chair and fanned herself. The rooms were warm, and the mixture of smells from flowers, perfume and over-heated bodies was making her head spin slightly. Mrs Northcott ignored her, and kept up a spirited and mildly slanderous conversation with a titled widow next to her. Sarah, watching Emily and Charles, was concerned to see that they appeared to be quarrelling. Emily was looking flushed and mutinous, and her partner seemed to be lecturing her.

'Not dancing, Miss Northcott? You will never get a partner if you frown like that.'

The minute he had spoken, St Ervan could have bitten his tongue out. Why did he always find himself making sarcastic remarks to her? He had meant to approach her in a neutral way, ignoring what had happened the day before, and now she was already looking angry and embarrassed.

'Lord St Ervan! I—I had not expected to see you this evening.'

'Nor had I intended to come. Forgive me, I am afraid I spoke without thinking.'

'It is of no concern to me if you choose to make fun of me, my lord.' Her voice was cold, but her cheeks were pink and she was surprised to find that she was pleased to see him. Since they were bound to meet socially, she was glad to find that his former manner towards her was unchanged. She had half expected him to cut her, and wondered why she was so glad that he did not. He glanced at Mrs Northcott, but she was still deep in her own conversation.

'The fact is that I have something of the greatest importance that I must say to you. Will you dance with me? We cannot talk here.'

'I cannot imagine what you can possibly find to say to me,' she said forbiddingly. With seeming reluctance, she rose and allowed him to lead her into the dance. There was a moment's silence as she waited for him to begin.

'Why were you frowning?' he asked abruptly.

'Was it so terrible? I suppose I was just thinking that it was too hot and stuffy.'

He did not believe her, for he had followed the direction of her gaze, and had seen it fixed on Emily and that young Guards officer, Dulverston. He recalled that he had often seen them together, and that as he had arrived a few moments before, they had been dancing, and had seemed engrossed in conversation. It occurred to him for the first time that others beside himself might find Sarah amusing and attractive. It was not a very good match, to be sure, but for a girl without a dowry and a younger son with few prospects, could either of them hope for anything better? He thought with a pang that marrying a soldier would appeal to Sarah. He could imagine her cheerfully following her husband round the Continent as she had done her father, undaunted by strange countries and customs, conjuring up a meal at a moment's notice and enjoying the freedom from restrictions that such a life would bring. Well, if that was what she wanted . . . He clenched his teeth. He had tried, and failed; he would not stand in the way of her happiness.

'Miss Northcott, I beg you to believe that I would not normally have intruded upon your notice had I not had something of the utmost importance to say to you. I would like you to know that I will never again refer to what passed between us the other day. I can only regret that I have to discommode you with my presence now.'

Sarah's heart sank. She had never known him to be so formal, so polite. Contrarily, she found herself regretting his usual outspoken rudeness. He had been brusque, insolent, annoying, yes, but he had been right when he had thought that at heart they were two of a kind, and her own unconventional spirit had responded to him in a way that had fuelled her annoyance with him. But if he could be formal, so could she.

'Thank you, Lord St Ervan,' she responded with dignity. 'I will endeavour to put it from my mind. Let it be as if it had never happened. What was it you wished to say to me?'

He led her on to the dance-floor. 'I would like to put you on your guard for your sister's sake. I heard something yesterday that made me think that she might be in danger of forming a most unfortunate alliance.'

Her eyes flew to Emily. 'An unfortunate alliance? To whom can you possibly be referring?'

'Mr Andrew Abbotsleigh.'

She could have laughed with relief. 'Mr Abbotsleigh! I do not think Emily is in danger of marrying him. She cannot abide him!'

'Nevertheless, my informant tells me that he is determined to marry her.'

'I was aware that his mother was determined, but I cannot think that he loves her. He does not appear to, though he is very attentive. He does not seem to me to be someone who is capable of caring for any woman, at least not enough to marry her.'

St Ervan sighed. 'Miss Northcott, you surely cannot be so naïve as to think that all marriages are made for love? Come now, you have lived abroad, and though you have been in London only a short time, you must be aware that in our set such things are the exception, not the rule. Marriages are made for position, and money. Particularly money. If there is love, or if that comes with time, then it is a bonus. Abbotsleigh is, I think, facing financial ruin. He has certainly been betting heavily, and with even less luck than usual. There was a rumour that his card-playing was not to be trusted, although no one has as yet made anything of it. If it is true, he faces social ruin as well. If, however, he can marry a fortune, he may pay off his creditors, and any other scandal would probably be forgotten, provided he did not do it again. Now do you see?'

She was shaken, but not yet very worried. 'Of course I can see that he would like to marry her, but I have told you that she does not care for him. Nor does her mother,

for whatever you may think of her, you may be quite
sure she will take no chances with Emily. Emily's money
is securely tied up. She will inherit only if she marries
with her mother's consent.'

'Consent may be forced, in certain circumstances.'
Sarah stared at him, uncomprehending. 'If she were in
some way compromised by him, she would have to marry
him,' he said impatiently. 'There would be no other
choice. Her reputation would be ruined, and she would
stand no chance of ever being received into society, let
alone of anyone else marrying her.'

'You cannot mean that he would abduct her!'

'I can only say that he has been heard to utter threats
of that kind. My informant was quite positive that he
meant it.'

'Who is he—or is it she?'

'I prefer not to tell you. It is someone who has no
liking for Abbotsleigh, yet has no reason to wish him
ill. I believe what I heard. Can you afford to take the
chance that it might be true?'

'What can I do?'

'You can watch her. You are with her almost
constantly. Try to be sure that she does not go out
without you, even if she has a footman with her. Servants can be bribed. Be sure that you know where she
is, or whom she is with.'

'Should I not warn her, or her mother?'

'I think not. I have no proof, and the person who
warned me might not be believed by Mrs Northcott. As
for warning her, I see no point in frightening her.'

'You do not mind frightening me.' Her voice was
almost petulant, and he looked down at her gravely.

'Believe me, if I could shield you from this, I would do so. But I do not think you are the kind of girl who would wish to be protected from the truth. I judged that you are used to facing up to danger, and that your courage would not fail you if it were a question of helping someone of whom you were fond. Did I misjudge you?'

He spoke with a gentleness of tone that she had not heard from him before, and with unquestionable sincerity. Her throat tightened.

'You did not,' she whispered.

'I thought I could not have done.' He smiled. 'A girl with a redoubtable vocabulary like yours should be more than a match for Mr Abbotsleigh, I think. You certainly did not seem afraid of me, either!'

'I thought we agreed not to speak of that again.'

'So we did.' His manner hardened to its usual sarcastic aloofness, and she wondered if she had only imagined the tender look in his eyes. They danced in silence after that, each lost in thought, and when the music finished he returned her to her chair and, bidding her a swift farewell, was gone.

CHAPTER TEN

SARAH WAS so stunned by the events of the evening that she completely forgot that she had seen Emily and Charles having, at least, a disagreement. That Emily was silent in the chariot going home she scarcely noticed, and it was not until she had completed her undressing and was tying the ribbons of her nightcap that the girl's stormy entrance reminded her. Emily had been crying, she saw, and noted without too much envy that the petal-fine skin remained free of blotches, and that even with reddened eyelids and nose her stepsister was still remarkably pretty.

'What ever is the matter, Emily?'

'Oh, Sarah, I am so unhappy!' said Emily unnecessarily, casting herself into a chair near the fire. 'Charles has been so cruel to me.'

'Now really, Emily, I cannot believe it,' said Sarah in rallying tones. 'Charles adores you.'

'Oh, I know you are great friends. I am sure he can do nothing wrong in your eyes,' retorted Emily crossly. 'Perhaps he is tired of me, and wants to marry you instead. I am sure he spends more time talking to you than he does to me.'

'My dear Emily, surely you cannot mean it? You do not think that Charles and I . . . Why, we hardly ever talk of anyone but you, except that he is too polite to do so all the time. He certainly thinks of no one else, and you cannot believe that I would betray you so?'

'I don't know what to believe,' wailed Emily, bursting into tears. 'I am sorry, Sarah. I know you wouldn't really do such a thing. But he was so horrid, saying he could not marry me because he has no money. As if that signified!'

'It must do, to any man of honour,' said Sarah gently, petting Emily like a child. 'You would not love him if he were interested only in your money, as so many are. You must understand that a soldier's life is not an easy one, nor is that of his wife.'

'That is what he said. I told him I should not mind that, and I shouldn't, really.'

'I know you would not. But life is uncertain for all, and even more so for a soldier. If he had to fight, you could be a widow before you are twenty. What then?'

'At least I should have happy memories to look back on. If he were killed, and we had not been married, I should have nothing.' Emily spoke with some dignity through her tears, and Sarah was impressed in spite of herself.

'Then it is up to you to convince him of that,' she said bracingly.

'But he said we should have to wait an age. A year, perhaps, or even two,' complained Emily, becoming childish once again.

'It is no more than many have to do. Most younger sons have to face several years of waiting before they can afford to marry. A year is not so long. At the very least I think you should wait until next autumn, until you have had at least one season. If nothing else, you owe it to your mother, who wishes so much for you. You cannot expect her to be pleased at your making such a match. Few mothers would be.'

'I shall not enjoy it,' said Emily petulantly.

Sarah laughed. 'I think you will, you know! Any girl with money and a pretty face is bound to. Think, Emily! Your mother has pinned all her dreams and hopes on you. She is bound to be disappointed if you marry Charles. Give her at least these few months to enjoy. You must know that she married my father only to help you.'

Emily was embarrassed. 'I know she did, but I wasn't sure if you did. I should have known you might. You do not mind, Sarah? And what of your papa? Will he be hurt, do you think, if he discovers it?'

'Knowing Papa, he knew it all along! He has had too much experience of the world to be taken in like that. No, if he married her, it was with his eyes open, and I do not scruple to tell you, Emily, that he did it because of your mama's money. It is a fair enough exchange: a good name for a share in a fortune, or at least the interest on it. You need not worry about Papa, he is well used to looking after himself. And as for me, how can you doubt it? I have never been so comfortable, or so well dressed, and never before have I had the pleasure of having a sister.'

'Mama is not always very—kind to you,' suggested Emily.

'I do not mind it, I assure you. I have been used to far worse treatment. No, I am happy enough, and I want to see that you are too.'

'Well, I shall be happy only if I can marry Charles.'

'Yes, I think you have made that sufficiently clear,' said Sarah drily. 'Nevertheless, I think you must do as he says and wait for a while. It will not be so hard, after all. You have plenty of young men willing to dance with you. By the by, who was that young gallant I saw you with this evening? The one who took your silver flower?'

Emily blushed, and laughed. 'Oh, that was only a piece of nonsense. He is not serious, I can assure you. We understand one another well enough. He says he adores me, but I am quite sure that if I were to take him at his word, he would be horrified!'

'Be careful you do not raise any expectations. High spirits are one thing, and will always be acceptable in someone of your age, but do not go beyond the bounds of what is pleasing.'

'I do not intend to. He, for one, would not let me, though he is willing to play at it.'

'What of Mr Abbotsleigh?' Sarah kept her voice casual.

Emily pulled a face. 'I would not be so sure about him. He sometimes goes beyond the limits of propriety. He is very pushing, but I am sure he does not really like me. I certainly do not like him.'

'No more do I. I think it would be as well, Emily, if we could cut the connection as far as possible. I cannot say anything to your mama on such a subject, but can you perhaps suggest to her that his attentions are not pleasing to you?'

'She has already talked of it to me. Someone told her he is not quite the thing, and she says that if he asks me to dance, I am to make an excuse. She does not care to have an open breach with Mrs Abbotsleigh, because she is related to so many people, but she does not wish me to be with him any more.'

Sarah was satisfied and relieved. She felt sure that she knew who had warned Mrs Northcott against Abbotsleigh. She wondered a little why he should go to so much trouble. Was *he* perhaps interested in Emily? The thought was somehow displeasing. She was beginning to think that in seeing him as an ogre, she had over-exaggerated. He had certainly been uncivil in Bruges, but though his words had been harsh his actions had been kindly, and he had kept her escapade secret from everyone. The thought that he might perhaps care truly for her crept into her mind, but she pushed it sternly away.

Her anger talked out, Emily went to bed in a happier frame of mind. Sarah, too, felt more cheerful than she had done for two days. Given time, she felt sure that Emily's affairs could be brought to a happy conclusion. Much though Mrs Northcott wanted her daughter to marry well, she was at the same time truly devoted to her, and would not stand in the way of her happiness for ever. If only Charles could begin to make his mark on the world, she would soon be persuaded that, with Emily's fortune behind him, he could achieve great things. As far as she, Sarah, was concerned, there was the beginning of a question-mark in her mind, which brought its own warming glow with it. She could not believe that he was in love with Emily, and found herself thinking that his concern for her sister reflected his feelings for her.

The following morning brought a letter from Northcott Hall. Lord Northcott, wrote his son, was still improving

in health. Time, and the realisation that he might not
have much longer on this earth, had softened the old
gentleman to the point where he thought he would like
to meet his only grand-daughter. He therefore invited all
three of them to join Mr Northcott at the Hall, there to
enjoy such seasonable festivities as might be devised.

Mrs Northcott was pleased. While there was no doubt
that Emily was enjoying a success in the Metropolis, the
fact remained that most of the smart set spent Christmas
in their country houses, and it was only a few dowdies
who remained in town for the festival. To pass Christmas
in a great country house, and on her return to speak
casually of it to her acquaintance, exactly suited her.

Sarah, too, was pleased. She had begun to miss her
father a great deal. She had never been apart from him
for more than a few days in her life. It was true that for
the last few years she had seen little of him, her days
being taken up with her teaching, but he had always been
there in the background, to laugh at the amusing things
which happened, sympathise with problems, and simply
to share her life with her. The thought of going to
Norfolk also heartened her. The prospect of seeing her
father's old home, and of being again under that wide
sky that can only be found where the countryside is flat,
filled her with joy. It was, as well, an escape from the
problems that seemed to be building up around them.

For Emily, however, it was an unmitigated disaster.
When Mrs Northcott, presiding over a late breakfast,
read the letter to them, Emily uttered a shocked protest.

'Leave London now? But we can't! I won't go!'

'Don't be silly, Emily, of course you will go! You have
been enjoying yourself, I know, but you will find that

all the best people are leaving London anyway. You will find it sadly thin of company for some weeks. In fact, it might well be better to stay in Norfolk until about April, and then come back in time to prepare for the season. The air in January and February is particularly smoky and unpleasant, I hear, and we might all be the better for being in the country.'

'I don't care about the company and what the best people do! I won't go. You cannot make me!'

'This is most unbecoming behaviour.' Mrs Northcott was heavily displeased. 'Of course you will do as you are bid, you ungrateful girl. We shall be very well at Northcott Hall, and there are sure to be other houses to visit. Besides, do you not want to see Mr Northcott, and make the acquaintance of Lord Northcott? I have heard that the Hall is very fine.'

Emily burst into tears, and fled from the room. Her mother pursed her lips disapprovingly, and looked at Sarah.

'I do not know what has come over the girl. She used to be so obedient when she was a child. Perhaps I was wrong to send her to that school in Paris. I have never trusted the French. Look at Napoleon, for example!'

Her lips twitching, Sarah suggested as tactfully as she could that the change lay less in the iniquitous influence of foreigners than in the fact that Emily was growing up, testing her wings as a young lady of beauty and fashion.

'It is not to be wondered at if so much attention has gone a little to her head,' she said carefully. Mrs Northcott, surprisingly, bowed to her superior experience of young ladies, and admitted that Sarah might well be right. 'If you will allow me, I might have a little talk with her, ma'am. She might be more prepared to listen to someone of her own age, perhaps.' Mrs Northcott agreed again, and they parted in better charity with one another than usual. Sarah reflected that social success had improved her stepmother's temperament. Maybe her father had not made such a mistake as she had at first thought.

As she had expected, Sarah found Emily in floods of tears in her room. Several pieces of blotched and crumpled-up paper bore mute testimony to the fact that she had been trying to write a letter.

'I can't bear it, Sarah,' she wept, flinging herself into the older girl's arms. 'To be so far away from him, perhaps for months. And then it is likely that he may soon be sent abroad! He will be killed, and I shall never see him again!'

Sarah did what she could to soothe her, and to direct her thoughts into more cheerful channels. At length Emily stopped her tears, but she was a woebegone figure as she sat close to Sarah.

'You cannot, you must not, allow yourself to be so overset by this. How will you ever be fit to be a soldier's wife if you behave so?'

'It would be different if I were with Charles. This will take me away from him.'

'For a few months only. Come, you must be sensible, and dry your eyes, and beg your mama's pardon for talking to her so. You will not improve matters by making her vexed with you.'

Emily obeyed, but grudgingly, and she declined to help with the bustle of preparations, retreating rather to her room. Sarah thought it best to leave her alone, and trust that her own sweetness of nature would bring her to a sense of her duty. It was decided that they needed at least three days to prepare, for clothes must be bought suitable for country wear, and the house closed. The servants were to be kept on at half wages at present, since it was not sure when they would return. Having found a suitable house at a good address, Mrs Northcott was reluctant to part with it, for she had a shrewd idea of how difficult it would be to find another as the season approached.

All was at sixes and sevens. Amid the bustle, one of the footmen, sent out in haste to purchase yet another indispensable item that had been forgotten, found himself hailed by a tall man well muffled against the cold. His face was almost hidden by a comforter, and his voice was low and hoarse.

'Here, you! Want to earn some extra money?'

The footman was suspicious. 'Depends what for. I won't do nothing wrong.'

'Nothing wrong, man, nothing in the world. It's an affair of the heart, see. All I want to know is what Miss Yarcombe does, where she goes, and so on. Can you do that for me?'

'You'll not harm her?' The footman was dubious. Emily's pretty face and ways had soon endeared her to the household.

'Hurt her! Didn't I just now tell you it was an affair of the heart? Look, here's a half-sovereign if you can tell me what she's doing today.'

'That's easy enough.' He pocketed the coin without reluctance. 'She's in her room, and like to stay there.

The family is off to Norfolk, and she don't want to go. Can't say I blame her, going to some windy old place in the country when she should be in London. Keeps crying, she does, and carrying on like you never saw.'

'Ah,' said the gentleman sentimentally. 'She does not want to be parted from me, don't you see? Of course she's unhappy.'

'Well, sir, if that's all...'

'Just a moment. Now you see I mean her no harm, don't you want to earn yourself a bit more? Just let me know if she's going anywhere, or anything like that.'

'I suppose so, sir. How shall I do that? Where shall I find you?'

'Leave a message for me at the tavern on the corner. No need for a name, just say you have a message for the gentleman. There will be someone there to speak to you.'

'Very good, sir.' Unsuspecting, the footman went about his errand, and his companion took himself off, well pleased with his success.

St Ervan had not exaggerated the depths of Andrew Abbotsleigh's misfortunes. He was being dunned on all sides for his numerous bills, he had several debts of honour incurred at the gaming table, and the shadow of disclosure of his dubious habits with cards hung over him, worse than all the rest. Even his few friends were beginning to look askance at him, and he knew that if the rumours came to the ears of his mother, the only person who still believed in him, it would be all up. It was, of course, annoying that Emily had confined herself to her room, but he was on the whole pleased to hear that they were about to leave London. He would stand a better chance of getting his hands on her while the house was overset by preparations to travel, and he would in any case have to leave town himself as soon as possible.

He was not particularly attracted to Emily. He preferred his women to be a great deal less innocent and, on the whole, coarser. Still, she was pretty enough, and the fortune a good one. One night with him, and her family would do anything to hush up the scandal. Afterwards, with a fortune in his pocket, he could do as he liked, and she could come with him if she learned to please him. If not, a house in the country out of the way, and a brat or two to keep her busy, would be cheap enough. The thought pleased him. He would check that his groom was in his place at the tavern, and go down to the Lyceum or the Haymarket and see what sport was to be had there. It was true that most of the girls had been reluctant to go with him recently, but there was that one, what was her name? who smiled at him and seemed willing enough. She was a bit ordinary, perhaps, but she would do. He quickened his stride.

Back at the house, Emily was desperate. Sarah had advised her to write to Charles's sister Lettice, but what good would that do? By the time Lettice wrote to Charles and he received the letter, they would be gone. To make matters worse, he had told her the last time she had seen him that he would not be attending any functions for a few days, as he had duties at the barracks. At last, knowing Sarah would not like it but unable to think of any other way, Emily sat at her desk and wrote a short, despairing note to Charles, folded and sealed it, and scribbled his name on the outside. Tucking it into the folds of her skirt, she went to look for a messenger. On the stairs she met one of the footmen, who was carrying a parcel for her mother.

'Oh, John,' she said desperately, 'have you been out? What a pity. I particularly wanted this letter delivered as soon as possible. The thing is,' she smiled shyly at him, 'that it is rather a private matter.'

He smiled at her. 'Don't you worry, miss. I quite understand. Just you give it to me, I know what to do. The gentleman himself was asking after you only this morning.'

'He was? How wonderful! Thank you, John. But ... you will be secret, won't you?'

'Trust me for that, miss! I shan't let on to a soul. And I'll bring you an answer, if I can.'

Greatly comforted, Emily went to help her mother and Sarah, who congratulated themselves on the success of their treatment of her.

'I thought she would come round if we left her to think about it,' said Sarah later. 'She is a dear, good girl at heart.'

'Her father spoiled her,' said Mrs Northcott gloomily, 'but I own she did apologise to me very prettily. I think we can say it is all forgotten.'

CHAPTER ELEVEN

THE LINES of communication being now set up, Emily was delighted to receive by John's hand a speedy reply to her note. She was a little surprised, for Charles had always been very particular that they should do nothing to cause any talk or do any harm to her reputation. She assumed, however, that he was as distressed as she at the prospect of their imminent parting. He certainly wrote with great feeling, and if the flowing compliments might have struck a little false to a critical eye, Emily blushed over them and pressed the paper to her lips.

Andrew, for his part, was beginning to enjoy himself. He had never imagined it could be so simple. Charles had never written to Emily, and though she had in the past seen his letters to his sister, it was some time ago. Each man had in childhood been trained to a similar style of writing, and it never occurred to Emily that the letters were not from Charles at all. Nevertheless, Andrew realised that he would have to take things carefully. If he tried to move too fast, Emily might well be startled and suspicious, for from the tone of the first letter it was obvious that Charles had strict ideas of propriety. He had hoped at first that it might be possible to persuade her to run away with him before they left for Norfolk, but he soon saw that there was not enough time. He contented himself with the thought that by following her to the country he would be escaping from his creditors.

The evening before they left, they went to their last party in London. It was quite an informal occasion, given by the family of another schoolfriend of Emily's, and she went to it quite happily. Sarah would rather have stayed at home, tired from packing and organising, but mindful of St Ervan's warning, she thought it better to go. To her relief, there was no sign of Mr Abbotsleigh, and indeed the general age of the guests was rather on the young side. By no means displeased, she took herself to the chaperons' corner and amused herself by watching the antics of the young people. The family's schoolroom children had been allowed to come downstairs for a while, as a Christmas treat, and presently, to her amusement, she found her hand being solemnly solicited by a young gentleman of about twelve years.

'It is very kind of you,' she said gravely, 'but would you not rather ask one of the younger ladies?'

'No, thank you. They are all Lucy's friends, and they might laugh at me. I am afraid I'm not very good at dancing.

'No more was I, at your age. In fact, I hated it.'

'So do I,' he confided, 'but Mama said that if I did not dance with any of the guests I should not get any ices. So I thought I'd ask you, because you're not dancing, and I thought you looked as though you would not laugh at me.'

Sarah's lips twitched at this disingenuous answer, but she obligingly stood up. She had to suppress another laugh at his expression when he saw how tall she was.

'I am a beanpole, aren't I?' she said cheerfully. 'I shall not be at all offended, you know, if you would rather ask someone else. You could escort me to the supper-room, if you like, and I could make sure you got at least one ice.'

'I don't think you're too tall,' he replied valiantly. 'Anyway, all the girls would be taller than me, so it doesn't make much difference.' He offered his arm with an air, and led her on to the floor. There were not a few smiles at the sight, but luckily he had to concentrate so hard on minding his steps that he had no time to look about him, and Sarah was quite unconcerned. They finished the dance very creditably, and he smiled at her with relief.

'You dance very well,' he said with the air of a connoisseur.

'Thank you. So do you. I was used to teach dancing, you know, so I consider myself well qualified to judge.'

'Are you a governess? You don't look like one. My sisters' governess never dresses half as fine.'

'Not any more. I am Miss Yarcombe's stepsister. Miss Yarcombe was at school with your sister, and her mama has lately married my papa. Before that, I lived in Ostend, in Belgium, and I taught at a girl's school there.'

His face lit up. 'Ostend! How famous! Did you ever visit Waterloo?'

'Yes, indeed, several times. Should you like to hear about it?'

'Wouldn't I just! The chaps at school will be wild with envy when they hear about this. It just shows you! I thought this party would be dull old stuff, all girls and soppy things, but wait till I tell them!'

'Then let us fortify ourselves with ices, and I will tell you everything I can,' said Sarah, who was also finding the evening more entertaining than she had expected.

Half an hour and several ices later they were the best of friends, and Edward had confided in her several of the small problems that beset him at school. Sarah advised him as best she could. He seemed to feel that he should earn his keep, or rather his ices, and asked her if she would dance again.

'Should you not ask someone else?' suggested Sarah gently.

'I suppose I should. But I know I can dance with you, and it doesn't make me nervous,' he confided.

Sarah could not resist such an argument and allowed him to lead her once again to the dancing. This time he had enough confidence to carry on conversing while they danced, and was highly pleased that at the end he had tripped only twice.

'Alas, that youth should succeed where I have failed,' drawled St Ervan's voice in Sarah's ear. 'I distinctly remember your telling me that you could not dance with the same gentleman twice in a row, and yet I hear you have honoured young Edward with your hand for two dances, and sat out with him besides. Should I perhaps advise Mrs Northcott to enquire what his intentions are?'

'Cousin Anthony, oh, Cousin Anthony! Miss Northcott has been telling me all about Waterloo. She has been there many times! It was ripping!'

'Lord St Ervan, why is it that I am never aware of you until you speak to me?'

'I make sure that you are not, for fear you will run away before I can have two words with you,' he said wryly. Sarah looked uncomfortable, but Edward, ignoring such dull adult conversation, tugged at his cousin's arm.

'Miss Northcott says I dance very well, Cousin Anthony. I hardly trod on her feet at all!'

'You are to be congratulated. You are aware, of course, that by spending so long in your company Miss Northcott has seriously compromised herself? You have done what no one else has ever succeeded in doing, and are now honour bound to offer her marriage.'

'Oh, pooh, she don't care for such stuff, do you, Miss Northcott? Besides, if it is true, I don't mind a bit. She's just the sort of girl I should like to marry; she's so jolly. Will you, Miss Northcott? Do say yes, and I'll leave school, and we'll go and visit Waterloo and all the battlefields!'

Sarah laughed, and relaxed. 'There is nothing I would like better, but I think you would soon tire of having a wife ten years older than you! Why, when you were a young man, you would find yourself pushing me about in a bathchair! Besides, though I made it as interesting as I could, there is not so very much to see at Waterloo, you know. Not worth getting married for. But I shall be happy to dance with you at any time.'

He was much gratified, and suffered her to kiss him before he went reluctantly, at his mother's summons, to bed.

'What a delightful boy! I have enjoyed this evening more than I thought I would.' She had for a moment forgotten to whom she spoke, as her eyes followed Edward across the room.

'And now come I, the spectre at the feast, to spoil it for you. Shall I go away?'

'How can you talk such nonsense, when I collect you are a relation. I did not know that.'

'Or you would not have come?'

She was silent, biting her lip, for that was exactly what she had meant. 'I do not know how it is that whenever I am with you I behave so uncivilly. I do not usually do so.'

'It is undoubtedly because I do the same to you. Do not stop on my account, I beg you! If find it most entertaining and instructive.'

'Like a visit to the Zoological Gardens?'

'Precisely. Now that we have complimented one another, may I ask you how Miss Yarcombe is?'

Sarah was annoyed to feel a pang of jealousy. Surely, she thought, she was not so ridiculous as to mind if he showed an interest in another girl? She nodded to where Emily was laughing with a group of other young girls.

'As you see, she is well and happy. We have not seen Mr Abbotsleigh for several days. You may not be aware that we leave tomorrow for Norfolk. My father writes that my grandfather is well enough to receive us, and we are to spend Christmas there, and maybe even stay until April. She will surely be safe there.'

'I hope so.' He looked serious. 'My informant tells me that he seems well satisfied with himself. He has some kind of plan in mind, although he has not divulged it. And he is aware that you are going away.'

'I suppose he might have heard that from his mother,' said Sarah dubiously, 'although I do not think Mrs Northcott has spoken to her recently. We have been very busy preparing to go to Norfolk. How else could he know?'

'That is what I mean. You may not be as safe as you think. Pray continue to watch her, as far as you can.'

'You seem very concerned for her,' said Sarah pettishly.

'As I would be for any young girl in danger. And also because you would be sad, I think, if she came to harm? Your situation is not altogether a happy one, is it? Mrs Northcott tolerates you if you are useful, and because her daughter is fond of you. If that daughter came to harm, how would she be then?'

Sarah was silent. Once again she was struck by his gentle and considerate tone. How could she ever have thought him harsh and rude? What had seemed displeasing before, now struck her as amusing, even pleasing. It occurred to her that he paid her the compliment of treating her as his mental equal, instead of some tender, half-witted little creature whose only function in life was to look pretty and pour the tea. He had said he would not refer to his proposal again, and had told her to forget it. Did that mean he no longer had any interest in her? Had he asked her merely as a sudden quixotic gesture, instantly regretted and abandoned with relief? Suddenly, she wished she could have those moments over again, and was shaken by her strong feeling of regret. So shaken that she was unintentionally brusque with him.

'I have managed for years without Mrs Northcott's approval or disapproval. I can do so now.'

'I am glad to hear it.' He spoke lightly and made as if to turn away from her.

She put out her hand to prevent him, and said, almost unwillingly, 'I did not mean to be ungrateful. You have been very good to Emily. I do thank you for that. I feel it is only right to tell you that Emily's heart is not entirely free.'

He could have told her that he hardly gave Emily a second thought, except that anything which harmed her would harm Sarah. Every time he thought of the way Mrs Northcott had spoken to her at the opera, his blood boiled. Brought up to think of himself first and other people a long time afterwards, if at all, he was not in the habit of caring what happened to those around him unless he was very fond of them. If Emily had truly been in danger that first evening in Bruges, he supposed he would have stirred himself to rescue her, but it would have been unwillingly. It was true that he would have helped any girl to escape from Andrew Abbotsleigh, if the opportunity presented itself and it did not cause him any inconvenience. Further than that he would not usually go. He was still surprised and almost annoyed at the depth of his own response to Sarah, and by the fact that since she had refused him he found himself, contrarily, more anxious to win her than before. He saw the mirror of his own uncertainty in her eyes, and smiled understandingly.

'If I promise not to tease you, will you dance with me?'

She put her hand in his and they danced in silence. Their bodies moved in time to the music without conscious thought.

'How well we dance together,' said Sarah without thinking, then blushed. Mindful of his promise, he responded with a civil platitude, and she was grateful. 'At least you do not count under your breath, as my last partner did,' she joked. 'We must have been a most comical pair, when I am so tall.'

'Not at all, a most elegant couple.'

'He is a delightful boy.'

'Yes, I am very fond of him. He is my godson, you know. You certainly made his evening a success; he could hardly tear himself away from you.'

They were silent for a few more turns, then he said diffidently, 'It is possible that I might see you in Norfolk, if you stay there for long. I have a cousin not far away, who has been inviting me to visit him for I don't know how long.' Her heart leaped, but she made no reply. 'May I call on your father, if I am in the neighbourhood?' he pursued.

'Of course—I mean—you would be most welcome...' She was flustered, and hardly knew how to answer him. To call on her father, he had said. Did he mean...?

'You know you may call on my help, at any time, if you have trouble with Abbotsleigh,' he continued. 'Send an express, if I am in London. I will give you my cousin's address in Norfolk.'

'You do think there is a danger, then?'

'I do.'

'I wish you would give me the name of your informant. Can you not trust me so far?'

'It is not that I do not trust you. If I tell you, you might think that information from such a source is not to be trusted. It is in any case not the sort of thing that one can speak of to a lady.'

'Then I suppose it should not be too difficult for me to guess, since I seem to remember you once told me I was no lady.' She pondered. 'It must be that your informer is an improper person, so I can only suppose that it must be a—a lady of easy virtue.' He nodded unwillingly, and she looked at him speculatively. 'Is she one of your...?' she enquired, with the air of one seeking after knowledge.

He gave a sound that was between a groan and a laugh. 'I should have known you would guess—and that you would not hesitate to say so! No, Miss Northcott, she is not one of my "particulars", nor, I might add, am I in the habit of availing myself of such merchandise, though Abbotsleigh is! I can see that I shall have to tell you how it came about that we met. This is not a subject that we can discuss while dancing. Will you sit with me for a while?'

He led her to a moderately secluded corner, a procedure which luckily Mrs Northcott did not see, for she would not have approved. His tale was not lengthy, and at the end of it she looked shocked and grave.

'I did not realise... That poor woman! Can we not do something to help her?'

If he noticed the pronoun, he did not remark on it. 'I fully intend to do so, but for the moment I need her where she is, keeping an eye on that blackguard. When he is in drink he talks to her, you see, and she might well be the only warning we get of his intentions. Afterwards, there is a cottage on one of my estates that she could have, or perhaps a respectable business could be found for her, if she does not want to leave London.'

He spoke with the careless good nature of one to whom such things meant little. She, accustomed to seeing life from the other side of the fence, thought how strange it must be to be able to dispense such largesse without noticing it.

'We cannot sit here any longer without attracting unwelcome attention,' he said, breaking in on her reverie. 'I will take you back to Mrs Northcott.'

'You seem to have a great many cousins,' Sarah said lightly as they crossed the room.

'Yes, the country's littered with them,' he said. 'My father had six sisters, and they all married. Eventually.'

'How fortunate for your grandmother,' she said seriously, for she had seen only too well what a disaster it could be, to have so many daughters to marry off.

'She certainly worked hard at it. My father always said that when the last one went up the aisle, she just gave up and died. He said it had worn her out, all those years of attending the season, all those late nights. But my mother said it was no such thing, that she had enjoyed every moment of it, and died of boredom when it was all over.

She was laughing as they reached Mrs Northcott. He made her a swift farewell, and was gone before the smile had faded from her face.

Mrs Northcott was not pleased. 'I had thought he would dance with Emily. He used to make such a fuss of her, and he hasn't been near her all evening. I hope you were not boring him, monopolising him like that?'

'We were talking of Emily most of the time,' said Sarah demurely. 'He says he has a cousin in Norfolk, and that he hopes to come and visit us when he is staying with him.'

'Does he, indeed.' Mrs Northcott looked thoughtful, and a little smug. 'To call on us in the country! Well! That puts quite a different complexion on the matter. I hope you told him he would be most welcome?'

'Oh yes, ma'am. Most welcome.'

CHAPTER TWELVE

THE JOURNEY to Norfolk was accomplished with much fuss but no problems. Emily was annoyed to find that her new coat had been marked by several blacks, but Sarah pointed out that such inconveniences as soot from the engine could not be avoided when one travelled by train.

'Papa told me that when he was a child a journey to or from London took two days, when they travelled in their own coach. We may accomplish it in a matter of hours! It is worth a little soot, to do that. Besides, Madeleine has already told you it will come off.'

'Yes, I suppose so. But I do hate being so dirty,' said fastidious Emily, regarding her gloves with distaste. 'I think it would have been fun to travel in one's own coach and stop to change horses at the posting-inns. And highwaymen too, Sarah, just think of that!'

'I do think of it, and am all the more thankful that we are in a train. Just think, you romantic goose, of how ill you were on the boat. I dare swear you would feel almost as bad sitting jolting in a coach all day. There is no way to remain clean when you travel. If it isn't blacks from the engine, it is mud and dust from the roads.'

Emily was not to be convinced. 'I am sure it all sounds the greatest fun when dear Mr Dickens writes of it. Oh, Sarah, I am quite excited at the thought of Christmas in the country. It will be just like *Pickwick*, when they are at Dingley Dell!'

Sarah had to laugh. 'I have never met my grandfather, but I cannot think that he is at all like Mr Wardle! Whatever gave you that idea?'

Emily was not offended. She did not mind when Sarah laughed at her. 'I never said Lord Northcott was like Mr Wardle! I am sure I should not dare! No, I merely meant that it would be a proper country Christmas. I have never stayed at a country house before, you know.'

'No more have I,' said Sarah. She was relieved to see that Emily appeared to have accepted their absence from London, and was looking forward cheerfully to the change. She did not look for the reason for her change of heart, assuming that Emily had seen the sense in what Sarah had said. She herself, now that the visit was about to begin, was looking forward with a good deal less pleasure than Emily. Her only memory of her grandfather being so unhappy, she could not imagine how he would behave with her now.

In Norwich her doubts were momentarily allayed by seeing her father awaiting them on the platform.

'Papa! Oh, Papa, I never thought you would be here to meet us! How very good of you.'

'I could not wait to see you all,' he said, embracing her warmly. His wife he greeted with a chaste salute, and Emily with a kiss and brief hug. 'I had my family for such a short time, and I wanted to be with you when you arrive at the Hall.'

Looking at him, Sarah thought that she had never seen him look so well. The smart new clothes bought for his wedding had been changed for country wear that looked somehow both well-worn and elegant. His tall form was held easily upright; gone was the defeated stoop she remembered so well. Even his face had changed. It was fuller, less drawn, and she saw with a shock that it had an expression of peace that she had never seen there before.

'Papa, you look so different!' she exclaimed. 'I feel quite shy of you!'

He looked surprised. 'Do I? I suppose I must do. Everything has changed so much, these last few weeks, I declare I hardly know myself. Come, is this all of the luggage?'

'By no means, Papa. You surely cannot think that we can survive with only these few small bags? The boxes are over there, just now being unloaded by John. We brought one of the London footmen with us to take charge of the luggage. We are ladies of fashion, you know, and must have several changes for each day!'

They laughed together, remembering the days when she had had but three frocks, for everything, and he a threadbare overcoat.

'I suspected as much. It is a good thing that I had the foresight to order the fourgon as well as the coach. I had thought Madeleine and your maid, my dear, could go in it, but I see you have brought only Madeleine with you. How is this?'

Mrs Northcott turned from overseeing the unloading of their numerous boxes. 'It is most vexing, Mr Northcott, but the wretched girl refused point-blank to accompany us. She said she did not wish to leave London. I had to tell her to seek another situation.'

'Never mind,' he soothed. 'It is a quiet life here in the country, now that my father is not well. If you need more help than Madeleine can give, I am sure we could get a girl from the village.'

Mrs Northcott sniffed disparagingly, but agreed. There was something pleasantly feudal about the thought of a girl from the village.

The luggage was safely bestowed in the fourgon, and Madeleine and John were to travel with it, so that they would not be crowded in the coach. This was agreed with reluctance by Sarah, and with complacency by Mrs Northcott, who did not wish to share the coach with a servant, and who always felt that Madeleine's manner was far too familiar. Mr Northcott transferred one of the foot-warmers to the fourgon, saying that Madeleine would need it more in the draughty old conveyance. The coachman shut the door, and the heavy old coach lumbered off through the Norwich streets and out into the countryside.

Sarah was content to sit in silence while Emily chattered of theatres, parties and balls. The short winter day was drawing to a close, and Sarah saw with pleasure the sunset colouring of the sky that was as wide and clear as that of her childhood. There was a feeling of homecoming as she passed the flat fields, the little villages, the ever-present cuts and ditches that drained off the water. When it was too dark to see any more, she withdrew her attention from the window. Her father was teasing Emily on her many conquests in London, and Emily was replying in kind, giggling happily as she enumerated their number. Mrs Northcott said little, and Sarah wondered if she, too, was asking herself what sort

of a welcome she would receive in her husband's an-
cestral home.

They had a fair distance to travel, and after an hour
and a half Emily's growing silence led Sarah to think
that her estimation of Emily's reaction to the swaying
motion of the coach had been quite accurate. Huddled
together though they were, and warmly dressed, the cold
was beginning to seep through the cracks in the old doors,
and to wrap icy tentacles round feet and hands. Sarah
wriggled her cold toes, and hoped that they were nearly
there. Then she considered again, and hoped that they
were not. Another half-hour passed, and the horses
quickened their pace.

'They scent their stables,' said her father quietly. 'We
are nearly there.'

Emily, at Mrs Northcott's instigation, tried in a half-
hearted manner to tidy her hair and dress. Sarah sat
quietly, watching for the lights that soon glimmered out
of the darkness, drawing ever nearer until she could
clearly see the outline of the great house against the sky.
As the coach drew to a standstill, a huge oak front door
was opened at the top of a flight of shallow steps. The
coachman opened the door and let down the carriage
steps, and they alighted stiffly. Sarah would have hung
back, but her father took her arm and hurried her
forward.

'You will forgive me, madam, if I take my daughter
in,' he said to his wife. 'I want her to see my old home,
after all these years.' Sarah had a swift impression of a
large brick façade, and then she was up the steps and
blinking in the lamplight. She looked about her, bewildered. The panelled hall seemed to be full of people,

faces staring at her. She clung to her father's arm, not
knowing that she did so.

'They all want to see you, Sarah. Many of them remember me when I was a boy here, and those who do
not have parents who do.' She was introduced in quick
succession to the butler, the housekeeper and Lord
Northcott's personal servant. They greeted her warmly,
but she looked beyond them, searching the large room.

'My father does not leave his room,' said Mr
Northcott, correctly interpreting her wandering gaze.
'You will meet him later.'

She was relieved, and presently followed her
stepmother and Emily up the stairs to their rooms, the
housekeeper talking volubly all the way. Mechanically,
as if in a dream, she washed and changed her dress,
swiftly brushing out and coiling her hair into a simple
knot once again. Then she went to help Emily, since
Madeleine, travelling in the slower fourgon, would not
yet have arrived. Emily was unwontedly subdued.

'I never realised it would be so big, and so grand,' she
whispered to Sarah.

Sarah, who was feeling a similar dismay, stifled it and
encouraged her with cheerful words. 'Nonsense, it is just
that you are a little tired. I am sure it cannot be as grand
as the Duchess's house, where we went to the ball.'

Emily looked dubious, but followed Sarah down when
they were called. Mr Northcott led them into the library,
explaining that his father spent most of his day there,
on a chair or a day-bed. Emily shrank behind Sarah,
but Sarah put up her chin and looked her childhood's
nightmare in the face.

He must, once, have been as tall as her father, but age and illness had shrunk him. There was still fire, though, in those blue eyes, and the bony nose and jutting eyebrows bristled with suspicion. In a voice that was stronger than his appearance, he apologised for not rising.

'My doctor forbids any effort,' he said grimly, and Sarah thought it must be a brave doctor who could forbid him to do anything that he wished to do. He greeted his new daughter-in-law politely but distantly, looking her over, as Emily later confided to Sarah, as if he were considering her for a position such as housekeeper or cook. Emily's pretty face brought a grudging smile. Then Sarah came forward.

'My daughter Sarah, sir,' said her father quietly.

Lord Northcott looked at her, neither smiling nor frowning, and Sarah, stifling an inner tremor, looked as imperturbably back. Reluctantly he held out his hand, and Sarah took it and made a small curtsy. He did not offer or invite an embrace. His grip was unexpectedly strong, and his eyes continued to regard her fiercely as he uttered a few words of greeting. Sarah refused to drop her own eyes beneath that stare and schooled her face into impassivity. As a child, she had thought of him as a huge, terrifying ogre. Looking at him now, she felt an unexpected stir of pity, which she knew would annoy him almost more than anything else.

Dinner was an uncomfortable affair. In their honour, Lord Northcott had himself carried into the dining-room and took the head of the table, Mrs Northcott taking the foot, to her obvious delight. Sarah was not yet used to living in such formality, and she found the bevy of footmen, the number of dishes and the echoing size of the dining-room unnerving. It was also extremely cold, and she was thankful that a quiet warning from the housekeeper had led her to wear a warm shawl, and to advise Emily and Mrs Northcott to do the same.

Of them all only Lord Northcott and, unexpectedly, Emily, were fully at their ease. Emily had never yet encountered an elderly gentleman whom she could not twist round her little finger. She expected to please, and she did so. Lord Northcott's craggy face softened when he looked at her, and her lively chatter hid the silences that would otherwise have filled the room.

They all retired early after the journey. Lord Northcott bade them a cool, non-committal goodnight, and appeared to forget them almost before they had left the room. Sarah told herself, as she went upstairs, that in the morning things would seem better. She hoped she was right.

They were, after a fashion. As the days passed, each of them found a niche, and settled into it. Mr Northcott was already fully occupied with learning about the running of the estate. As a younger son, he had never concerned himself with it. He was dismayed to find much had been neglected, in the last few years, and happily applied his energies and some of his new income to putting things to rights. Mrs Northcott, after a few days of mutual suspicion, allied herself with the housekeeper. That good woman, at first afraid that there were to be criticisms and changes, soon learned that Mrs Northcott knew less about running a great house than she did. A tacit acceptance of this, never put into words but clearly understood on both sides, led to a harmonious relationship, while the possibility of replacing worn linen and buying new curtains and hangings cemented what could almost have been a friendship.

Emily, to everyone's surprise, was happy as well. At first she had feared that she would no longer be able to continue her correspondence with, as she supposed, Charles, but it was decided that John, having travelled down with them to care for the luggage, should stay for the time being and make himself useful in the house. This, since he was young and ambitious, he was happy to do, and Emily was thus assured of her postman. That problem solved, she was happy to live a country life, saying with some truth that she was tired after all their socialising. Much to her mother's surprise, she showed no sign of missing the excitements of London, and instead took to spending much of her time with Lord Northcott. In him she found a replacement for her father, who had been elderly when she was still a schoolgirl. She proved herself skilled in caring for and amusing him, and for his part he was happy to have a bright young face about him, and lost no opportunity of saying so.

Of them all, it was Sarah who found herself at a loss. Accustomed to being busy and useful, she found that here there was no role for her to play. The running of the house was more than taken care of by the housekeeper and Mrs Northcott, while her father was happily occupied with the estate. She felt herself to be useless, a situation with which she was totally unfamiliar. What saddened her most was that her natural role, as nurse and companion to her grandfather, did not come about.

Try as she might, she could not feel comfortable or at ease in the old man's company. He was unfailingly courteous, but never ceased to treat her as a stranger, and while she was happy to see Emily so well received, she could not help but feel hurt when she saw her bend over his chair, caressing and caressed, and knew that she herself was not loved like this. Feeling awkward and in the way, she spent less and less time in the library, and Emily soon commented on this.

"You do not spend very much time with Lord Northcott, dear Sarah. Is it my fault? Would you like me to leave you with him sometimes? He is your grandfather, not mine, and I do not want to be pushing in.'

'Of course you do not, Emily. If I do not spend much time with him it is not that I do not want to, but that he does not seem to be happy with me. He is still far from well, and I cannot see that it will do him any good to be fretted by my presence, when he is happy and relaxed with you.'

'You must not think that he dislikes you, Sarah. Indeed, he speaks of you always with great kindness, but with a sort of sadness, too. I know he always likes to hear me speak of you. He likes to hear about how we met, and what we did in London, but when I spoke of your life in Belgium he did not wish to hear of it. It seemed to make him very sad. I think he wants to love you, but does not know how to.'

Sarah guessed that her grandfather was feeling guilty about his former treatment of her. With his son it was easier. They had shared memories of his childhood; they could quarrel and make it up, but she was a stranger to him, the child he would have denied and cast out. Her very appearance, resembling as she did her despised mother, was an affront and a reminder. He had wronged her, and the fact that she was ready to forgive and forget did not make it any easier for this proud old man to accept her. Knowing that he had been wrong and unfair in his treatment of her, seeing her made him feel both guilty and irritated.

Because of this, Sarah confined her visits to her grandfather's room to duty appearances morning and evening. After the night of their arrival he had reverted to his former practice of taking his meals there, since the effort of coming to the dining-room was too much for him. Emily spent much of her day with him, reading, chatting, sewing and singing, and Sarah found herself very much alone. At her father's suggestion she started riding, an accomplishment she had never had the opportunity to master. She seized on this as a new occupation, and on every fine day made her way to the stables. For the first few days her aching muscles protested, but soon she became more accustomed to the exercise, and more proficient. The elderly groom who taught her pronounced himself satisfied that, providing she had a quiet horse and did not attempt to jump anything, she was safe enough to go out with a groom to take care of her.

Such freedom was an unfamiliar joy. Mounted on a quiet old grey who had been brought out of semiretirement for her use because he was as safe to ride as an old sofa, and about as fast, she took to roaming around the countryside with a youthful groom in attendance. The weather remained fine, cold and crisp but with no more than a sprinkling of snow, and she rejoiced in the wide clear skies and the homely familiarity of the flat landscape.

She took to visiting the villagers, finding that in many ways they resembled the Flemish fishermen and peasants she had known. They had the same sturdy independence, and the same almost incomprehensible dialect. Viewing her at first with suspicion, once they found that she came neither to patronise nor to preach, they made her welcome. Material assistance they had little need of, for she soon found that her grandfather was a good and conscientious landlord. There was even a small school, and while she was aware that her own experience of teaching was far removed from the needs of this little community, still Sarah hoped that in time she might be of use there.

On sunny days she rode down to the beach, not more than three miles distant, and left her horse by the dunes with her groom while she walked on the wide, empty sands. She could easily imagine herself back in Belgium, and chided herself for being homesick for it, now that she had everything that she had once longed for when they were poor and friendless. From these excursions she returned much refreshed, her hair tangled, her skirts heavy with sand, and her pockets full of seashells that made Madeleine scold her for her careless ways.

Her mind returned ceaselessly to St Ervan. She found it impossible to understand why he had proposed to her. Their relationship had been such a stormy one, whenever she saw him he seemed to delight in teasing her, and making her behave her worst. Could it be that it was merely a joke? If so, how it would have backfired if she had taken him at his word, and accepted him! For a moment she allowed her mind to dwell on the prospect, until she realised with a flush of shame that she was actually imagining him kissing her. He could not have meant it. And yet ... there had been a look in his eyes, sometimes ... She gave herself a shake. She would not allow her mind to dwell on him any longer.

CHAPTER THIRTEEN

CHRISTMAS WAS almost upon them. Emily had confided in Lord Northcott her expectations of a Pickwickian Christmas, and he, laughing heartily, had promised to do what he could. The house was in a bustle from dawn till long after dusk. Food must be procured, not forgetting the barrel of oysters, and seasonal delicacies were prepared in the kitchens, from which emanated a heady aroma of baking and roasting. The surrounding countryside was ransacked for greenery, and the house decked out with it. In the full flush of his enthusiasm Lord Northcott decided that they must have a party, and accordingly sent out invitations to all his neighbours. His family worried that it was too much for him, but his doctor cast a knowledgeable eye over his patient and said that it would do more harm to oppose his wishes than to allow him to have his way.

Unknown to them all, St Ervan was to be among those invited. On the point of leaving his home one evening several days before, he had been surprised to hear sounds of altercation from the front steps of his house. Making his leisurely way thither he had not been altogether surprised to see Oyster Sal in vigorous verbal conflict with his butler, who was sternly denying her entrance to the house.

'I tell yer, 'is lordship told me to come. 'Ere's 'is card, if yer don't believe me, you old...' Her epithet, somewhat to the Marquis's regret, was silenced as the wranglers saw him standing in the doorway.

'I beg your pardon, my lord, for this unseemly affray,' began the butler, only to find himself shoved aside by Sal.

''E wouldn't let me in, me lord, but I 'ad to see yer!'

'That will do.' His quiet voice was enough to halt them both. 'I beg you will not be so zealous in protecting me in future, Harding. If you will cast your eyes over that card, you will see that it is indeed mine, and that I have written on it.'

The butler took the card reluctantly between thumb and finger. It was certainly rather dirty and dog-eared, but the writing on it was unmistakable. 'I beg your lordship's pardon. I could hardly have thought that this—person—came at your lordship's invitation,' he said stiffly.

'I do not pay you to think, Harding.' The voice was gentle but cold, and the butler hastily banished the look of disdain from his face.

'No, my lord. I am sorry, my lord. If you will come this way, er, miss.'

Tossing her head, Sal followed him into the house and, at St Ervan's gesture, went into the study that led off the hall. The Marquis shut the door in his affronted butler's face, and set a chair for his unusual guest, waiting politely for her to be seated before he sat himself. Careless though he might be in the observance of the proprieties when with his equals, he seldom behaved with anything but punctilious courtesy with his inferiors in rank.

'You have news for me, Sal?'

'Yes, me lord. Oh, me lord, I'm sorry, but 'e's gorn!'

'Gone? Gone where?'

'That's just it, me lord, I don't know. You got me message, didn't yer, what I sent by my Tom?'

'Yes, I did. That's a good boy you have there, Sal.'

She smiled, willing to be sidetracked for a moment into maternal fondness. 'Yes, 'e's a good boy, right enough. 'Elps out in the market, 'e does, and brings all 'is money 'ome to me, and a nice bit o' fish, and all.'

'He told me our friend was planning something, and seemed to be preparing for a journey.'

'That's right. 'E didn't want anyone to know, see, 'cos they was all dunnin' 'im for 'is bills, but I kept me ears and eyes open, and I could see 'e were gettin' ready to do a flit. But I never thought 'e'd go so quick, or I wouldn't 'ave let 'im out o' me sight. 'E must 'ave gone in the night. I looked for 'im this mornin', like, and they said as 'ow 'e'd clean gone, packed up 'is things and all. 'Is landlady was in a fair old taking, I can tell yer. Owed 'er six months rent, 'e did. I could 'ave told 'er not to trust 'im, but she said as 'e was a gent, Gawd 'elp us, so she believed 'im when 'e said 'e'd pay 'er soon. 'Ow 'e got 'is stuff out without 'er knowin', I'll never know, but 'e did. Stripped bare, 'is rooms were, and 'er sleepin' like a baby all the while.' Sal seemed torn between scorn at the landlady's lack of acumen, and reluctant admiration for the skilled manner of his departure.

'He gave you no hint of his departure? Or of where he was intending to go?'

'Like I told you, 'e didn't want me to know nothin'. I knew 'e was goin', see, but 'e never knew I knew. And as for *where* 'e was going, it's obvious, ain't it? After that poor girl of 'is, what's gone to the country. You'd best get off after them, me lord, if you wants to stop 'im. Now 'e's left London, there'll be no comin' back for him, not without 'e's got some money to pay his whack.'

'You are right, Sal. I shall have to go after him. You have done very well to let me know so quickly. He cannot be very far ahead of me, for I fancy I know well enough where he has gone.' He stood up, and took some money from his pocket. 'Here, Sal, this will give those children of yours a good Christmas, and some over besides. I shall be off almost immediately, but I shall want to see you when I return. I will send you a message. There is no time at present, but I should like to see you out of that—profession—of yours, and I fancy you would not be sorry either.'

'No, me lord! Yes, me lord! Thank you, me lord!' gasped Sal, gaping at the largest amount of money she had ever seen in her life in her own hand. 'Leave off that—I should just think I would like to! And me old Mum, too, she wouldn't 'alf be pleased. Always on at me, she is, but like I says to 'er, what else can I do with 'er and two kids to feed?'

He gave her a gentle push towards the door. 'Go home, then, and tell her. I must make haste, now. I shall see you again when I return.' She departed in a daze of happiness, and at once he shouted for his butler.

'Harding! Tell that man of mine I want my things packed at once. I shall be going to Lessingham directly. No, I do not know how long I shall be staying, not above a fortnight, I suppose. And Harding, bring me the *Bradshaw*.'

The arrangements were quickly made, and a suitable train looked up. It was, he decided, too late to be leaving that evening, for to arrive at his cousin's house, unannounced and in the middle of the night, would occasion some surprise and might lead to the sort of gossip he particularly wished to avoid. St Ervan arranged for his groom to take his horses and his curricle down to Norfolk, and told his valet to wake him early as he intended to catch the first possible train. It was lucky, he thought, that he had a cousin living in such a convenient situation, and doubly lucky that he and his wife were of such an easy-going nature that they would accept his sudden arrival with equanimity and, probably, pleasure.

He was right. Arriving at his cousin's in time for luncheon the following day, he was greeted with pleasure by his host and his family, who accepted without question that he had taken a sudden whim to visit them. As a young man he had often behaved in this way, and while it might not have happened recently, well, it was just Anthony's way, and he had not grown out of it yet.

His cousin's house was not above ten miles from Northcott Hall. As soon as his groom arrived, the Marquis sent him round all the local villages with instructions to ask, discreetly, for news of any strange gentlemen who might be staying in the neighbourhood. It was of no use for him to go himself, for he was too well known both to Abbotsleigh and to the local people, and he had no wish to frighten his opponent into precipitate action. Sooner than he had hoped the groom was back, having run the quarry to earth in a secluded inn about five miles away.

'Calling himself Mr Andrews he is, my lord,' the groom told him. He had been with St Ervan for many years and was completely in his confidence.

'You did not let him see you, Jacob?'

'Oh, no, my lord. I never went near the place. I was asking in the next village, and one of the women at the inn there has a sister who works where he is, and she told me. Described him, she did, and said he was a proper nuisance to the maids.'

'Abbotsleigh to the life!' grinned St Ervan. 'Do you think he would know you if he were to see you?'

'Not he, my lord. One of those who never sees servants, not unless they've got pretty faces, that is.'

'Then I want you to stay there, Jacob. Keep him under your eye, and be careful, for he's a slippery customer. Whatever he does, I want to know of it. If he makes any move, or even looks as though he might, then you must send for me at once. Do you understand?'

'Yes, my lord. Don't you worry, my lord. He shan't take a breath without you hear of it.' With that, Anthony was content.

His cousins, meanwhile, were full of the new arrivals at Northcott Hall. Henry's unhappy marriage and untimely end were spoken of with some pity, although Henry had never been popular locally. They had called on Matthew when he had returned, and had found him much changed, but pleased to be home and reconciled to his father. When Lady Jane Lessingham found that her husband's cousin had actually met the rest of the family, and had known them in London, he was made to tell all that he knew, a task which considerably exercised his tact. Of Mrs Northcott he spoke at length, not altogether kindly, for he was still angry with her treatment of Sarah. Sarah herself he described merely as tall and dark, then he waxed eloquent over Emily's beauty.

'Sounds as though he's caught at last,' remarked Sir Julian in the privacy of the marital bedroom that night. His spouse was surprised. She had not thought him so perceptive. 'Not that I grudge it, mind, but it seems unfair, in a way, when he's as rich as Croesus already. What does he want with another fortune?' he asked her.

'Another fortune? Whatever do you mean? She will get something, of course, but the Northcotts are not rich. Most of the new money is tied up in the girl, my dear.' Sir Julian was regarding her in some confusion. Lady Jane tied the strings of her nightcap securely under her chin. 'You look puzzled. You surely did not think that he was interested in the heiress?'

'But he did nothing but talk about her! And he hardly mentioned the other girl at all!'

'Precisely.' Lady Jane climbed into bed with a look of feminine superiority on her lace-framed face. 'My dear Lessingham, Anthony is not a child, to be babbling of his newest interest. It is the very fact that he hardly mentioned her at all, when by all accounts he is well acquainted with her, that I find significant. Why else should he choose to visit us at this time? Not but what I'm very glad to see him, of course, but a family Christmas in the country is hardly my idea of Anthony's form of pleasure.'

'Well, it sounds like a lot of flim-flam to me,' he grumbled, thumping his pillow hard before blowing out the candle.

His wife smiled into the darkness. 'Yes, dear. That is because you are a man,' she said fondly. With this enigmatic but incontrovertible statement he had perforce to be satisfied.

The invitation arrived on the following day and was accepted with alacrity, the more so since Mrs Northcott, ever on the look-out for unattached young gentlemen, had thoughtfully included in the invitation any guests who might be staying at the house. To be sure, as Lady Jane remarked, ten miles was a long way to be driving on a winter night, but the moon would be almost at the full, and the coachman was to be trusted, so providing the weather stayed clear, it all seemed possible.

Sarah, who helped her stepmother with the arrangements for the party, saw St Ervan's name included in the reply from Lessingham Court. She felt a strange fluttering sensation, half pleasure, half almost fear, and schooled her face into impassivity.

Mrs Northcott was delighted. 'St Ervan! Down here, and we not here above ten days! It does seem as though...' She floated off into a happy dream.

'He has a cousin living near by,' remarked Sarah prosaically.

'So he might have, but why should he choose to visit there just at this moment, if not for being near us?'

Sarah could not deny it, but she wondered privately whether he was merely protecting Emily, or whether he also wanted to see her again. Since she found it hard to believe that Andrew Abbotsleigh could abduct Emily while she was in the safety of this country house, there seemed grounds to believe—to hope—that he had come for her.

Fortunately for the success of the party, the weather continued clear. The roads, though frosty, were dry and free of ice, and the moon shone brightly. By London standards it was a small affair, since Lord Northcott's health no less than the limited number of suitable neighbours precluded a large gathering. An elegant supper, cards for the older guests and games for the younger, with perhaps a little informal dancing, were the order of the evening, though this in itself was pleasure enough to set many a young heart into a hopeful flutter, and to brighten older eyes with the joyful anticipation of gossip.

Piqued by his wife's assumption of superior knowledge, Sir Julian was careful to observe his cousin's behaviour. As he did so, he felt more and more convinced that she must be wrong. St Ervan spoke little to Miss Northcott, and only with a serious face, whereas with Miss Yarcombe he was cheerful and smiling, encouraging her at the games, and dancing twice with her while an obliging governess played for them.

Sir Julian was not the only one who was watching. Mrs Northcott, too, her suspicions aroused by his sudden appearance in Norfolk, let no move or smile pass unnoticed. She was well satisfied with what she saw, and that night informed Mr Northcott of her suspicions.

'St Ervan? I would not have said he was the type of man to be attracted to Emily.'

Mrs Northcott bridled. 'I do not know why you should say such a thing. I am sure my little Emily is good enough for anyone!'

'I did not say she was not good enough. If anything, rather the reverse. He has a certain reputation, you know, and is nearly twice her age.'

'What nonsense! If he has a reputation, I am sure all that sort of thing is in the past. He has behaved with perfect propriety every time I have met him. To be sure, he is a little overbearing, but he is a Marquis, after all.'

'You must know best, my dear. At least he is wealthy enough not to be after her for her money. I suppose he thinks it is time he settled down. If it is so, it is a great match, and you are to be congratulated. But what of Emily? What does she think of him?'

'I hope Emily has been too carefully brought up to think anything of him, or of any other man, until I inform her that she may. In any case, I do not see how she could possibly object. He is charming, and so handsome!'

Mr Northcott wondered privately whether Emily might not have more ideas on the subject than her mother supposed, but wisely held his tongue on the subject. It did not seem to him that Emily held any of the young men of whom she spoke in particular regard, and though Sarah had not mentioned the subject since, he could not help remembering that evening in Bruges—how long ago it now seemed—when Emily had strayed from her hotel to meet someone.

Both Sarah and St Ervan would have been pleased to know that their own conversations had passed unremarked, though he might not have been so pleased had he known of the other hopes his behaviour had given rise to. Sarah had found herself not knowing how to talk to him. She had never felt uncomfortable in his presence before, because she had never cared what he thought of her. Now she found that she wanted him to like her— yes, to love her. His face was unreadable, and she treated him with a cool civility that he found almost daunting. He thought her indifferent, and began to speak of Emily, warning her that Abbotsleigh was in the neighbourhood. For one brief moment she felt a pang of jealousy that his only thought had been for her sister. She suppressed it, but he had not missed the flash in her eyes, and his heart leaped. He could not resist the temptation to punish her a little.

'Miss Yarcombe is looking particularly lovely this evening,' he remarked blandly. 'I can see I must hurry if I am to be sure of a dance with her.'

'Yes, indeed. You should not be wasting time here with me.'

Her face was calm, but there was a little shake in her voice that did not escape him. He could have swept her up into his arms there and then, but he merely turned in well simulated surprise to her. 'Come, Miss Northcott. How can you think me so uncivil? I meant, of course, when I have had the pleasure of a dance with you.'

'Please do not trouble yourself. I had not really intended to dance this evening.'

'That will not do, Sarah. I have already seen you dancing with someone else.'

Without giving her more time to demur, he swept her into the waltz. His strong hand clasped her waist, holding her closer than was usual, whirling her round the room as the music speeded up. Her white skirts swirling behind her, she was forced to lean on to his supporting hand and arm as they spun. She was dizzy and breathless, but not from dancing, and at that moment they could have been alone together, the rest of the room forgotten. His eyes caught and held hers, and her lips parted in a smile.

Her hand trembled in his, and she knew that he felt it. She was silent in his arms, and he resolved to put his luck to the test again very soon. When the dance was over, however, he merely bowed his thanks and took her back to her chair before leaving her for Emily. He knew that Mrs Northcott was going to be bitterly resentful of his interest in Sarah, and until he was in a position to be able to protect her from her stepmother's tongue he had no wish to expose her to unpleasantness. Sarah wrenched her eyes from his retreating back, and concentrated on replying with composure to the remarks of her neighbour.

CHAPTER FOURTEEN

THE FOLLOWING morning St Ervan arose early. His first task was to meet with his groom at a pre-arranged place. The isolated barn was not far from the inn where Abbotsleigh was staying, and at this time of year it was unused. Usually there was a note left on a convenient shelf just inside the door, but today there was nothing. He scarcely had time to wonder when he heard footsteps approaching, and recognised the whistling as that of his servant. His momentary anxiety was allayed when he saw that Jacob was in no hurry, but was strolling along with the appearance of a man taking a pre-breakfast walk on a fine morning.

'Good morning, my lord. All's quiet, so I ventured to come myself and speak to you.'

'You are quite sure he will not give you the slip? He is a crafty customer.'

'Not so crafty as I am, my lord,' came the complacent reply. 'We're by way of being friends, you see. We sat and drank together. And when I say drank... I've never seen a gentleman put it away like that. I was paying, you see, and I get the feeling he's very short of money. The landlord is giving him funny looks, and asking for money before he will serve him. Seems to me he's shot his bolt.'

'You may well be right. He certainly left a mass of debts behind him in London.'

'The thing is, my lord, now we have him nice and settled, we don't want to lose him. If the landlord throws him out, he'll go I don't know where, and he would be suspicious if I followed him.'

'No, we must keep him here. We can scarcely pay his shot for him, but there must be some way of getting him some money.'

Jacob grinned. 'Nothing easier, my lord. Like I said, him and me's by way of being cronies. A hand or two at cards, and there you have it. Bored silly, he is, and missing his old haunts. Nothing he'd like better than a few hands of cards with me.'

'The very thing! If he knows you have money, he'll have it off you, one way or another.'

'No doubt of that. We had a few games last night, just for shillings, and I know a sharp when I see one.'

'What does he think you are? What reason have you given him for staying there?'

'I told him I am a horse-dealer. He could see I'm at home with horses. Said I was looking for likely young horses for a customer, and taking a few days off at his expense over Christmas. He swallowed that right enough.'

'And he was in his cups last night. Did he talk?'

'Nothing useful, my lord, but then I never asked him much. Didn't want to put him on his guard, asking too many questions. He wasn't that keen to sit with me; it was only the free drinks that tempted him, I reckon. By the time I put him to bed he was dead to the world, and he won't be awake yet, not by a long chalk. And when he does wake, he won't be feeling so wonderful, I shouldn't think.'

'You must have a remarkably hard head yourself, Jacob.'

'Bless you, my lord, I hardly had a drop! Brandy, he was on, and the gin for me. I had one or two at first, to keep him happy, but once he was fuddled you may guess that it was more water than gin in my glass, and him none the wiser. I had a bottle all ready. He never saw me change them over.'

'Well done, my friend. So you put him to bed, did you?'

'I did, my lord. Leastways, I put him on his bed and took his boots off. Landlord helped me. I had a quick look through his things, too, after the landlord had gone. Funny old collection it was, too. One or two small things that might not belong to him at all, I'd say, and a bit of jewellery I could swear I've seen on his Ma, once.'

'Nothing in writing, though? No letters?'

'Afraid not, my lord. There was writing things out on the table, though, looked as though they'd been used. He's too fly to keep anything like that lying around. I couldn't search too well, as I didn't want the landlord to start wondering where I'd got to.'

'Never mind. You have done very well, Jacob. Here is some more money. Make friends with him if you can, but be careful. He will be very much on his guard, if I am right in what he intends. He will not want to leave any clues behind which might help anyone to catch up with him before it is too late. Send for me at once if anything happens. I will try to stay at the Court as much as I can, but if I have to go out, I will leave word where I may be found.'

Watching his groom walk whistling back whence he had come, the Marquis wished that he did not have this added responsibility thrust upon him, when all he wanted to do was to pursue his wooing. If only Jacob had been able to come up with more substantial proof, he would have taken the whole thing to the Northcotts and left them to deal with it. As it was, he had no idea why Abbotsleigh should be so confident that he could get Emily away, and no way of proving that such was his intent. The word of a woman such as Oyster Sal would not carry much weight with Mrs Northcott, he knew. Besides, he wanted to be rid of Abbotsleigh once and for all. Knowing what kind of man he was, he could not have it on his conscience to leave the man at large.

As he rode home he mused that it ought to be possible to discuss the matter with Matthew Northcott. He, at least, was a man of the world who would know as well as he himself did the depths of villainy to which such a man could sink.

As he considered this, St Ervan also thought of the night before when he had resolved to try again to win Sarah. Wise in the ways of females, he felt sure that she was not as indifferent to him as she had claimed. The main trouble was likely to be her pride. Having told him that she disliked him, it was not going to be easy for her to back down. There again, her father might be able to help. He knew that she was very fond of him, and that his opinion was bound to carry weight with her. If her father could talk to her, persuade her that he did indeed care for her... He kicked his horse into a canter and hurried back for breakfast.

Escaping with some difficulty from his cousin's hospitable plans for the day, he made his way to Northcott Hall, and arrived by mid-morning. Matthew Northcott was alone in the estate-room, and explained that his father, tired by the party, was keeping to his rooms, and that the ladies of the family had all taken advantage of the fine weather to go to Norwich for the day to do some Christmas shopping. Matthew led the way to the library, apologising profusely for their absence.

'It is of no moment,' said the Marquis, accepting a glass of sherry and seating himself near the fire. 'It was really you whom I wished to see, sir.'

Matthew looked and felt startled. It crossed his mind that perhaps his new wife had more perspicacity than he had given her credit for. His astonishment grew as his guest, far from launching himself into a request for Emily's hand, proceeded to warn him that she was in danger.

'My dear St Ervan, I cannot but feel that you exaggerate,' he said soothingly. 'There can be no danger to Emily here.'

'I do not think you can be acquainted with Abbotsleigh,' replied St Ervan grimly. 'He is a most unpleasant type of man, ruthless and unpredictable. If even half of the whispers I have heard about him are true, he would stop at nothing to lay his hands on Miss Yarcombe's money. He is, I believe, a desperate man. And he has been seen in the neighbourhood.'

While making allowance for the natural anxiety of a lover who fears for his new-found beloved at every turn, Matthew had himself heard enough about Abbotsleigh to think that there might indeed be some risk. 'What should I do?' he asked helplessly.

'All you can do is be watchful. I myself am keeping an eye on Abbotsleigh, but it is after all no crime to stay in the country, even under an assumed name. Oh yes, he is calling himself Andrews.'

'Should I not warn her?'

'I think not. It would only alarm her. She does not like the man, so she is unlikely to go with him of her own volition. As long as she does not go out of the grounds alone, she should be all right. But if she does leave your land, she should be accompanied by someone you can trust, and if possible by a strong man-servant as well.'

'Good heavens, she is at this very moment in Norwich!'

'With her mama and Miss Northcott, who can be trusted to take care of her. He cannot do much in a crowded street, and besides, I understand he is a trifle under the weather today.'

'But we cannot lock her up here for ever!'

'It should not be necessary. I will exert myself to the utmost to be rid of him. He is bound to make a mistake, and as soon as I have some proof, I will use it.'

'You are putting yourself to a great deal of trouble for my family,' said Mr Northcott innocently.

His guest rose to his feet and took a turn about the room before answering. 'I cannot deny that I have an interest in your family, sir. I have another reason for calling on you this morning.'

'Yes, I was beginning to think you might have,' said Mr Northcott slyly.

St Ervan was surprised, but let it pass. 'I have the honour, sir, to request permission to pay my addresses to your daughter.'

'Have you, by Jove!' Matthew Northcott reflected that he was not really the one to be asked, but since his guest was being so formal, he supposed that as the man of the family it was for him, and not the girl's mother, to receive the first request. 'It's not really for me to say you yea or nay. I don't know what the girl thinks. I suppose no parent in his right mind would turn you down as a son-in-law, but I'm fond of the girl, and I want to see her happy. I'll be blunt with you, St Ervan, and tell you that I've heard some things about you that make me wonder whether you'd be a good husband for a gently-bred young girl. No offence, mind,' he added hastily, eyeing the Marquis's height and build in some alarm.

To his relief, his prospective son-in-law smiled. 'It's true that I've led a pretty wild sort of life. But it's also true that there was never anything serious in the gossip about me. I won't deny that I've been in a good many scrapes, but there was never any real harm in them. Utkinton, for instance...'

Mr Northcott interrupted him. 'I heard all about that at the time, and I must say he deserved everything he got. I suppose, if you're wanting to settle down... but as I've said, it's not for me to decide. I don't know what she thinks of you. It doesn't matter how eligible you are, if she don't care for you.'

St Ervan grimaced. 'I am afraid she has taken me in dislike, sir. It's my fault; I have this dashed bad habit of saying what comes into my head without thinking about it. When we first met I made her very angry with me, and now I have to live with the consequences.'

'She didn't look angry with you last night,' remarked Matthew, remembering Emily's laughing face as she danced with the Marquis.

'Not altogether,' admitted Anthony, remembering the flash of jealousy he had discerned, and the tremble of Sarah's hand in his. 'That is what gives me to hope. I cannot deny to you that I have spoken to her on the subject, and she turned me down flat.'

'You don't want to worry about that,' said Mr Northcott comfortably. 'These young girls can be very missish when it comes to proposals.'

St Ervan reflected that missish was hardly a word he would have used in connection with Sarah, but made allowances for a father's partiality in seeing his only daughter as younger and more delicate than she really was. 'I am afraid that she did not think me sincere. She does not seem to believe that I love her.'

'Want me to have a word with her, eh?'

'If you would be so kind. I prefer to handle my own lovemaking, but she will respect your judgement. I can assure you that I do most sincerely love her.'

'Well, I shall have to tell her that you called to ask my permission to speak to her again, and I will tell her that in my opinion you are sincere. Further than that I will not go. I will have no pressure put on her.'

'I would not expect it. Thank you, Mr Northcott. I will take my leave now, for I am sure you are busy. May I return tomorrow or the day after? I have been a poor sort of guest, I fear, always disappearing on my own errands. It might be necessary for me to postpone my visit for at least a day. I believe my cousin has planned some excursion for tomorrow, and he would be upset if I were not to take part.'

'By all means, return when you like.' They parted on excellent terms, neither aware that the other had been speaking and thinking of a different girl. The truth was that Matthew Northcott had been so accustomed to hearing his daughter say she had no interest in marriage that it had not occurred to him that the Marquis had been speaking of her. Emily was his daughter, in law if not in fact, and since they had earlier been speaking of her, it seemed obvious that she, pretty, rich and eligible, should have been the one to catch the Marquis's fancy.

As soon as the three female members of the family returned from Norwich, tired out and laden with parcels, Mr Northcott made haste to take his wife aside and tell her what had happened in her absence. She was triumphant.

'Did I not tell you, Mr Northcott? Did I not say he was interested in her? And now you see that I am right. Oh, my dear, dear Emily a Marchioness! I never thought she would do so well—never! And he is rich, too—not that it signifies, precisely, but at least he is not marrying her for her money. A Marchioness! How happy she will be!'

'But does she care for him?'

'Care for him? Of course she will care for him. How can she not do so? He might be any girl's dream, so handsome as he is, besides the title and the money. Where is she? I must tell her.'

As luck would have it, Emily was alone in her room, putting away her purchases. She looked up smiling as her mother came in.

'I think these gloves will do very well for Papa Northcott, do not you, Mama? And I am particularly pleased with this book for Lord Northcott, for it is newly published, and I know he will enjoy it. What is it, Mama? You look at me so strangely. Is anything amiss?'

'Amiss? My dearest child, how can you think so? Come and give me a kiss, for I have something wonderful to tell you.'

Obediently Emily planted a kiss on her parent's cheek. 'Something wonderful? Whatever can you mean, Mama?'

'My dear Emily, I bring you the happiest tidings that any mother can bring her daughter. Today, Mr Northcott has received an offer for your hand in marriage, and such an offer! Even now I can scarcely believe your good fortune! My dear Emily, what do you say to being a Marchioness?'

'A Marchioness? I do not understand you, Mama. How can this be?' She had turned quite white, a fact that Mrs Northcott put down to excess of emotion, and it did not displease her.

'A Marchioness, dearest girl, because you are to marry a Marquis. Lord St Ervan has done you the honour of wishing to make you his wife. I see you are surprised; I am glad to see that you have such true delicacy of mind that you have not previously thought to interpret his very distinguished attentions thus. Now, my child, it is otherwise. You have my—our—permission and blessing to think of him as your future husband.'

Emily burst into tears.

Mrs Northcott fished in her reticule for a handker-chief and her smelling-salts, and pressed them both on her daughter, sitting her in a chair and hanging over her solicitously. 'My poor child, the sudden excitement has been too much for you! I should have broken it to you more gently. Pray, my dear, calm yourself. Had you no idea of his preference for you?'

'He has never thought of me!' sobbed Emily. 'It is not me he loves at all, but Sarah!'

'Nonsense, my dear, you have imagined it. Sarah, indeed! How could she possibly be preferred to you?'

'I tell you, Mama, he does not love me.'

'I believe he said to Mr Northcott that you might be under that impression, and he begged him to inform you that his sentiments were as sincere as any female could desire. I understand he spoke with the greatest warmth. You may safely trust your heart to him.'

'But I do not want to!' cried Emily angrily. 'I will not marry him, Marquis or no Marquis. Do not ask it of me, Mama, for I do not love him, and I will never consent.'

'Foolish girl, how can you say such a thing?' Mrs Northcott could not believe what she heard. 'Have I not told you he has my permission? I will not allow you to throw away such a chance as this. You are overwrought; all this has been too much of a shock. You will stay in your room and rest. I shall tell them you are not to be disturbed.' With that, she swept from the room, leaving her daughter a prey to the most dismal reflections.

CHAPTER FIFTEEN

WHEN MRS Northcott returned an hour later, she was shocked to find that her daughter, far from having calmed down and come to a proper realisation of her good fortune, had hardened her determination not to accept the Marquis's very flattering offer. When her mother entered, she was sitting very upright in a chair, dry-eyed, and with one glance Mrs Northcott could see that she had a battle on her hands. She hardly recognised her usually meek and obedient daughter.

'Now, Emily, you are being very foolish,' she began.

'Yes, Mama, I suppose I am, in a worldly sense. But Mama, you have always been very kind, so surely you do not want me to undertake a marriage that will make me so unhappy? I cannot believe it.'

'Of course not, my dear child. But I cannot see that marriage to a Marquis with a handsome face and fortune is likely to bring you anything other than joy. I should be a strange mother if I did not encourage you into such a splendid match.'

'Even though I tell you that I do not, I cannot, love him?'

'What can you possibly know of such things, at your age? You cannot tell me that you dislike St Ervan? You have always seemed perfectly happy in his company.'

'I like him well enough as a friend.'

'Then you are luckier than many girls in your position,' returned her mother drily. 'Do you imagine that I was in love with your father when I married him, so young as I was? I liked him and respected him, and I knew that I was a lucky girl to have such an opportunity to rise in the world, for you know that my own parents were in a very small way and had very little money. Yet you cannot deny that we were happy together. You will find, my dear, that love between husband and wife is something that, if you are lucky, grows after marriage.'

'But I am not like that! Since I have money of my own, why must I marry against my own heart?'

'The possession of money brings with it yet more responsibilities. In the society to which we now belong, marriage for love is even rarer than in the lower orders. You are fortunate, indeed, that such a man should have declared his love for you, for you may be assured that he is sincere, and not merely a fortune-hunter.'

Emily sighed. She still feared to tell her mother that her affections were already given. She knew that everything her mother said was true, and that marriage for love was something that rarely occurred outside the pages of a novel. Nevertheless, she could not agree to such an engagement. St Ervan had, she knew, a character totally dissimilar from her own. While he might, she thought, have been momentarily dazzled by her face, he could never be happy with such a girl as she knew herself to be. To enter into such a marriage would be to ensure a lifetime of misery for them both, but she found herself unequal to the task of explaining this to her mother. She thought that perhaps, having been refused by Sarah, he had decided that it did not matter whom he married, as long as she were a suitable match.

'I cannot marry him. I do not love him,' she reiterated helplessly.

Mrs Northcott lost her temper. 'I have tried to be patient with you, and understanding, for I know that girls of your age are subject to moods and strange ideas. Nevertheless, if you continue to defy me, I have to tell you, miss, that it will not do. How can you be so ungrateful, after all that I have done to introduce you into good society? For no reason at all, that I can see, you turn down a suitor that most girls would give their eye-teeth for. I tell you that I will not stand for it. You shall stay in this room, seeing no one, until you come to a proper realisation of your duty to me. Obedience is what you owe your parents, and obedience I will have.' She swept from the room once again, leaving Emily dissolved in tears.

On the landing she found Sarah, attracted by the sound of quarrelling voices, hovering anxiously. She knew nothing of what was afoot, for her father had withdrawn to the estate-room at the first hint of dissension in the household, and Mrs Northcott did not choose to discuss the matter with her stepdaughter, the more so as Emily seemed to have some maggot in her head that the Marquis had a preference for Sarah. She was more than half inclined to blame this new rebellion on Sarah's pernicious influence, telling herself that Emily had never defied her mama before.

'Oh, what is wrong, ma'am? I could not help but hear Emily crying. Is she unwell?'

'She is not, but she is a disobedient, unnatural girl to upset her mother so,' replied Mrs Northcott, her own spirits finding relief in a burst of tears.

'Come, ma'am, surely not? I know how sincerely attached she is to you, and how she strives to please you. What has she done?'

'I am afraid that is something that I am unable to discuss with you, as it is of a very private nature. I have told Emily that she is to stay in her room until she has seen the error of her ways, and I would thank you, Miss Sarah, to be obedient to my wishes, and not speak to her.'

Sarah was hurt, but made allowance for her stepmother's overwrought state. 'Of course I will do whatever you say, ma'am. I fear you are very upset— may I fetch you anything? At least let me take you to your room, and send for something to restore you.'

Mrs Northcott was a little softened, and allowed herself to be led to her chamber, where Sarah persuaded her to undo her stay laces and lie on a couch while some tea was brought. The mother wept quietly into her handkerchief. To have all her hopes and dreams so overset was more than she could bear, but she had a feeling that for once her biddable daughter was not going to change her mind. She was adamant, however, that she would not discuss the matter with Sarah, nor would she permit her to visit Emily in her room. Sarah, therefore, spent a solitary evening, dining alone since none of the rest of the family put in an appearance. She was worried about Emily and longed to go to her, but she could not go against Mrs Northcott's stated wishes. She felt sure that Emily must, for some reason or another, have con-

fided in her mother her love for Lieutenant Dulverston.
Sarah could understand only too well the dismay that
so ambitious a parent must feel on hearing of her
daughter's wish to ally herself with a second son of no
fortune and few immediate prospects.

Emily, alone in her room, abandoned herself to tears
for a while. Then she sat up, blew her nose and wiped
her eyes, and set herself to think. She was under no illusions that she would be able to continue to defy her
mother for long. While she could not be forced into an
unwilling marriage, the pressure that a parent could bring
to bear was considerable, the more so since there was
no reason in the eyes of the world, and of the rest of
the family, to turn down the chance of such a brilliant
match. Mr Northcott, she knew, would not dream of
interfering between them, and Lord Northcott, whose
opinion her mother would be more inclined to value,
could only view with pleasure the alliance of his family
with that of the St Ervans.

Her only hope, as she saw it, was Charles. Surely, now,
he would accept the need for action? Unwilling though
he might be to compromise her, or to allow her to ally
herself with him while his fortunes were so unsure, surely
he could not, if he loved her, allow her to be talked into
this marriage. With many pauses for thought, and much
scratching out, she composed a letter, blotching it with
her tears as she wrote, containing an impassioned plea
that he save her from this dreadful pass. When her supper
was brought to her, the letter was ready and folded in
her hand, and to her joy it was John himself who carried
up the tray.

The servants, as usual, had a very much better idea of what was going on than anyone realised, and were certainly more aware of the situation than Sarah was. John felt sure that Miss Emily would be wanting to communicate with her lover, and he was happy to think that he would be able to perform this service for her, and to put her mind at rest. He was sincerely attached to his young mistress, and was young enough himself to see no harm in carrying their correspondence. Emily jumped to her feet as he entered the room, and hurried towards him. Hastily he raised his eyebrows and jerked his head towards the door, knowing that the butler was within earshot.

Emily was quick to understand him. 'Oh, John,' she said carelessly, 'I do not think I could eat anything. Please take the tray away again.' She moved round out of sight of the doorway, and showed him the letter. 'Please take it away quickly,' she said with meaning, and he nodded.

'I'm sorry you're not hungry, miss. I'll get this out of here at once,' he said. 'Will you be wanting anything later, miss? A nice cup of tea, or some hot milk? I'm sure Cook would be happy to send up something in an hour or so.'

She raised her eyebrows at that. She had thought that her letters were being sent to and from London, for Abbotsleigh had realised that she would not expect Charles to be able to leave his duties and follow her to Norfolk. John nodded vigorously to her, however, and she slipped the letter into his pocket. 'Yes, I might fancy some hot milk later on. Whenever it is convenient to Cook,' she said.

John himself was unable to leave his duties, but he had arranged with one of the grooms that he would take messages with him when he went home in the evening, since he lived not far from the inn where Abbotsleigh was staying. John had explained that he had an uncle, a warm man with no heirs, who was visiting the neighbourhood, and that he, John, was anxious to keep in with the wealthy relative, and thus be remembered in his will. The groom, who was not over-bright, had seen nothing strange in this, and unquestioningly delivered the letters to the inn.

Andrew Abbotsleigh was feeling remarkably cheerful. The inn, if not perhaps all that he was accustomed to, was not uncomfortable, and the innkeeper's wife was no mean cook. In addition, it was stocked with some good wines and a surprisingly palatable brandy. To crown it all, he had just refilled his purse with some much-needed money, and he need no longer fear that the innkeeper would treat his lordly demands with rudeness, or even a downright refusal.

Fate, he thought, was playing into his hands. He had established a useful correspondence with the heiress, who was ready to fall into his hands at any moment, and then, just when he most needed money, along had come that bumpkin, his pockets full of money given to him to buy horses, and willing to play cards with this chance-met stranger. Abbotsleigh had no compulsion in emptying his purse, for he was nothing but a vulgar fellow, a mere horse-dealer or some such, who was foolish enough to think that he could play cards with a gentleman and win. It had scarcely been necessary even to fuzz the cards, and under the influence of a few glasses of brandy he had skilfully relieved his opponent of his money, apologising all the while. As he mused before a handsome fire, a glass in hand and breathing the aroma of what promised to be a good dinner, the innkeeper came in.

'Letter for you, Mr Andrews. Young Sam brought it from Northcott Hall.'

'Very good, landlord. That will be all—oh, stay, you may bring me some more of this brandy. It is not bad.'

'Yes, sir.' The landlord swallowed the insult. He set no store by this London fellow, with his lordly ways and his empty pockets, but while he was prepared and able to pay, he could stay. Times were hard, and a customer who would order and pay for the choice delicacies his wife was at this moment working over in the kitchen must be humoured.

When the new bottle of brandy had been brought and the landlord had withdrawn, Abbotsleigh opened the letter idly and began to read it. After a few words he sat up straight, and read with more attention. The writing was shaky, the words blotched with tears, but that was of no interest to him. What did move him to excitement was the news it contained.

First of all, he was alarmed to hear that St Ervan was in the neighbourhood, and even more that he had cast his eyes in the heiress's direction. He found it almost impossible to believe that he had proposed, for to his certain knowledge the Marquis had resisted the blandishments of young women both lovelier and richer than Emily. He found it even harder to believe that she was prepared to refuse him. However, that was what she had written, and also that her mother was exerting some pressure to make her accept. That did not surprise him!

It was not the first time he had encountered such a match-making mama, and he mentally congratulated her on her success.

Except, of course, that she was not going to be successful. For here was this goose of a girl, with the world before her feet, begging him to rescue her! She was even proposing what he had never dared suggest as yet, an elopement! It was almost too good to be true, and for a moment his head almost swam with delight. Certainly coming to this inn had been an inspired decision, he told himself. Here he was with the heiress almost within his grasp, and thanks to last night's success with the cards he even had the means to carry it through.

Pouring himself another glass of brandy, he set himself to thinking. Tomorrow, he realised, was Christmas Eve, a day when every household in the country would be preparing for the festival on the morrow. An ideal day, he thought, for everyone would be too busy to notice what was going on around them. His plans were soon made, and he rang for pen and ink.

He re-wrote the letter twice before he was satisfied with it. It would not do to frighten her off now by appearing too eager. Better, if anything, to be reluctant, to speak of her reputation. Then to agree—in so gentlemanly a fashion—to what she wanted. He counselled Emily to appear more submissive, so that she might be allowed to take a walk in the garden. That would be their moment to make an escape. He closed with protestations of tender care and undying love, and exhorted her not to make the sacrifice unless she were sure, really sure, of her own heart.

The letter finished to his satisfaction, he ordered it to be carried at once to Northcott Hall and delivered to John. Then he set himself to perfecting the rest of his plans. His servant had, according to his orders, taken possession of a cottage some few miles away, in an isolated piece of woodland. It was to this cottage that he intended to carry Emily. His design hinged on her failing to recognise him until he had her safely there, where her cries could not be heard and he could keep her hidden for at least one night, maybe two. During that time he aimed to seduce her, for he felt sure that once her ruin were thus accomplished, her mother would have no choice but to agree to her instant marriage.

In her bedroom at Northcott Hall, Emily waited. At last came the knock she had been waiting for. John came in with her cup of hot milk on a tray. He did not speak, but nodded meaningfully at the tray as he laid it down. As soon as the door had closed behind him, she snatched the cup from the tray and found her letter, hidden under the embroidered cloth.

As she read it, she was torn by different emotions. Part of her was pleased and excited at the thought of running away with Charles. Part of her, though, was sad, almost hurt, that he was willing to elope with her with so little argument. He, who had always been so strict with her, not allowing her even the minor indiscretion of writing to him, was now prepared to countenance a runaway match. She felt somehow lost, as if the floor on which she stood had suddenly become unstable beneath her. For a horrible moment she wondered whether the Charles she thought she knew really existed, or whether he was just such a fortune-hunter as her mother had always warned her against. She pushed the disloyal thought away from her, but it lay coiled like a nightmare monster in the deeper levels of her mind.

It was perhaps unfortunate that Mrs Northcott decided not to bid her erring daughter good-night. If she had done so, Emily might well, in the turmoil of her heart, have admitted everything to her. As it was, she spent an almost sleepless night packing a few jewels and such money as she possessed into her reticule, since it was clearly impossible to carry anything larger away. She awoke from a fitful sleep unrefreshed, but in a more determined frame of mind. When Mrs Northcott came to see her, she was gratified to find that her daughter had come to a more dutiful mood. She was greeted with an apology and a burst of tears, both of which were heartfelt and genuine.

'I will try to love Lord St Ervan, if that is what you wish, Mama,' she said, all contrition.

'That's my good girl! I knew you could not remain obdurate for long. A period of quiet reflection has shown you how very foolish it would be to turn down such an offer, has it not?

'Yes, Mama,' Emily replied meekly, hanging her head, and blushing with shame at her falsehood.

'You are looking pale, my love. It will not do for you to be receiving your distinguished suitor until the roses are back in your cheeks.'

'Yes, Mama, I have a little headache,' admitted Emily, snatching at this heaven-sent opportunity. 'I think perhaps a little fresh air, this afternoon, would help.'

'A nice walk in the garden, with Sarah?'

'Yes, Mama. Only, do you know, I think I would rather be alone. It would be a chance to think things over...'

'Very well, but just in the garden, mind. And do not stay out too long; this is no time to be taking a chill.'

'Thank you, Mama,' said her dutiful daughter.

In high good humour Mrs Northcott swept downstairs to supervise the last-minute preparations for Christmas.

CHAPTER SIXTEEN

IN LONDON, Lieutenant Charles Dulverston was worried. He had heard no news of Emily since she had left for Norfolk. His sister wrote that she had received no letter from her friend. Emily was accustomed to write to Lettice two or three times a week, with the express intention of sending messages to Charles. Now, for the first time, he found himself regretting that his own punctilious regard for the correct forms had made it impossible for him to write to Emily, or to receive letters from her.

He knew that she must have been disappointed, perhaps even annoyed, that he had been unable to see her before she left London. Perhaps, he thought, she was punishing him for what she might see as a lack of attention. At the same time, he had never known her to behave in such a way, for she was nothing if not direct, and if she was angry with him she was more likely to say so in no uncertain terms. So long a silence was most unlike her.

In the end, he took his problem to his Colonel. He, though unwilling to allow his junior officers to tie themselves up in marriage at such a relatively young age, was yet man of the world enough to feel that it would be improvident, to say the very least, to allow such a notable heiress to slip, as it were, through his fingers. Charles was therefore granted a week's leave, and he set off at once.

As he travelled, he pondered on how he was to present himself at Northcott Hall without exciting too much speculation. Not being acquainted with Lord Northcott or his son Matthew, he could scarcely arrive as a guest, particularly so close to Christmas. He must find himself accommodation near by, then visit as casually as he could, saying that since he was in the neighbourhood he had taken the liberty of calling on his friends from London. He had no acquaintance in the vicinity, so he must put up at an inn, but he would have to make it appear that he had some business in the county that necessitated his presence there. He could only hope he would not be questioned too closely on the subject. It did not, fortunately, occur to him that Mrs Northcott saw him as a suitor for Sarah, and would inevitably see his visit as having matrimonial intent.

On reaching Norwich, he hired himself a horse without any loss of time, and without much difficulty discovered a comfortable inn at a small town some few miles from the Hall. Having seen his few belongings bestowed, for he had travelled with the minimum of luggage, he called for pen and ink and wrote what he hoped was a suitably bland note, saying that as he was by chance in the neighbourhood he would give himself the honour of calling on them the following afternoon, to wish the family the compliments of the season. He chose the afternoon, knowing that Mrs Northcott generally retired to her room for an hour or two after luncheon, and he would be more likely to see the young ladies on their own.

His letter arrived on the same evening as Emily's one purporting to be from him. Mrs Northcott, perplexed and worried, was not much interested in it. 'Lieutenant

Dulverston?' she replied in a preoccupied tone to her husband's query, 'Oh, yes, quite a pleasant young man. His sister was Emily's great friend at school, and I believe he called a few times in London. I had an idea that he might be interested in Sarah,' she added carelessly.

'What sort of a young man is he?' enquired Mr Northcott, not unnaturally interested.

'I hardly know. A younger son, of course. Good family, but no prospects. She could probably do better for herself now that your father has relented towards you.'

'Did she seem to care for him?'

'I could not say. I suppose she liked him well enough. They seemed to dance together, and converse, and she did not repulse him. He might do well enough.'

'A second son... But if she cared for him...'

Mrs Northcott was impatient with the conversation. She had little interest in Sarah's matrimonial prospects at the best of times. Privately she thought the girl too old, too headstrong and too tall to attract any good match, while her mother's birth and her own upbringing would, she thought, disgust any man of good family.

'It seems to me most likely that this is no more than a courtesy visit. If, however, he should declare himself when he comes tomorrow, I would advise you not to turn him down, second son or no. Until that time, I see no need to discuss the matter further.' Mr Northcott would have liked to sound Sarah out, but he thought it might be unfair to raise hopes in her breast until they knew for certain whether the Lieutenant had any intentions towards her.

Meanwhile, Emily was preparing for her flight with some care. Knowing how little money Charles had, she was determined to go to him as well provided as was possible under the circumstances. After some thought, she contrived to stitch two stout petticoats together so that they formed a huge circular pocket. Into this she was able to put several changes of underwear, two night-gowns and an evening dress. The full-skirted fashions of the day meant that she had merely to leave off her stiffened and padded underskirt that usually held her skirts in their wide bell shape, and she looked much as usual.

At her own request, her luncheon was brought to her on a tray. Her mouth was so dry that the cold chicken stuck to the inside of it, but she forced down as much as possible. A soldier, and, she supposed, a soldier's wife, must eat when the opportunity presents itself, and already she thought of herself as a soldier's wife preparing for manoeuvres. It helped her to subdue the feeling that she was doing something very wicked.

When the tray had been removed, she dressed herself carefully, putting on two dresses, a shawl, and then a warm, enveloping cloak and stout boots. She managed to tuck a pair of shoes into her muff, thankful that the cold weather made it possible for her to wear such garments. Letting the hood of her cloak hang down, she donned a bonnet, hung her reticule over her arm, and anxiously inspected her appearance in the looking-glass. She looked rather bulky and stiff, she thought, but while she might have attracted attention in London, here in the country no one was likely to remark it, and indeed she hoped to gain the garden without seeing anyone.

Before leaving the room, she picked up the letter that she had spent some care over during the morning. It had cost her not a few tears, and several attempts had been thrown on the fire before she was satisfied. Now she looked for somewhere to leave it. It would not do to have it in open view, for who knew whether her mother or Madeleine might not take it into their heads to come into her room before she was safely away? She re-read the letter with dissatisfaction, but there was no time to write another, and so it must serve.

> Dearest Mama,
>
> I am so very sorry, but I <u>cannot</u> marry Lord St Ervan. I must tell you that my heart has long been given to Lieutenant Charles Dulverston. I know you will not like it, Mama, but I can never be happy with anyone else, so I am going away with him. I pray that you will forgive me, and that Lord Northcott and Mr Northcott will not be too angry with me. Let me always continue to be, as I shall always think myself, your loving daughter,
>
> Emily

After some thought, she put the letter into her jewel-box. It was quite possible that she would not be missed until Madeleine came to help her dress for dinner, since she had expressed a wish for solitude. In a house as large as this one, no one would be surprised if she were not to be seen for a few hours. Once her absence was established, she felt sure that Mrs Northcott would examine her jewel-box to see whether anything was missing.

Stopping several times to listen for footsteps, she made her way down the stairs and out of a side door into the garden. As she had hoped, she met no one. Her mother had, as usual, retired to her room, the servants were in their hall enjoying their own meal, and Mr Northcott was with his father. Sarah, the person Emily most feared to meet, was nowhere to be seen. Emily closed the door softly behind her, and hurried down the path, eager to be out of sight of the house.

The gardens round the Hall were laid out in formal parterres, the beds for the most part empty at this time of year, though here and there the small green snout of a bulb showed itself through the soil. Further away were shrubberies with gravelled walks, designed so that the ladies of the house might take their exercise without soiling their footwear or their skirts in wet or muddy grass. Beyond the shrubbery the garden was less formal, wooded parkland surrounded by a brick wall. The public road ran along the far side of the wall, and there was a small door, bolted on the inside, set into the wall for the convenience of those within, for it was a useful short-cut to the village for those on foot. It was here that she was to be met.

She was not to go through the door until she heard the sound of wheels and hooves stopping on the road. There was no sound, and she sat down on a convenient log, trying to compose herself. It was only three o'clock, but it was already gloomy in the shadow of the trees. The ephemeral winter sunshine of the morning had been swallowed up in a thick blanket of lowering cloud, and a vicious little wind stirred the dead leaves at her feet and made her shiver. Hurrying along in her double layer of clothes had made her hot, but now she felt clammy and uncomfortable. The tight garments made her arms stiff and unnatural, and her head and face felt hot and throbbing although her feet were already almost numb. The sound of approaching hooves made her start to her feet, but they did not stop and she subsided once again, only to jump up after a few moments and pace backwards and forwards by the door, unable to sit still and hoping to warm her feet again.

At last came the sound she had been waiting for. The rattle of wheels and trotting of a horse approached and slowed. The heavy bolt slipped in her icy fingers as she tugged at it, and her eyes blurred with tears. She wished longingly that Charles were there, ready to take her into his arms and reassure her, but he had said that it was safer to send a servant to fetch her, and she did not question his commands. Andrew Abbotsleigh was making quite sure that should anything go wrong and the escape be apprehended, he would not be there to take the blame. His servant was a boor, but clever enough to know that he would be in some danger should he reveal his master's name.

The bolt slid back and the door opened. Emily swallowed convulsively and peeped round it. A shabby gig, driven by a heavily muffled man who had climbed down and was waiting for her, met her eyes. Glancing swiftly up and down the road, Emily darted out, pulling the door shut behind her. Swiftly she climbed into the gig, ducking under the tattered cover. Without a word the servant returned to his seat, and in a moment the gig was bouncing down the road. Emily pressed her cold, clammy hands to her burning cheeks, and struggled to suppress a feeling of nausea.

Sarah was puzzled and concerned. Never before had Emily been unable or unwilling to talk to her. She knew very well that some kind of upheaval had taken place, but her stepmother refused to discuss it, and out of loyalty to her, Mr Northcott's lips were also sealed. Sarah felt awkward, and kept herself out of the way as much as she could. At the same time she could not forget St Ervan's warnings. Strictly forbidden by Mrs Northcott to have anything to do with Emily, she could not risk any harm coming to her because she was not careful. In the end she turned, as she had so often done in the past, to Madeleine.

'Mrs Northcott is displeased with Miss Emily, and has forbidden me to see her,' she said bluntly. Knowing Madeleine, she was quite sure that she knew as much, if not more, of what was going on than Sarah did.

'Yes, she is very angry with her. Annie said she came out of Miss Emily's room with a face as black as Nooger's Knocker,' said Madeleine with relish.

'I am quite sure she said nothing of the sort,' giggled Sarah, momentarily distracted. 'Wherever did you get that wonderful expression from?'

'I learned it in London. What is Nooger's Knocker, Miss Sarah?'

'Newgate's Knocker, I should suppose, where the debtors are imprisoned. But enough of that. I should not ask you this, but do you know what caused the quarrel?'

'Of course!' Madeleine was surprised that Sarah should doubt it, and Sarah thought wearily that it was impossible to have a secret in a house full of servants, particularly when those servants were devoted to their employers. 'It was because she would not marry the Marquis!'

'The Marquis? Not—Not Lord St Ervan?'

'That's the one. He came and asked your papa's permission very correctly, and of course Madame was delighted, only she won't have him.'

Sarah was silent. A pang shot through her. For the first time she saw and acknowledged that she had mistaken her own heart. And so, it appeared, had he. Well, Emily was certainly more suited to being a Marchioness, and it was hardly surprising that her mama should be angry at her turning him down. She now knew, she thought, why he had been so concerned about Emily's safety. Well she had had her chance and lost it, and he had not wasted much time in forgetting her. He had probably been relieved that his impulsive offer had been turned down. She was glad for him, and glad for Emily, and as for herself, she would be an old maid, as she had always intended, and care for her papa.

Meanwhile, in case St Ervan was right that Emily was in danger from Abbotsleigh, it was up to her to keep her safe for him. If she could not watch over her herself, then Madeleine must do it. She turned to her old friend and servant with a deep feeling of relief, knowing she could rely on her completely. 'Madeleine, have you heard of Mr Andrew Abbotsleigh?'

'Yes, Miss Sarah. In London they said he was after Miss Emily for her money. I have heard some bad things about him, Miss Sarah.'

'So have I, and one of them is that he may try to run off with Miss Emily.'

'Run off with her? How could he do such a thing?'

'I do not know, but I have heard that he means to try. I may not watch her while her mama is displeased with her, for I am forbidden to see her, but you could. Will you do that for me?'

'I certainly will, for you and for her both, the pretty dear. Just let him try it, that's all. He'd have me to reckon with! I'll guard her, never fear.'

'She must not know,' said Sarah anxiously.

'I'll keep my distance, don't you worry.'

Sarah had perforce to accept this. Madeleine hurried off, and Sarah resigned herself to spending the rest of the day in her room. It was not hard. Somehow, try as she might, her eyes kept filling with tears. She despised herself for such weakness, but whenever she thought of St Ervan, and Emily, she was hard put to it not to throw herself on to the bed and weep.

She was trying to occupy herself with some much-needed mending, a job she detested, when she heard hurrying footsteps approaching, and the door burst open to reveal Madeleine, still in her outdoor clothes, panting for breath.

'Miss Sarah! Oh, Miss Sarah! She is gone!'

'Gone!' Sarah jumped to her feet. 'How can this be? Gone where?'

'I followed her, as you said, but I could not get too close in case she should see me and be alarmed. She went through the garden, and I thought she was walking fast, but I never realised... It was cold, and I thought... She went down to the park, and I hid behind a tree. Then all of a sudden she opened the little door—you know, the one in the wall—and went out! I never expected... You said she might be taken, but she went of her own accord! I ran, but when I reached the gate she was gone, and only some wheel-marks in the road left behind. Forgive me, Miss Sarah, but how could I have known?'

Sarah thought furiously. 'I must go after her. Do you go to the stables and order a horse—a fast one, mind, while I change.'

'But, Miss Sarah, you cannot go alone! It will be dark very soon!'

'What else can I do? No one must know of this, or she will be ruined. If only I can find her, get her back... Oh, hurry, Madeleine, hurry!'

Quickly she stripped off her dress and bundled herself into her habit, snatching her purse from her drawer, and pulling her old warm cloak out of the wardrobe. She ran lightly down the stairs, praying that she would not meet her father or Mrs Northcott. The great hall was deserted, and as she struggled to open the door she was startled by a sudden pealing of the bell. She pulled again at the door, and opened it to find the Marquis, attired with exquisite elegance, gazing at her in astonishment.

'You!' she gasped.

CHAPTER SEVENTEEN

SARAH GAZED at St Ervan in horror.

'Yes, Miss Northcott, it is indeed I,' he responded urbanely. 'Can it be that you are adding the duties of butler to your already numerous accomplishments?'

'Of course not! I was going out. I wish you would not be so silly.'

'You do not seem at all pleased to see me. I assume that my errand is not destined to meet with success. Are you running away? I trust I have not driven you from the house?'

'Your errand? I don't know what you are talking about. It is not I whom you have driven from the house, but Emily.'

At once his teasing manner vanished, and he grasped her arm, propelling her back through the door. The butler, summoned by his peal on the bell, was waved peremptorily away, and vanished in some dudgeon, his stiff back expressing just what he thought of young ladies who opened the door themselves to gentlemen callers, and received them in riding-clothes and a cloak.

'We cannot stand discussing things on the front step like a pair of washerwomen. Let me at least close this door. Now, what are you saying, that I have driven Emily away?'

Even in her own misery, she shrank from hurting him. 'Well, not that, precisely, only Emily was upset, I suppose. I have to tell you that she loves Another!'

'In the name of heaven, stop talking like a French romance and tell me what she has done!'

'I very much fear she has eloped with Charles Dulverston,' said Sarah baldly, abandoning all attempt at breaking it to him gently.

'The devil she has! I'd wager it was not with Dulverston, however, but with Abbotsleigh she has gone.'

Sarah was horrified. 'How can that be? She cannot bear him! She would never go with him. I have to tell you that I set Madeleine to watch her, since I have not been allowed to see her for the last day. Madeleine could not get very close to her, but she saw her slip through the door in the boundary wall, and she seems to have gone off in some kind of conveyance, for there were wheel-marks in the road. But she definitely went by her own choice. I was going to go after her, if I could, and persuade her to come back.'

For the first time, he took in her appearance, and smiled. 'Miss Northcott to the rescue once again! Gallant, but I fear an ill-advised exploit. Can you really believe that young Lieutenant Dulverston, whom I have always understood to be a stickler for correct behaviour, would consent to take part in such an escapade? She may have thought she was going with him, but you can stake your life that it was Abbotsleigh outside that gate— or some servant of his. I have told you that he is staying near by. I had word this morning that he has been receiving correspondence, and replying to it, from someone in this house. The boy who brought it said that it was for one of the men-servants—a fellow called John.'

'John? He is the footman who came with us from London. He has always seemed quite devoted to Emily: I cannot believe he would harm her. I will ring for him at once.'

'Should we not be advised to move to a less public place?' He glanced around at the big, shadowy hall.

Sarah nodded and led him into a little-used sitting-room, lighting a lamp on a table, and rang for John. The footman was soon induced to tell his story, and after he had done so, she dismissed him and stared at St Ervan, her eyes wide with shock.

'So she has been writing to him, thinking that he was Charles! And now she has gone... There is no time to be lost! We must go at once!'

'I agree, but not "we". *I* will go after them. I have my curricle outside. I will leave at once.'

Sarah hurriedly put herself between him and the door. 'You must let me come, do you not see? You must have another female to lend her countenance, or it will be of no use to have saved her from Abbotsleigh. If I am there, we can make up some story that people will believe.'

'But do you not see that you will be in just the same pickle if you come with me now? It will not do, my dear. I have no wish to push you into marriage if such a notion is displeasing to you, but if it became known that you were driving round the countryside alone with me, after dark, you would have no other choice.'

He thought she looked at him strangely at that, he could almost have said longingly.

'Push me into marriage? I do not understand you, but there is no time to be discussing it now. If you will not take me on my own, then I will bring Madeleine. That will make all quite proper.'

He sighed. 'If you must, then let it be so. It would be better if only your maid were to come, but I suppose you will not consent to that. You had better call for her at once. We have wasted too much time as it is. You had better leave some kind of message for your family, also.'

Sarah hurried away, and St Ervan told her to meet him at the stables. The scandalised butler was hovering in the hall. Since he had obviously heard the Marquis's last instructions to Sarah, St Ervan informed him that he was taking Miss Northcott and her maid on an important errand.

'But the dressing-bell, sir! It will shortly be ringing, for we dine at six!'

'It is only a quarter past four, and it is a matter of some urgency. Should we be delayed, however, I leave you to make my apologies to the family. I shall see that Miss Sarah is safely back before too long.' With this the butler had to be satisfied, for the Marquis strode towards the door and he was compelled by force of habit to open it for him.

It was fortunate that there had not been time for his horse to be unharnessed, and in a few minutes the curricle was in the yard. He looked round impatiently for Sarah, and at that moment there was a clatter of hooves, and his groom rode into the yard, flinging himself from his horse at the sight of his master.

'Thank God you're still here, my lord! I went looking for you at Lessingham, and they said you were here. The game's afoot, my lord!'

'So I have just heard. The young lady has gone, and I was expecting to see you at any moment. Quick, man, what can you tell me?'

'If she's gone, then it's not him that's taken her, for I've had him under my eye all day. I told you there were letters back and forth last evening, and this morning he paid his shot and was off. I had some trouble following, for I didn't want him to know I was there, but I saw the road he took and galloped round to the next crossroads and hid. That way I saw how he went next, and that was a winding road, so I kept just out of his sight and rode softly on the verge, so I could hear his horse up ahead. I kept with him all the way, till at last he took a track through some empty countryside. I had to tether my horse and follow on foot. There's a little cottage, my lord, in a patch of woodland, far away from any other house, and that's where he's gone to ground. I crept up and saw he had stabled his horse in a shed, and looked as though he would stay there awhile, so I took the chance and came away to tell you. He had someone there, a man; I heard them talking, but I couldn't get near to hear them. I can lead you there, my lord.'

'Excellent, Jacob. He must have had his servant there, and sent him to fetch the young lady. If we hurry, we should be in time. He will not risk taking her anywhere else, for once she sets eyes on him there will be no question of her going willingly with him. My guess is that he means to hold her there. Ah, there you are. Miss Northcott and her maid will be coming with me, Jacob.'

He bundled them into the curricle, remarking that it was a tight squeeze for three but that they would not get so cold that way. Then they set off briskly, following Jacob. As they travelled, he told Sarah what Jacob had said. She was immensely encouraged to hear that the hiding-place was known, and felt some of her immediate anxiety leave her. As it did, she found herself suddenly very aware of the man at her side. Pressed up against him as she was by Madeleine on her other side, she could feel the play of his muscles as he controlled the horse, and the warmth of his body against hers. She found herself scarcely heeding what he said, becoming absorbed in watching his hands on the reins. They were strong and shapely in their tan gloves, and she found herself remembering the feel of them as he clasped her in the dance. Deep inside her she felt a shiver that was both painful and pleasurable, and when the bend of the road swung her against him she did not stiffen against the pull.

Sarah became aware that he had asked her a question, and recalled her wandering thoughts sternly. 'I beg your pardon! I fear I was not attending.'

'I asked, why did you say I had driven Emily from the house?'

Sarah glanced up at him, and looked away. 'Because, as I told you, she is in love with Charles Dulverston, and she was afraid that she would be forced into marrying *you*.'

'Forced? I hope I would have no such unwilling bride. But I do not see how she could have been forced into marriage with *me*. Do I not have any say in the matter, or were they going to force me as well?'

'But—But you wanted to! You asked Papa's permission!'

He gave a shout of laughter. 'Lord, what a mare's nest! I asked permission, my dear little goose, to have another try at wooing *you*! Come to think of it, I suppose your name was never actually mentioned. I did say to him that I wished to marry his daughter, but I thought I had made myself clear.'

'I suppose, legally, she is that. Emily's mama is so anxious to marry her well, that I suppose he never thought you might have meant me.'

'Does he not wish you to marry? Surely, now that he has a home and a position again, to say nothing of a wife, he does not mean to tie you to his side?'

'Of course not! Only he has not been accustomed to think of me like that. Do not forget he was never with us in London. But he wants me to be happy, and to marry. He has often said so. I think that is why he married Mrs Yarcombe, to give me a chance.'

He turned his head to give her a swift, piercing glance. 'And you—what do you want?'

Sarah was thankful for the darkness that hid the rush of colour to her cheeks. 'I want that too,' she said shyly. Her face was lowered, and she felt rather than saw him glance at her again. One of his hands left the reins and took hers in a fierce clasp.

'Sarah, perhaps I should not ask you this, but when you were told I wanted to marry Emily, what did you think?'

'I did not hear it until this afternoon, for my stepmother did not want me to know, and so Papa did not tell me. It was Madeleine who told me just now, when I asked her to watch over Emily. I thought that, perhaps, it had been Emily you had wanted all along, and you just asked me out of—I don't know, pity, or pique perhaps. I thought that was why you were so concerned about Emily. I was hurt,' she said frankly, and felt his fingers tighten bruisingly on hers, glorying in the pain. 'I thought Emily was a more suitable bride for you.'

She heard the smile in his voice. 'Do you still think so?'

His teasing no longer worried her. She felt that she had hurt him by her previous manner of receiving his proposal, and wanted nothing so much as to make amends.

'No, I do not! I'll be—be damned if I let you marry anyone but me!' she said boldly, lifting her head to look him in the eyes. Her unladylike language had no power to shock him, as she very well knew, and their eyes met and held for one burning moment. Then he reined in the horse and gathered her into his arms, his lips coming down on hers with a bruising force that sent a wave of shock through her body. Her response was as ardent as he had known it would be, and for a long instant they remained locked together. He raised his head and looked down at her, the moonlight bleaching all colour from her face so that she was all ivory and ebony, a living statue.

'To hell with Emily,' he said huskily. 'Let us go away together now!'

'For shame, my lord, to make such an improper suggestion,' she smiled, knowing he did not mean it.

'Then we must hurry now, for Jacob is nearly out of sight.' He released her from his arms and shook up the horse, continuing in a conversational tone, 'Your maid has a strong interest in astronomy?'

Sarah came down from the heights, turned to look at Madeleine, and giggled. The maid, her face averted, was studying the sky with a deep, if spurious, interest. 'A fine chaperon you are!' said Sarah with mock indignation, in Flemish.

Madeleine looked at her calmly. 'He is a Marquis,' she pointed out with earnest practicality. 'And I think,' she continued in response to her nurseling's indignant look, 'that you do not want to be protected from him, do you?' She responded in her native tongue, and was surprised to hear the Marquis reply, haltingly, in the same.

'She needs no protection when I am here,' he said.

'Where did you learn to speak Flemish?' asked Sarah, momentarily distracted. 'I have wondered ever since the first evening we met how it came about that you understood what I was saying.'

'I have spent much of my life roaming the world. I spent some time in the Dutch East Indies, and the Dutch they speak there is not so very different.'

Sarah forced her mind to return to the matter in hand. 'Will we find them in time, do you think?'

St Ervan looked grim. 'I very much hope so. I am counting on the fact that he is not likely to try to travel any further with an unwilling bride, but will stay at the cottage where Jacob is taking us. Nevertheless, if I know anything of Abbotsleigh, he will not be content with merely keeping her away from her friends. I am sorry to have to speak to you of such matters, but you should know that I think he will not hesitate to ravish her, if he thinks that by such means she will be forced to agree to marry him.'

Sarah shuddered. 'Hurry, oh, please hurry,' she begged, knowing he was already making as much speed as was safe on a dark, unknown road.

'We should be in time. They cannot be so very far ahead. I think they cannot have had more than half an hour's start, and this horse of mine is far superior to any that he would have been able to hire.'

'She will be so frightened,' mourned Sarah.

She was right. Jolted along in the ill-sprung gig, Emily had ample time to reflect on the possible consequences of her behaviour. Slow tears crept down her cheeks as she saw herself an outcast from society, denied by her own family, and worse, Charles's career in ruins. If he had but been there beside her she would have forgotten cold, discomfort, the musty smell of the dirty vehicle and everything, but as it was her nerves became almost unbearably frayed, so that when at last she felt the driver pulling up the horse she could almost have screamed in terror. She had been so taken up with her own thoughts that she had paid no heed to the roads they had taken or the countryside they passed. Now she peered through the gloom to see a small, ill-kempt cottage standing on its own in a clearing of a scrubby woodland. There was no other house in sight, and the only sounds that met her ears were those of woodland creatures disturbed by their passage. She shivered.

There was a glow of candlelight from one of the small windows. The servant opened the door of the gig and helped her down. She wondered why Charles did not rush out to her, but found herself hurried towards the cottage. The door opened, and she was inside before she had time to think. The meagre light of two candles was enough to show her that the gentleman with his back to her was not Charles. He turned, and she gave a gasp of horror. The door closed behind her, and she glanced wildly round for a means of escape. There was none.

'There must be some mistake,' she gabbled, thinking furiously. 'Mr Abbotsleigh, what can you be doing here? I had thought you still in London.' He gave her a sardonic look, scrutinising her in a way that made her feel smirched by his glance. She clasped her hands under her chin, feeling at the same time under her cloak for the large cameo brooch she had pinned to the neck of her gown. She continued to babble inanely and breathlessly into the silence, and felt with relief the clasp of the brooch come undone and the heavy disc with its long pin slide smoothly into her hand. It gave her the courage to continue. 'I do not know why you are here, for I do not at all wish to see you. I should like to be taken back to Northcott Hall at once.'

'I expect you should,' he agreed unpleasantly, moving slowly towards her. 'But I am afraid I cannot allow it. I have—shall I say—a matter of business to settle with you.'

'I do not understand you. What business can there be between us?'

'I mean to marry you,' he said carelessly.

'Never! I would never do so! And it would do you no good if I did,' she continued shrewdly, 'for if I marry without Mama's consent, I will get nothing. I assume it is my fortune you want, and not myself?'

'She'll give her consent fast enough. She'll go down on her knees and beg me to take you after I've made a whore of you,' he said coarsely. He pinched her chin painfully, forcing her to raise her head. 'You're pretty enough. It will be no great hardship for a day or two, though I prefer my meat riper, in general.'

Her flesh crawled, and with all her strength she drove the pin of her brooch hard into him. He cursed and drew back a pace. She whirled round and shook the door, and when she found it locked she dodged round the wooden table that was one of the few pieces of furniture that the room possessed.

'My God, you'll be sorry for that!' He looked at the hand he had pressed against the wound she had made, and saw it spotted with blood. With a vulpine grin he moved towards her again, laughing as she dodged away from him round the table. 'It seems this could be more entertaining than I had thought.'

It would be only a matter of time before he caught her. She could have screamed, but restrained herself, knowing that she needed every ounce of energy to evade him, determined to do so for as long as possible. She stifled a sob, and whispered, almost as a talisman, 'Charles! Oh, Charles!'

CHAPTER EIGHTEEN

LIEUTENANT DULVERSTON had set out in the early afternoon of that same day full of high hopes. He knew from local gossip that the family were all at the Hall, and felt that he was fairly sure to be able to see Emily; even, if he were lucky, to have some private conversation with her. After riding for about a quarter of an hour at the best speed he could get from his hired horse—not a very good one, it seemed unwilling to be forced even into a shambling trot—he was annoyed to find that the creature had gone lame. Dismounting, he found that the wretched creature had cast a shoe. Not knowing the countryside, he could not risk going on, and was forced to retrace his steps to the town.

By the time he was remounted, the afternoon was almost gone. Even so, he set out once more, determined to make his visit. He could hardly have the audacity to present himself on Christmas Day, and thus two days of his leave would have been wasted. He made what speed he could, trusting that he would not find the family just about to sit down to dinner.

In the event, dinner was the last thing on anyone's mind at Northcott Hall. He arrived to find the place in an uproar. Matthew Northcott stood in the hall shouting orders, frequently contradicting each other, to his scurrying servants, while Mrs Northcott alternated between shrill scolding and fits of hysterical weeping. The front door was open wide, and Charles was in the house before they were aware of him. He stared aghast at the scene, wondering what was amiss, until Mr Northcott turned and saw him.

'Who the devil are you?' he asked with unusual acerbity.

'Lieutenant Charles Dulverston, sir. I had the honour to write to you yesterday. I was in the area, and...'

He was interrupted by a shrill scream from Mrs Northcott. 'Dulverston! Then she is not gone with him, thank God!'

'I don't see what you can find in that to be pleased about,' said her husband testily. 'Who knows where she is, if she is not with him?'

'I will never permit it—never! He is a nobody, a mere Lieutenant. It is all a plot. He has hidden her somewhere, and I will never see her again! Wicked, evil man, where have you taken my daughter?'

She flung herself at Charles, shaking his arm fiercely as a terrier with an oversized rat. He, having no idea what was going on, stood looking from one to another in silent amazement. At her last words he started, and brushing Mrs Northcott from him strode to Mr Northcott, who was telling the servants that they must all look for Miss Emily, but that no one must know that she was missing.

'What are you saying? Emily is missing? Lost? You must, you shall, tell me. For God's sake, sir, what has happened?'

'A trick! A lie! He has stolen her away!'

'Calm yourself, my dear.' Matthew Northcott summoned up his patience as his wife continued to shriek.

'Can you deny that you have been in secret correspondence with Miss Yarcombe?'

His look was stern, but Charles met it with frank indignation. 'Deny it? I most certainly do! I would never permit her to do anything so underhand.'

Mr Northcott's face relaxed some of its severity. He took Emily's letter from his wife's unresisting fingers and handed it to the Lieutenant, who read it with surprise and growing alarm. At the end of it he drew himself up straight, and spoke frankly.

'I cannot deny, sir, that I love the young lady, and that I would give anything to make her my wife. At the same time, I am only too well aware that my situation in life is not such as to recommend me to any parent as a suitor. That she loves me I am perfectly sure, but I would never permit her to cast her lot with one who has yet to prove himself in his chosen profession. I love her too well for that. If I thought that she wished to wed another, someone with whom she could be happy and could love, I would wish her well and try to be happy for her. Nevertheless, if she is in trouble, I claim the right to go to her aid.'

Mr Northcott was regarding him with a fascinated eye. 'Seems to me you're wasted in the army,' he remarked. 'With speeches like that, you should be in parliament. Make them up as you go along, do you?'

'I must confess, sir, that if it had been possible to find a patron, I should have liked to serve my country in that way. But Emily... Miss Yarcombe, I should say...'

'Do not speak to him, the fiend!' ordered Mrs Northcott. 'Ask him what he has done with her!'

'I regret, my dear, that I cannot comply with both those requests. I think we should rather ask this young man's help in finding her, if may be.'

Charles looked round the hall. 'Where is Miss Northcott? I do not see her here.'

'Of course she knows the girl's mind, if anyone does! I cannot understand why she is not here.'

At this point John, who had been hovering unhappily in the corner of the room, stepped reluctantly forward, holding out another letter.

Mr Northcott scanned it and looked up in amazement. 'I do not understand it! Here is Sarah writing that she has gone with St Ervan!'

At these ill-advised words, his wife shrieked again. 'The hussy! She shall not have him!' and fell into strong hysterics.

Mr Northcott attempted to soothe her. 'It is not what you think, ma'am! Sarah writes that she fears that Emily is in danger, and that she is going with St Ervan to try to save her. We are not to be alarmed, for she has Madeleine with her, and they will do their best to see that no harm comes to Emily or her reputation.'

Mrs Northcott was not to be comforted, and it was with relief that the men saw the arrival of the house-keeper, a sensible woman who lost no time in removing the overwrought mother to her room, where she plied her with remedies and sympathy.

At this point another servant hurried in, saying that he had heard something he thought might be important. He dragged behind him a young stable-lad, who pulled bashfully at his forelock and stared about him dumbly.

Charles strode up to him, and the boy's eyes widened at the sight of his resplendent uniform.

'Now then, boy, you have something to tell us?'

'Yas, sir, oi heard where they wur gowing.'

'Miss Emily? Or Miss Sarah?'

'Yas, sir. Near moi grandad, it were.'

Charles looked helplessly at the servant who had brought the lad.

'Begging your pardon, sir, but he's a bit shy-like. He told me he heard the gentleman—that'll be his lordship, sir—talking with his groom, who knew where Miss Emily might have been taken. He's a bright lad, sir, and he recognised what they said because it's near where his grandad lives.'

'You know where they are gone? Can you take me there?'

The boy grinned, wide and gap-toothed. 'Yes, sir, easy. Oi knows a quick way, too.'

'Splendid. Mr Northcott, have I your permission to go after them?'

'Yes, go at once, go at once. You can hardly make anything worse, at least. I will come with you.'

'Forgive me, sir, but I think you would do better to stay here and reassure your wife. You may trust me to do all that is necessary. Only lend me one of your horses.'

'Take whatever you need, only make haste!'

Charles hurried away, leaving Mr Northcott distracted in the hall, and reflecting thankfully that his father had chosen to remain in his room all day and had missed the entire scene. If only Emily and Sarah could be returned safely, they might perhaps be able to avoid his hearing about it at all.

Charles picked himself a sturdy bay, already saddled by servants who had been bidden to search for the young lady, and the stable-lad was put up on another horse, which he swore he knew and could handle. The truth of his statement was soon proved, and Charles found himself being led at some speed down a narrow track between open fields. His youthful guide led him at such speed that at any other time Charles would have been alarmed. Now, however, he followed recklessly, heedless of the danger to himself or his horse in taking an unknown route at speed in the treacherous moonlight.

When they came to the edge of the woodland, they had perforce to check their horses. The boy indicated to Charles that the place was not far away, and that among the trees it would be easier to dismount, and lead the horses. Thus they reached the cottage quite quietly, and were treated to the edifying spectacle of two men, one of them a peer of the realm, grappling viciously, but almost silently, on the grass outside the door of the cottage.

Charles strode forward, and the two figures were more clearly to be seen as the Marquis and another man in rough clothes. The silence was explained by the fact that St Ervan's hand was held firmly over the servant's mouth, so that he could do no more than grunt. At the same time, the need to prevent the man from warning his master meant that the Marquis was unable to subdue his adversary easily, and was suffering a number of painful kicks and blows.

Charles's arrival meant that the contest was very soon over. In no time at all the servant was overpowered, gagged, and was being tied up with a piece of rope from the old shed where the man had been seeing to the horse. As they worked, the Marquis informed Charles in a low whisper that he had Sarah and Madeleine, in the care of his own man, just a short distance away in the woods.

Charles looked up, and grinned. 'Left them there safely, did you? Miss Northcott is not one to be left behind, it seems.'

Following his gaze, St Ervan looked up and saw Sarah and Madeleine, followed by an anxious Jacob, drawing near. He frowned and went to them, drawing them away from the cottage.

'I thought I told you to keep the young lady and her maid out of the way,' he muttered crossly to Jacob.

'I'm sorry, sir, but they would come,' Jacob mumbled his apology, glancing deprecatingly at Sarah.

'Pray do not be angry with him. He would have stopped me if he could,' Sarah pleaded for him. 'But I could not stay there wondering what was going on, you know. I had to come.'

'Abbotsleigh is a dangerous man. This is his last chance, and he knows it. He will not take kindly to being thwarted. But we are wasting time. I cannot make you remain behind, but I beg you not to get in the way.'

'I promise I will not, but please be careful,' she begged.

It was at that moment that Emily, goaded beyond endurance and knowing that she could not dodge Abbotsleigh for much longer, screamed out. 'Charles! Oh, Charles!'

All were for an instant frozen at the sound, except Charles himself who, galvanised by the sound of his own name and by the desperation of the cry, charged to the cottage. The door was locked, but he crashed the full weight of his body against it, and it flew open almost immediately.

Inside the cottage his sudden entrance caught both Abbotsleigh and Emily unawares. The gust of wind from the open door immediately extinguished the candle flames, and they were plunged into darkness. Emily was transfixed with terror, for she did not know whether his sudden interruption was friend or foe. Abbotsleigh, knowing that it must be foe to him, was quicker to recover. While Emily still stood trembling, he slipped round the table and caught her, twisting her round so that her back was pressed against him, with his left arm across her and his hand gripping her throat. By the dim glimmer of the fire he shuffled his way backwards, pulling her with him, to a rough dresser a few feet away. Pulling open a drawer he snatched up a pistol, which he pressed against her head. The figure in the doorway froze at once.

'I don't know who you are, but if you value this young lady's life, you will come no nearer.'

'Harm one hair of her head, and I will make you rue the day you were born,' growled Charles.

At the sound of his voice Emily felt her knees buckle beneath her. 'Charles!' she whispered.

'Do not worry, dearest. I will not let him hurt you,' he soothed.

She did not notice the two other figures that now stood behind Charles in the doorway, for her whole attention was fixed on him, but Abbotsleigh did. He tightened his grip so that she cried out, and shouted, 'Back! Stay back, or I fire, and be damned to you!'

Charles put out a hand, and pushed St Ervan and Joseph back. 'He means it. We must take no chances,' he said in an agonised murmur. 'The pistol may not be loaded, but we cannot take the risk.'

'We are three to your one,' said St Ervan in a calm, almost conversational tone. 'You cannot hope to succeed now. If you kill the girl, you will hang for it, if Dulverston here does not save the hangman his labour, as I suspect he would. Have done now, and if you do not hurt her, I guarantee you your freedom.'

'Freedom? What good is that to me without money? Give me my freedom and money to enjoy it with, and you may have her. She is no more than a milk-and-water miss, when all's said and done.'

Charles stirred angrily, and felt St Ervan's restraining hand on his arm.

'Hold hard. We can do nothing while he has that pistol,' the Marquis whispered. 'Leave me to speak to him.'

Charles chafed, but acknowledged the sense of this, and held his tongue. It would do no good to antagonise Abbotsleigh, or to drive him to desperate measures.

Outside the cottage, Sarah listened anxiously. She felt desperate to see what was going on and crept closer, unnoticed by the men. Keeping her body out of sight of the doorway, pressed against the wall, she peered cautiously round the entrance, crouching down so that she was looking through the space between Jacob's arm, raised to grasp the door-frame, and his body. The fire was no more than a glow of red embers, but it gave enough light to illuminate the tableau within. It struck gleams from the barrel of the pistol, and from Emily's

wide open, terrified eyes. The wooden table, the dresser
and a settle against another wall were all the furniture
the room contained. Sarah studied it carefully, noting
the wide fireplace and the broad chimney that led from
it. Then she withdrew silently, pulling Madeleine with
her.

'I want the boy, the boy who came with Charles. He's
still with the horses, I think. Don't you see, he thinks
there are just the three of them? He doesn't know we
are here, too. We are the only ones who can do anything. If they move, he might shoot.'

'He might do that anyway,' Madeleine's solid peasant
common sense was quick to point out, but Sarah did
not heed her.

They had reached the boy, and Sarah was hurriedly
explaining her idea to him. 'Can you do it, do you
think?'

'Think oi could, miss,' he replied obligingly, and they
hurried back.

The boy eyed the water-butt, a huge barrel against the
side wall, and nodded. Swiftly he unlaced his boots,
pulled them off, and climbed barefoot on to the lid of
the barrel. Sarah pushed Madeleine towards the shack
where the horse was stabled, and by the time she returned with the wooden bucket of water provided for
the horse to drink, the boy was already on the roof, his
bare toes digging for purchase into the old thatch.
Madeleine's strong arms made light work of lifting the
bucket up to him, and holding it in one hand he inched
his way cautiously up the shallow slope until he reached
the chimney, when he was able to stand upright, hanging

on to the stack with his other hand and waiting for Sarah's signal.

It was impossible for her to tell the three men in the doorway what was afoot, for to do so would reveal her presence to Abbotsleigh. She could only hope that they would be quick-witted enough to take advantage of the surprise. Standing again beside the doorway she looked up at the boy, raised her hand, and dropped it sharply.

CHAPTER NINETEEN

WITH ONE neat movement, the boy tipped the bucket of water down the chimney. For a second it caught a sparkle from the moonlight that glimmered through the shifting clouds, then it fell on the glowing coals in the fireplace. There was a sharp hiss, and immediately the dim glimmer of the fire was doused in a billow of steam. The sudden noise and the blanking out of all vision startled Abbotsleigh, and for a second he relaxed his hold on Emily as he swung his pistol towards the source of the noise.

That second was all she needed. With a swift twist, she was out of his hold and throwing herself across the room towards Charles. He was already moving to find her, and hearing her sobbing breath caught at her, pulling her into his arms and clasping her in an agony of relief. He held her up as she clung to him, half fainting.

Abbotsleigh, cursing fluently, stumbled after her, only to knock heavily into the table, which tipped over with a crash. St Ervan moved warily forward towards the noise.

'Take care, my lord, he still has that pistol,' muttered Jacob, moving forward in his turn.

'I had not forgotten it,' came the calm reply. 'But while Abbotsleigh may be a blackguard, he is not a fool. He knows as well as I that we are too many for him. He cannot shoot us all, and should he shoot even one of us, he knows he must hang for it.'

Abbotsleigh did not speak, but St Ervan heard his breathing, rapid and hoarse. He took another step forward, and at once felt rather than saw his opponent jerk up the pistol. He stopped.

'Do not move, my lord. I believe he is mad enough for anything,' said the servant urgently.

'He is right, my lord,' came a whisper from the darkness. 'I should know that voice, I think. Is it not my friend the horse-dealer?'

'No horse-dealer, but my groom Abbotsleigh. I have had you under my eye for longer than you think. There can be no escape for you. Give yourself up now, and it will go easier with you.'

'Easier? You must think me an idiot, St Ervan! So you have been watching me, have you? Wanted the girl and her fortune for yourself, I suppose. Well, you may have her now, and welcome to her. The money, though, is another thing. I must have money, you know. It is all up with me here. What are your terms?'

'I have no terms at pistol-point. Lay down your gun.'

'Do not bargain with him, St Ervan. He has only the pistol, and he cannot use that against three of us.'

'Who is that? Another of your servants, my lord? They are very familiar with you, if so. I suppose you did not care to come without a bodyguard.'

'I am Charles Dulverston, as you very well know, Abbotsleigh.'

'So? I should have known you, for I have been making free of your name for some while. If you think I have nothing to bargain with, think again. I hold your young lady's good name in the palm of my hand. You do not know, perhaps, that she has been writing to me? I have her letters safely put by.'

'Writing? To you? What is this, Emily?'

She lifted her head from his shoulder. 'I thought he was you! I never meant any harm. Do not be vexed with me, Charles!'

'Never, my pet, but you must make me understand how all this came about. How was it that you thought he was I? You know I have never wished to carry on a clandestine correspondence with you.'

'It was when I knew we must leave London, and I would not be seeing you any more. Mama said we might stay for three months in the country, and I could not bear it, for I thought I might not even see you to say goodbye, so I wrote to you. Somehow he must have got hold of the letter, for he wrote back almost at once. I was so pleased that I never thought it might not be you at all.'

'But how came you to run away with him? Surely you could not think I would suggest such a thing?'

She hung her head. 'It was not he who suggested it, but I. I was desperate. I begged you—I mean him—to run away with me. It was very wicked and foolish, I see that now, but I did not stop to think. I was so very unhappy.'

'And you actually thought I would agree to such a disgraceful proceeding? I am astonished at you, Emily. I would have thought you knew me better than that.'

'I know! I must have been mad!' she wept. 'It was just that I was so miserable, and I thought since you had changed your mind about writing to me, you might agree to this. And you did! I mean, he did, only of course I thought it was you. And we should have been married, and so happy, and surely that cannot be wrong. You do want to marry me, after all. Or at least, you did,' she finished dolefully.

'I still do, foolish one, but not in such an underhand way. Could you really be happy, do you think, cut off from all your friends and family? I could not do that to you, Emily. When we marry, it must be with the consent of your friends.'

'Of course it must,' put in Abbotsleigh in a sneering aside. 'You won't see a penny piece of her fortune else!'

Charles ignored the interruption. 'And you wrote that in your letter? You asked me to run away with you?'

'Yes. I could not think what else to do.'

'But I do not understand why you were so unhappy. It was not so very bad, surely, at Northcott Hall? They were kind to you there, were they not? Even if it meant waiting a few months apart, you knew you would see me again in London. Why could you not wait?'

'I am afraid you must hold me responsible for that,' St Ervan put in. He was still standing in the middle of the room. The fire was completely out, and the only light was a faint gleam from the doorway. He could not see Abbotsleigh, but knew that he was backed into the corner. While he still had his pistol undischarged, he was reluctant to make any sudden move that might push his quarry into an act of desperation. He was under no illusions that the normal code of civilised behaviour would restrain this man who had, after all, so little to lose.

At the sound of the Marquis's voice, Emily shrank. Charles was puzzled.

'You, St Ervan? I do not understand you. What have you to do with all this—except that you have protected Emily, and for that you have my eternal gratitude. That fellow seemed to think that you had an interest in the lady yourself.'

Emily drew herself out of his arms. 'I am very sorry, my lord, if what I must say should cause you pain,' she said with a belated attempt at dignity, 'but I regret to have to decline your most flattering offer. I cannot marry you.'

Even in these trying circumstances, St Ervan could not prevent his misplaced sense of humour from coming into play. 'Madam, it has been made clear to me that your heart is given to Another. Far be it from me to press upon you a suit that is clearly repugnant. Go! I renounce my claim! Henceforth, though my life be a desert, I shall count myself fortunate in calling myself your friend!'

'Th—Thank you, my lord,' faltered Emily, taken aback by the accents of high tragedy he had suddenly assumed. 'I see now that I should have spoken to you sooner, and then all this need not have happened. But I was so frightened, and I am afraid I did not think very clearly.'

'Frightened of me? You wound me to the core. I did not know I was so alarming.'

'Not of you, precisely. But Mama said you wanted to marry me, and she was so pleased, because I would be a Marchioness, that I thought she would compel me to accept you—not by force, you understand, but by duty, and not wishing to disappoint her when she has always been so good to me. It was not that I did not like you,

ou know, for I am sure I like you very well, only I do
ot love you as I love Charles.'

'Enough! Speak no more! My life is blighted, my
opes are gone. I see now that even my title and my
vealth are not enough to win me a wife. I shall seek a
fe of retirement, withdraw myself from the world, bury
1yself away from the sight of my fellow man...'

'I say, steady on!' interrupted Charles, as with a wail
f dismay Emily cast herself once more on to his chest.
There's no need to carry on like that! You never showed
hat much interest in her, that I could see. In fact, if
nyone had asked me, I should have said you were more
nclined to favour Miss Northcott than Emily, although
ou always seemed to be quarrelling with her!'

'Dulverston, you are a man of perspicacity and I am
nore than ever convinced that you should go far! My
lear child, dry your eyes. I am afraid I was teasing you.
t is Sarah's hand I was requesting, not yours. Unfor-
unately I cannot have made myself clear to Mr
Northcott, and so the misunderstanding arose. You may
ave the Lieutenant with my blessing, if that is needed.'

'But not with mine.' Abbotsleigh had grown tired of
eing ignored while these explanations were made. 'You
orget, my lord, that I have those letters. If I should
hoose to reveal them, Miss Yarcombe will never be re-
eived in society again. It seems I may have done you a
ood turn, Dulverston. They may be glad to marry her
ff to you after all, for no one else would have her once
have had my say. She had, after all, been alone with
1e for a while before you all arrived. Her reputation is
n my hands. Will you still want her then, I wonder?'

Beside herself with fear and fury, Emily broke from Charles's restraining grasp and stepped towards her to mentor. As she did so, she was clearly outlined against the gleam of moonlight that came through the open door Hardly knowing what he did, Abbotsleigh swung hi pistol towards her. The moonlight gleamed on the barrel and as his finger tightened on the trigger, Charles too one swift stride, grasping Emily and swinging her roun to interpose his body between her and that faint, deadl glimmer of light. There was an explosion, magnified i that enclosed space so that the crockery on the dresse rattled. Emily screamed, and clasped her arms roun Charles as he reeled against her.

St Ervan was in motion almost before the pistol fired In two steps he was within reach, and had knocked th pistol from Abbotsleigh's hand, his other hand reachin to grasp him. He heard Jacob following him.

'Help the Lieutenant, Jacob! I think he is hurt. I ca manage this one.' His hand closed on a neck-cloth, an with savage strength he caught and twisted it, ignorin the flailing fists and kicks of his opponent. It did no take long for these to become weaker, and then to ceas altogether. At once he slackened his hold, and droppe Abbotsleigh to the floor, where he lay motionless, th breath rasping in his throat. Then, with his usual prac tical good sense, he groped on the floor by the over turned table until he found the candle which he kne had been on it. It was a matter of seconds to light it an locate its candlestick, then he took it hurriedly over where Charles stood, still on his feet but patently un steady in Emily's grasp, and with an ominous stai spreading across his coat front. Jacob hurriedly pulle open coat and shirt, and Emily closed her eyes and swayed at the sight of the wound that was thus revealed.

'Hold hard, miss. Let's get him to that settle.' Jacob slipped his arm round Charles, and supported him to the seat.

His lips were tightly pressed together, and he was very pale. Emily, anxious to prove herself a good soldier's wife, opened her eyes again and drew herself up straight. Sarah and Madeleine hurried in with the bucket, which the stable-lad had filled again at the well behind the shed.

'It is freshly drawn,' said Sarah tersely. 'We will try to get the fire going again.'

'Good girl.' St Ervan smiled briefly at her. 'Courage, Miss Yarcombe! He is not dead yet, nor will he be, if I have my way. Jacob! Your late acquaintance is stirring over there. You had best see about tying him up. Then I shall want you to support the Lieutenant. As far as I can see, the bullet has passed straight through his shoulder, and should have missed any vital organs. We must stop the bleeding, if we may. There is a flask of brandy beneath the seat of the curricle, Sarah. I think a sip of that would do him good.'

Sarah brought the flask, and in trembling haste Emily poured some into the earthenware cup that Sarah found on the dresser. Emily held it to his lips, and he sipped. A little colour returned to his cheeks and he looked up at her. He gave a weak smile.

'Don't worry, sweetheart. You are not hurt, are you?'

Her gown was stained with blood, but it was his. Her lips trembled so that she could not speak, but she shook her head and tried to return his smile. Sarah, meanwhile, rummaged through the dresser until she found

two more candles, which she lit at the first so that St
Ervan would have more light to work by. Madeleine had
found some dry wood and a few glowing embers still
buried in the ash at the edge of the fire, and was blowing
them into life. Joseph returned from tying Abbotsleigh
up just as his master was pressing a pad made from his
handkerchief on to the wound.

'All trussed up like a chicken, my lord.'

'Good. Now I want you to lift the Lieutenant so that
I can take a look at the back of his shoulder. Gently,
now. Yes, I thought so. You are in luck, young man.
We will not be needing to ask the surgeon to cut the
bullet out of you, for it has passed clean through. We
must bind it in some way, and get you back to civilis-
ation. I shall need a good pad of clean cloth.'

'Wait, I have the very thing!' exclaimed Emily, turning
up the hems of her two skirts and pulling at the stitches
she had put into her petticoats. They came undone in a
rush, and out fell the clothes she had hidden there.

St Ervan raised his eyebrows in some admiration. 'Very
ingenious! You will make a capital wife for a soldier,
my dear! We will wash the wound as best we may. Tear
me a piece of linen. Is there any hot water?'

Sarah brought the pan that Madeleine had been
heating over her small fire. With scissors that Madeleine
produced from her capacious pockets, he cut away coat
and shirt, washed the wound as clean as he could, and
bound it up. Charles bore the operation with great for-
titude, gripping Emily's hand. At the end of it he was
as white as she, but after another nip of brandy, he smiled
and said that he was a great deal more comfortable.

'We shall soon have you in bed, and call a doctor to you, but first I think we must decide what is to be done with...that.' St Ervan nodded his head to where Abbotsleigh lay half propped against the wall, firmly tied up. They all looked at him, and he glared back with a mixture of terror and defiance.

'If you ask me, my lord, the world would be a better place without him,' growled Jacob. 'He would have killed the young lady, no question, if the Lieutenant here hadn't saved her. You just leave him to me. I'll deal with him, and no questions asked.'

Both Sarah and Emily gave inarticulate sounds of protest, but St Ervan quietened them with a look.

'I am much inclined to agree with you, but I am afraid it will not do. It is not for us to take justice into our own hands. If we did that, we should be no better than he. What we may not do, however, the law of the land may do in our stead. He could well hang for this night's work. Abduction, attempted murder, the shooting of an officer in the Queen's army—I think the list against him is long enough. There is also, of course, the matter of a young woman in London who is thought to have died under mysterious circumstances not unconnected with him. I have no doubt that there would be plenty who would be willing to come forward and testify against him, now that he is safe caught.'

Abbotsleigh blenched. 'No! You can't! They wouldn't! I never had anything to do with that girl, I swear it!'

'I do not think your word carries much weight in this company, Abbotsleigh.'

A film of sweat broke out on his sallow, bony face. His eyes darted desperately from one to another, looking for a sign of clemency.

'Oh no, not hanging!' broke in soft-hearted Emily in distress. 'His poor mother! She would never bear it! Whatever he may have done, surely he has not deserved that.'

'You are kinder than he would have been to you. Nevertheless, I am prepared to deal with him, if only because if the matter came to trial it would be impossible to keep your name out of it, and I would not wish to inflict that on you or your family. However, Abbotsleigh, there is to be no bargaining. You will accept, or not accept, my terms. Is that clear?' Abbotsleigh gave a reluctant nod. 'Very well. You leave this country, at once, and you may not return, ever. You may not go to Europe, but beyond that I place no restriction. Australia, the Americas, the East, you can choose. That is in exchange for your life. Do you agree?'

'Of course I agree. There is no choice in that. But what am I to live on?'

'I should say that you must earn your living as you may. However, lest you be tempted by want to fall into worse crimes than you have already committed, I am prepared to allow you one hundred pounds a year. It will be sent to the bank of your choosing, when you have decided where you will stay. In return, I demand your silence, now and for ever, on what has occurred. If you dare so much as to breathe Miss Yarcombe's name, you may be sure I shall come to hear of it, and you will regret it. Furthermore, you will give me every letter of hers that you have in your possession. Do you agree?'

'I cannot live on one hundred a year.' The fear of death was receding, and a calculating look had replaced the abject terror in his eyes.

'It will keep you from starving. If you want more, you must work for it. No bargaining, I said. Come, I have no time to waste. Do you agree, or not?'

'I agree, damn you to hell!'

'Then I think we may dispense with the pleasure of your company. Joseph! You will see him on to the boat, and his servant with him, if he chooses to accompany his master. Be sure that he gives you all the letters. Use the money I gave you for tickets. You may write to me when you have the name and address of a bank for your money, Abbotsleigh. Do not think to break your word. I will see that you hang if ever you set foot on these shores again.'

CHAPTER TWENTY

CHARLES, THOUGH he did not complain, was obviously in some considerable pain, and it seemed essential that he should be taken elsewhere immediately. St Ervan, running the possibilities rapidly through his mind, could see no better place to take him than Northcott Hall. It was, for one thing, by far the nearest house. He could scarcely expect his cousin to take in, on Christmas Eve, a complete stranger with a large bullet hole in his shoulder without a rather better explanation than the Marquis was prepared to give. The fewer people who knew of the night's adventures, the better. Then again, the girls should be returned to their parental roof as soon as possible, and it was quite obvious that Emily would not allow herself to be parted from Charles without a severe struggle. As well as that, St Ervan had taken a liking to the Lieutenant, and hoped to be able to use what influence he might have with Mrs Northcott to induce her to agree to Emily's betrothal.

That being decided, he made his dispositions swiftly. It was fortunate, he thought, that they had Abbotsleigh's hired gig as well as his own curricle and several extra horses.

'Joseph, you stay here with our scoundrels. You had better take Abbotsleigh's man into the cottage so you can keep an eye on them both. If he chooses to go with his master, so much the better. You might tell him that the penalties for assisting in a kidnap are likely to be pretty severe. I will send someone else back to help you, and in the morning I will send a conveyance to get them to the port. Better to travel that way. I do not want them going on the railway, where they might have an opportunity to talk.'

'Very good, my lord. I will harness up the gig for you, my lord. Can you drive a gig, lad?'

''Course oi can! Oi'm a stable-lad, an't oi!'

Charles was placed tenderly in the curricle, and Emily insisted on going with him. St Ervan chose to drive them, leaving Sarah and Madeleine to follow in the gig with the lad. He took the time to hand Sarah in, retaining her hand for a moment in his firm clasp as he bent over her to speak in a low voice.

'Bravely done, my girl! There is no time to speak now, for I must get that young man back as quickly as may be. It seems to me that it is time to make an end to all this confusion we seem to have landed ourselves in. Will you trust me to unravel it all, and bring us safe home?'

'I think you are the only person who might be able to achieve it! I tremble to think what my stepmother will say!'

He did not answer, but lifted her hand to his lips for a brief moment. In the stuffy darkness of the gig Sarah lifted her hand, where his kiss still seemed to burn, to her cheek, and shivered with a mixture of joy and anxiety. To love and to be loved was still so new an experience that she scarcely dared trust her own memory.

They made what speed they could, with due regard to Charles's wounded shoulder. Northcott Hall was ablaze with lights, and the front door was open before the curricle and the gig had finished pulling up. Matthew Northcott hurried out, all feelings of anger submerged in his relief at seeing both Sarah and Emily safely returned. He hardly knew whom to embrace first, but hugged both indiscriminately, with incoherent exclamations.

'My dear girls! My dear, dear girls! We have been so anxious! And you are positively all right, no harm has come to you? Is not that blood on your gown, child? Not your own, thank God, thank God! Your mama has been beside herself... Come in, come in to her. She will not be satisfied till she sees you with her own eyes.'

Emily, however, would not enter the house until she had seen Charles carried in by two strong footmen. At St Ervan's quiet but authoritative orders, a rider was dispatched in haste for a doctor. Mr Northcott, quite at sea, watched while Emily took charge of things, telling the men to lay the Lieutenant on a sofa, and impatiently casting the extra cushions on to the floor so that he could lie stretched out. Once this was done to her satisfaction she hung over him, holding his good hand in her own and gazing into his face, oblivious of all else.

Matthew Northcott plucked anxiously at Sarah's sleeve. His wife's entrance could not be long delayed, and he wanted to be au fait with what had been happening before she arrived. 'What has happened? Are you both all right? Where did you find her?'

Sarah looked helplessly at him, hardly knowing where to begin her explanations, and St Ervan glanced up at them.

'Let us leave the explanations for the moment, sir. The young ladies, particularly Miss Yarcombe, have sustained a very shocking experience, and would be none the worse for a little restorative. Some wine, perhaps, or even something stronger. I have sent for a doctor for the Lieutenant, and I think he should do well enough, but he has lost some blood and has sustained an uncomfortable journey. I do not like to give him much until the doctor has seen him, but a small brandy would not come amiss, I think.'

'Brandy, yes, to be sure. That's the thing. I could do with some myself. I'll go and find...' His watchful butler, ever on the alert and longing to find out what was happening, appeared at his elbow with a tray.

'I have taken the liberty of anticipating your orders, sir.'

'Good man. We will all have a drop, I think, Bates. Then you had better see that all is prepared above stairs. The Lieutenant will be staying, of course.'

'Of course, sir. If you please, sir, there is bound to be some talk in the servants' hall. What would you wish me to say has happened?'

Mr Northcott looked helplessly at St Ervan.

'For the moment it will be sufficient to say that the Lieutenant sustained his injury while going to Miss Emily's rescue. I imagine the whole household knows that she was...out?'

'Yes, my lord. We have all been most anxious for Miss Yarcombe.'

'I am sure, Bates, that you will do your best to see that there is as little talk as possible. You would not wish any harm to come to Miss Yarcombe through any sort of loose talk in the servants' hall. Miss Yarcombe was so unlucky as to be lost in the countryside, but here she

is safe home, and no harm done. Let that be sufficient
for all. For yourself, of course, your master will wish
you to have a fuller explanation, when the time is right.'

Much gratified, the butler took himself off, vowing
eternal silence on the least of the kitchen-maids and
garden boys. The Marquis poured two small glasses of
brandy, and obliged both Sarah and Emily to sip them.
Sarah, for her part, was glad to feel the bite of the spirit
in her throat, and feel its warmth spread through her
limbs.

Thus it was that Mrs Northcott, roused from her
uneasy sleep by the bustle of their arrival, came down
from her chamber and found her daughter, dishevelled
and bloodstained, clasping the hand of the man whom
she had stigmatised as a nobody, and sipping from a
glass, as were her stepdaughter, her husband and the
Marquis.

'No one has seen fit to inform me that my daughter
has returned, and now I find you indulging in what I
can only call a carouse! Emily, leave that young man
alone, and explain yourself to me at once!'

The brandy had made Emily bold.

'In a moment, Mama. I must be sure that the bleeding
has not started up again.'

'If he is bleeding, I am sure he has no one but himself
to blame. To be writing to you, in this underhand
fashion! And for you to run away with him! I am mortified, Emily, that you should treat me so. As to what
his lordship must think...'

'All I am thinking at the moment, ma'am, is that I
believe I hear the doctor arriving. All other explanations
must wait on him. I am sure you can see, ma'am, that

it is of the first importance that he should not take away with him any undesirable ideas as to what has been afoot here. You must not allow him to think that anything is amiss between yourself and your daughter.'

'He is right, my dear,' put in Mr Northcott earnestly. 'If he realises that Emily has been—well—away from home, it will be all round the district by the day after tomorrow. I beg you to hold your peace.'

The presence of the doctor effectively silenced Mrs Northcott, and she was forced to hold her tongue, only continuing to glare at her daughter and cast darkling glances at the bloodstained patient.

The tubby doctor, summoned in haste from his Christmas fireside, wasted little time in examining the wound. He professed himself satisfied with it, saying that it needed but a little cleaning before it was bound up properly, and that the young gentleman should be carried up to bed and undressed. Mrs Northcott was unable to protest as the injured man was taken away, but she took up her station beside her daughter. Emily, once Charles was gone, seemed to shrink within herself. The courage induced by the need to care for him, and in part by the brandy, evaporated, and she sank into a chair. Sarah would have gone to her, but encountered such a blaze of fury from her stepmother that she stopped in her tracks.

The doctor accepted a glass of brandy from Mr Northcott, and fixed him with an enquiring eye.

'What I have just seen, sir, is a wound from a firearm, and I feel compelled to ask you how the gentleman came by it. I would not wish to be a party to anything underhand.' As he spoke, he glanced curiously at the

Marquis, who was also looking tousled after his fights with Abbotsleigh and his servant.

The Marquis grinned wickedly. 'I am afraid the good doctor suspects us of duelling, sir.'

'No such thing, I assure you, doctor,' blustered Mr Northcott. 'I should not dream of allowing such a proceeding. The fact of the matter is, er...' He cast a wild, imploring look at the Marquis, who came to his rescue.

'The fact is, that our friend the Lieutenant was instrumental in rescuing the young ladies here from the attentions of some footpads, who had waylaid them as they returned from a walk. They had gone rather further than they should have done, and being as you know unfamiliar with the countryside, had become lost. With darkness coming on, you may imagine their fright, and also the concern that was felt by Mr and Mrs Northcott, who were already anxious that they had not returned. Lieutenant Dulverston, an old friend of the family'— here he quelled Mrs Northcott with a look when she stirred angrily—'had ridden over to visit, and heard that the young ladies were missing. He at once volunteered to ride out to look for them, as did I myself. As they wandered, the ladies encountered a pair of ruffians and, thinking no harm in it, requested their aid in finding their way home. The fellows, seeing that they were ladies, lost no time in asking them for money and jewels, in exchange for their assistance.'

'You shock me, sir! I had not thought that such a thing could happen here!'

'So the young ladies had thought, also, and they tried to run from the ruffians. They, however, were more determined than might have been expected, for they came after the ladies and would have laid violent hands on them, had not the Lieutenant, hearing their cries, come instantly to the rescue. Seeing that they had a man to deal with, and an officer at that, one of the men drew a pistol and threatened the ladies with it. In the ensuing affray the Lieutenant received the wound that you have seen, and I, hearing the shot, arrived in time to lend my assistance in subduing the rascals. My servant and I were soon able to overpower them, and we conveyed the ladies and Lieutenant Dulverston back here.'

The doctor was amazed and alarmed. 'To think that such men should be roaming here, where everyone is known and we are accustomed to think ourselves safe! The authorities should be notified at once! Where had they come from? Not locally, surely.'

'No, they must have been travelling the countryside searching for employment—or so they said. There is no need for alarm. They were but two, and I have myself dealt with the matter. The miscreants are under lock and key, and will be gone from here in the morning. My servant will remove them from the district, and will see that they do no further mischief.'

'But the magistrate, surely...'

His wandering life had made Matthew Northcott quick to follow a lead. 'I believe you are not acquainted with the Marquis of Berrington, doctor?' he said suavely.

The startled doctor abandoned all thought of the footpads, and bowed low. 'I beg your pardon, my lord! Of course, if you have dealt with the matter yourself, there is no more to be said. If I may make so bold, my lord, as to congratulate you! You will forgive me for saying that your appearance proves you to have taken a brave part in the fray. If you should be in need of medical attention...?'

St Ervan saw with resignation that this must be the price for the doctor's acquiescence in the story.

'Perhaps, when you have seen to the Lieutenant, you would be so good as to check me over? I have sustained some bruises, at least, and would be glad to have them attended to.'

This tactful speech sent the doctor off in haste, much gratified by the thought of treating so noble a patient, and planning already how he would bring it casually into the conversation in the future. Having struggled for some years to be accepted by the higher levels of country society, he could not be blamed if he seized on this wonderful chance.

Emily would have followed the doctor from the room, eager to supervise anything that was connected with Charles, but her mother caught hold of her, and it was impossible for her to leave without making an undignified scene. As soon as the door closed behind the doctor, Mrs Northcott burst into speech, no longer able to contain herself. 'This talk of getting lost while out walking, and ruffians, is all very well, my lord, but it will not do for me! I cannot deny it is a good enough story for the countryside, and I own I am grateful to you for thinking of it, but I insist on being told the truth, at once!'

St Ervan raised quelling eyebrows. 'My dear madam, no one denies that you have every right to hear the truth. Now that we have, I think, dealt with the problem of local talk as far as we are able, I am only too willing that you, and of course Mr Northcott also, should hear the plain tale.'

Unheard by them all, another door had opened. A small door that led from the saloon to the library, which had in fact been ajar for some time, now swung wider. Resplendent in a silk dressing-gown of gorgeous hue, Lord Northcott walked in. His stance was upright, though he leaned on a silver-headed stick, his linen gleamed like snow, and the candlelight caught sparks from the old-fashioned silver buckles on his shoes. At once, without any effort, he dominated the room, and even Mrs Northcott's quick tongue was stilled.

'I, too, should like to hear the plain tale. Perhaps you would be good enough to tell us all.'

CHAPTER TWENTY-ONE

THERE WAS a moment's silence. St Ervan, seeing that the rest of the company was struck dumb with surprise, or horror, or both, rose to the occasion. 'Lord Northcott? I believe I have not previously had the honour of making your acquaintance. I am Anthony St Ervan.'

'So I had gathered. I should perhaps make it clear that, being disturbed by a great deal of noise and, I have to say, screaming, I came down to my customary place in the library. By that time the noise had died away, and since all appeared to be well, I did not do anything. Being tired, I sat in my usual chair and must have dozed off. The next thing I knew was that there were voices coming from this room. It seemed best that I should not, at that time, appear, so I have kept myself out of the way until the doctor was gone. I have gathered that all is not as you would wish him to believe, and I had no desire to make myself a party to a deception.'

Lord Northcott looked around the room as he spoke, studying the faces of his family. Of them all, it was Sarah who met his eyes the most easily. He stared at her, and her colour rose, but she would not drop her steady look. He gave her a grudging look of respect that encouraged her to come forward to him.

'I am sorry that you should have been disturbed, Grandfather. Now that you are here, will you not sit down? I am sure it is not good for you to stand, and the explanations will take some while, I fear.'

He suffered her to lead him to a comfortable chair, and settled himself, gesturing her to a chair near by.

'Would it not be better if we all sat down? Mrs Northcott, will you not take this sofa, and Miss Emily may join you, perhaps.' Once again, St Ervan prepared to take the lead. At his direction, the whole party was seated, and Mr Northcott gave his wife and his father a glass of brandy. She waved it away with a look of disgust, but he placed it on a small table within her reach. It seemed to him that she might have need of it.

'If you have been in the next room, Lord Northcott, you will know that both Miss Northcott and Miss Yarcombe had been missing for some while. The facts of the matter are these. Miss Yarcombe was abducted by a man whom she had met in London, one Andrew Abbotsleigh, who was desirous of gaining control of her fortune. He, representing himself to be someone else, tricked her into leaving the grounds of the Hall, and carried her off. I had suspected for some time that Abbotsleigh was up to no good, and had in fact warned both Miss Northcott and her father that he was in the neighbourhood. When Miss Northcott heard that her sister was missing, she at once guessed who was responsible. I arrived, and together with her maid we went after Miss Yarcombe, for my groom had been watching Abbotsleigh and knew where he had gone. I own that I feel myself greatly at fault to have allowed Miss Northcott to accompany me, but for the sake of Miss Yarcombe's good name it seemed best to have female companions. As it turned out, it was well that she did come, for it is almost entirely owing to her quick-witted actions that we were able to free Miss Yarcombe from one who turned out to be even more dangerous than I had thought. Your grand-daughter acted with the greatest presence of mind.'

Lord Northcott turned his eyes to Sarah's blushing face. Their look was veiled, and he did not speak.

The Marquis turned to Mrs Northcott. 'I think it best to say at once, Mrs Northcott, that at no time have I wished to marry your daughter.' He held up his hand as she gave an affronted gasp. 'Do not mistake me. She is a wonderful girl, and the man who marries her will be lucky indeed. It is simply that we would not be suited. I am afraid that the whole misunderstanding arose because I asked Mr Northcott for his leave to pay my addresses to his daughter.'

Mrs Northcott stared at Sarah in disgust. 'You! You sly, deceitful girl! After all I have done for you, to spoil my daughter's chances! She would have been a Marchioness!'

Emily exclaimed in horror, but Sarah forestalled her. 'You are very right, ma'am, it is too bad! I cannot but see that Emily would make a better Marchioness than ever I will. I can only assure you that I did nothing to encourage him.'

'She certainly did not. Indeed, she was positively repulsive towards me. You can comfort yourself, however, that Miss Yarcombe has chosen a better man than I am ever likely to become, and one who will make her truly happy.'

'But a younger son! And no fortune at all, or any title!'

'To be a younger son is a misfortune shared by many, but I see no reason why this should hold him back. He seems to me to be a young man of estimable character and worth. By making a good marriage and allying himself to your family, he will put himself in a position to attract much favourable attention. I think that with the help of his friends—and I count myself among them—he should go far.'

A stubborn look came over Mrs Northcott's face. It was hard for her to give up her dream of her daughter's greatness, which had implanted itself so firmly into her mind. 'I cannot agree to it. She is far too young to be tying herself down in marriage just yet! She has not yet had a proper season in London.'

'She was not too young for marriage when you thought St Ervan wanted her,' said Lord Northcott, voicing what nobody else dared to say. She glared at him impotently, but Emily gave him a grateful look. 'Should we not hear the rest of this stirring tale?'

'No tale, sir, but the unvarnished truth.'

'No need to take me up so sharply, St Ervan. I meant to cast no slur on your veracity. May we know how the rescue was effected?'

'By all means. We found the cottage easily enough, and subdued Abbotsleigh's servant, who was stabling the horse. Lieutenant Dulverston arrived at that moment, and when Miss Yarcombe cried out, he burst in at the door.'

'She cried out? Did he hurt you, then?' All Mrs Northcott's maternal feelings rose, and for the first time she turned a look of real anxiety on to her daughter.

'No, he did not, but he said—he said he was going to—oh Mama, I cannot say it!' wept Emily, re-living the terror of the moment. 'I stuck the pin of my brooch in his arm, and ran away from him, but the door was locked and I couldn't get away. I kept the other side of the table, but I knew he would catch me in the end, and so did he. It was terrible! And when Charles broke the door, he grabbed me, and held his pistol to my head. He said he would shoot me if they moved!'

Mrs Northcott forgot her anger, and clasped her daughter to her in an agony of protective love. 'My poor girl! But how did you get away?'

'I do not know how it happened, but it was Sarah who managed it.'

'Miss Northcott got the stable-lad who had come with Lieutenant Dulverston to climb on the roof,' explained St Ervan, seeing that Sarah was not going to relate it herself. 'He tipped a bucket of water down the chimney. The sudden noise and cloud of steam was enough to make Abbotsleigh loose his grip, and Miss Yarcombe made her escape.'

Honest tears stood in Mrs Northcott's eyes, and she held out a hand to Sarah, who quickly came to her side. They clung together for a moment in the only embrace they had ever truly given one another.

Emily, seeing her mother so softened, nestled up to her. 'Forgive me, Mama. I never meant to hurt you,' she said simply. 'Forgive Charles, too, for he saved my life this evening.'

'That is very true,' said St Ervan, as all looked to him for confirmation. 'Abbotsleigh was beside himself when he realised he had lost all chance of keeping her. He would have shot her in cold blood, I think, had not Dulverston put his own body between them. He is a brave man, and deserves to win her.'

Mrs Northcott looked down at her daughter's face, lifted imploringly to hers. It was pale and dirty, and there was even a smear of blood on her cheek, but it held a look she had never seen there before. With a little sigh she abandoned her former dreams, and prepared to build new ones. If St Ervan was not to be her son-in-law, he might still benefit her daughter. It went against the grain to see her plain stepdaughter marry so well, but with his influence she might yet see her daughter up on the heights of Olympus with the great ones.

'I see you will have your way whatever I say. I only hope you do not live to regret it,' she said with a sad smile.

'I see no reason why she should,' put in Lord Northcott unexpectedly. 'Young Dulverston—I knew his grandfather, and his father, a good family—has shown himself both courageous and quick thinking. I may be old, but I still have friends who would help a promising young man on his way, if I should ask them. With my help, and St Ervan's, he may yet surprise us all. As for the girls, your daughter and my grand-daughter have both shown their mettle today. I think we may be proud of them.' For the first time he smiled, an open, warming smile, at Sarah, and she smiled back through a mist of tears. It was an apology, none the less sincere for being unspoken, and she knew that she would never again be looked at askance by her family.

Mrs Northcott was still a little concerned. 'Whatever happens, today's events must be kept a secret. If it ever got out that you ran away with Abbotsleigh...' She shuddered.

'I think you may make your mind easy on that score. I have seen to it that he will have no chance to speak to anyone, and within a day or two he should have left this country for good. I have told him that I will see him hang if ever he returns, and he knows I mean it. My own servant is to be trusted completely, and I assume that yours will not talk either. I think we should keep to the story I gave the doctor, that Lieutenant Dulverston saved the young ladies from footpads.'

'I am all at sea,' grumbled Mr Northcott. 'I still do not understand how Emily came to run away with that scoundrel Abbotsleigh, or why she should think he was young Dulverston when, as far as I can tell, they bear not the least resemblance to one another. And then, how did you come to know of it, St Ervan? I wish someone would explain, for it passes my comprehension.'

'It does not at all surprise me, and I think that you should have a full explanation at once,' agreed the Marquis heartily. 'Miss Yarcombe is, I believe, the proper person to do this, and I am sure her mama is as eager as you to hear what she has to say. You will not, of course, wish to run the risk of anyone hearing, and as this is rather a public room, you will doubtless want to retire to a more secluded chamber. Perhaps Lord Northcott's room? I feel sure he should be resting. The presence of a stranger, or rather an outsider, would be invidious on such an occasion. I shall remain here with Miss Northcott, who I am sure will entertain me in your absence.' He looked blandly at Lord Northcott as he spoke, and was answered by a sharp twinkle and a slight smile.

Lord Northcott held out his hand to his grand-daughter. 'Goodnight, my child, and God bless you. I think I shall keep to my room tomorrow, but be sure you come and see me. We have some catching up to do, you and I.'

'Perhaps I should go with Emily, to support her?' suggested Sarah wickedly as her grandfather left the room. At this the Marquis gave her a smouldering look that boded ill for her future well-being.

Emily tactfully said that she did not need Sarah with her. 'I have so much to explain and apologise for,' she said, taking her mother's hand once more. 'I have been very wicked and foolish, and I long to confess all to you, Mama. Let us go upstairs, where we can be private.'

'I think you will do better without me,' said Mr Northcott hastily, foreseeing a session of tears and recriminations.

'Nonsense, Papa Northcott. Of course you must come. I owe you an explanation also, and Mama needs your support.' She shepherded them to the door, pausing to glance back in a conspiratorial fashion. Her look reminded Mrs Northcott of her duties.

'Should we be leaving Sarah alone with him?' she whispered to her husband. She could not quite believe that this rich plum should pass by her own beautiful, amply dowered daughter and fall into the lap of her stepdaughter.

St Ervan heard her. 'If I still have your permission to speak to your daughter, sir? You did grant it once before, after all!'

'I suppose I did, though it was for a different daughter! I don't suppose I have much to say in the matter, though. These women will sort things out to suit themselves.' Nevertheless, he came back to kiss Sarah's cheek, and look into her face. What he saw there must have satisfied him, for he left the room without further speech.

St Ervan looked at Sarah, who suddenly felt unaccountably shy and unable to meet his eyes. She looked down and fidgeted with a fold of her skirt. She heard him walk towards her, and saw the buttons on his coat before her eyes. One of them had been ripped off in his fight, and she put out her hand absently to smooth the tear. He caught his breath.

'Sarah, look up at me.' His voice was kind, and serious as she had never heard it. With a beating heart she raised her eyes until they met his. For an instant his look burned into her, then he snatched her into his arms and kissed her, gently at first and then more fiercely as he felt the warmth of her response. She felt her body melt into his, carried away by a tide of feeling such as she had never experienced or even imagined.

Minutes or hours later, Sarah had no idea which, they were seated close together on a sofa. The sound of a log shifting in the fireplace recalled her to the present. 'Oh dear, I wonder if Mrs Northcott will ever really forgive me,' she murmured.

'I expect she will, in time. At least you are keeping me in the family,' he pointed out, finding a place that he had not yet kissed by the corner of her eyebrow, and rectifying the omission. 'After all, I shall be able to help Dulverston when we are married.'

'Oh, it is marriage you have in mind, then?' she questioned demurely. 'Only you have not precisely asked me yet, my lord.'

'Don't call me "my lord",' he insisted, looking down at her. 'I have every intention of proposing to you in form, when I have the leisure. But just now I have something much more important to do.' Once more his lips met hers, and with a sigh of exasperation and pleasure she met his kisses with her own. 'I should have done this when we first met,' he murmured wickedly. 'It would have saved so much time!'

Sarah refused to allow herself to be taken in by this shameless provocation. 'Yes, it would, wouldn't it?' she agreed.

'Hussy! You would have slapped my face for me! I was terrified of you, so angry and cold. I could hardly get a word out of you.'

'You force me to remind you that your reputation, as far as I had heard of it, was not such as to inspire confidence in a girl situated as I was, alone in a strange town with no money, and no one to protect her.'

He was instantly serious. 'Were you frightened of me? My poor darling, I left any libertine tendencies behind with my giddy youth. I would never have done anything to dismay you.'

'I think I sensed that,' she said, shyly raising her face to kiss his cheek. 'I mean, you made me angry, but I was never frightened of you in that way. I should not have gone with you in your carriage if I had been, even with that silly girl.'

'Nevertheless, it was brave of you. I admired you for standing up to those boys, and to me, though you stung me when you said I was no gentleman! You seemed more—more real, than any of the girls I had met before. I think I knew even then that you were the one for me. What luck, that we should have met like that!'

'The devil looks after his own,' she suggested, smiling at his softened face.

'Was that for me, or for you?' he teased.

'For me, of course. Who would have believed that the despised English teacher would rise to such dizzy heights! A Marchioness, as my poor stepmother keeps remembering. Will she ever forgive me, I wonder?'

'Not completely, but you need not worry about that. Whatever she might feel, you may be sure that she will treat you with the greatest amiability. How could she not? She will come round to poor Dulverston in the end, particularly when your grandfather takes him under his wing. With his influence, and mine so far as I have any, he will go far. But why are we talking of them? We have a great deal of lost time to make up, after all. Let us start our honeymoon at Bruges. We might stay at the inn where we met? I feel a great affection for that place, now.'

'Next you will be suggesting that I call on Madame Duval at the school, and visit all my old pupils!'

'If you want to, though it sounds rather boring. Would they be pleased to see you?'

'I shouldn't think so. They would just say I had the devil's own luck, and probably be very resentful.'

'Then we shall forget them. I shall take you from Bruges to Venice. They say Bruges is the Venice of the north, and I want to show you the real one. All this talk of luck is foolishness. If anyone has been lucky, it is I, that my own bad manners have won me the one woman in the world who can make me happy!'

There could be only one answer to this, and Sarah gave it with her kiss.

BETRAYALS, DECISIONS AND CHOICES...

BUY OUT by David Wind   £2.95

The money-making trend of redeveloping Manhattan tenement block
sets the scene for this explosive novel. In the face of shady deals and
corrupt landlords, tenants of the Crestfield begin a fight for their
rights – and end up in a fight for their lives.

BEGINNINGS by Judith Duncan   £2.50

Judith Duncan, bestselling author of "Into the Light", blends sensitivit
and insight in this novel of a woman determined to make a new
beginning for herself and her children. But an unforeseen problem
arises with the arrival of Grady O'Neil.

ROOM FOR ONE MORE by Virginia Nielsen   £2.75

At 38, Charlotte Emlyn was about to marry Brock Morley – 5 years
her junior. Then her teenage son announced that his girlfriend was
pregnant. Could Brock face being husband, stepfather *and* grandfathe
at 33? Suddenly 5 years seemed like a lifetime – but could the
dilemma be overcome?.

**These three new titles will be out in bookshops from
MAY 1989**

W●RLDWIDE

*Available from Boots, Martins, John Menzies, W.H. Smith, Woolworths
and other paperback stockists.*

AROUND THE WORLD WORDSEARCH
COMPETITION!

How would you like a years supply of Mills & Boon Romances ABSOLUTELY FREE? Well, you can win them! All you have to do is complete the word puzzle below and send it in to us by October 31st. 1989. The first 5 correct entries picked out of the bag after that date will win **a years supply of Mills & Boon Romances** (*ten books every month - **worth around £150**) What could be easier?

```
R D N A L R E Z T I W S
E O N M C H I N A A C C
G M U I G L E B N N U O
Y E C E G W H I Z C B T
P D R H S E R I A Z A L
T N S M P E R U N D D A
N A W I A T P I I E N N
Y L A T I N A N A N A D
N G S T N H Y D E M L Q
W N O J A M A I C A L A
R E L A D A N A C R O R
T H A I L A N D D D K H I
```

ITALY	THAILAND	SCOTLAND	SWITZERLAND
GERMANY	IRAQ	JAMAICA	
HOLLAND	ZAIRE	TANZANIA	**PLEASE TURN**
BELGIUM	TAIWAN	PERU	**OVER FOR**
EGYPT	CANADA	SPAIN	**DETAILS**
CHINA	INDIA	DENMARK	**ON HOW**
NIGERIA	ENGLAND	CUBA	**TO ENTER**

HOW TO ENTER

All the words listed overleaf, below the word puzzle, are hidden in the grid. You can find them by reading the letters forward, backwards, up or down, or diagonally. When you find a word, circle it or put a line through it, the remaining letters (which you can read from left to right, from the top of the puzzle through to the bottom) will spell a secret message.

After you have filled in all the words, don't forget to fill in your name and address in the space provided and pop this page in an envelope (you don't need a stamp) and post it today. Hurry - competition ends October 31st. 1989.

Mills & Boon Competition,
FREEPOST,
P.O. Box 236,
Croydon,
Surrey. CR9 9EL

Only one entry per household

Secret Message _____

_____

Name _____

Address _____

_____

_____

_____ Postcode _____

You may be mailed as a result of entering this competition

S COMP 6